LOVE
and
RAIN

ESSENTIAL PROSE SERIES 209

ONTARIO ARTS COUNCIL
CONSEIL DES ARTS DE L'ONTARIO
an Ontario government agency
un organisme du gouvernement de l'Ontario

Canada Council   Conseil des arts
for the Arts   du Canada

Guernica Editions Inc. acknowledges the support of
the Canada Council for the Arts and the Ontario Arts Council.
The Ontario Arts Council is an agency of the Government of Ontario.
We acknowledge the financial support of the Government of Canada

CARMELA CIRCELLI

LOVE
and
RAIN

GUERNICA
EDITIONS

TORONTO · CHICAGO · BUFFALO · LANCASTER (U.K.)
2023

Guernica Founder: Antonio D'Alfonso

Michael Mirolla, general editor
Julie Roorda, editor
Interior and cover design: Rafael Chimicatti
Guernica Editions Inc.
287 Templemead Drive, Hamilton, ON L8W 2W4
2250 Military Road, Tonawanda, N.Y. 14150-6000 U.S.A.
www.guernicaeditions.com

Distributors:
Independent Publishers Group (IPG)
600 North Pulaski Road, Chicago IL 60624
University of Toronto Press Distribution (UTP)
5201 Dufferin Street, Toronto (ON), Canada M3H 5T8

First edition.
Printed in Canada.

Legal Deposit—Third Quarter
Library of Congress Catalog Card Number: 2023930382
Library and Archives Canada Cataloguing in Publication
Title: Love and rain / Carmela Circelli.
Names: Circelli, Carmela, 1954- author.
Series: Essential prose series ; 209.
Description: Series statement: Essential prose series ; 209
Identifiers: Canadiana (print) 20230139140 | Canadiana (ebook)
20230139191 | ISBN 9781771838139 (softcover)
ISBN 9781771838146 (EPUB)
Classification: LCC PS8605.I73 L68 2023 | DDC C813/.6—dc23

Life is an adventure of our own design,
intersected by fate and a series of lucky
and unlucky accidents.
> —**Patti Smith**

Every illness is a musical problem,
its cure a musical solution.
> —**Novalis**

For my late father,
Francesco Circelli

HALF
THE PERFECT
WORLD

IT WAS AFTER THE WORLD was supposed to end, after they discovered the "God particle," after Hurricane Sandy wrecked the Jersey Shore, after Lhasa de Sela died. That's when the *Thing* entered my life, cracked it, then reconfigured it in a whole new way. It was like a collision of fate and chance, and then, a crashing wave from an unknown past.

From this vantage point, it all seems foreshadowed by a series of storms. The first was in midwinter, the night I decided to leave my boyfriend Daniel and move back to my own apartment. He was out that night at his martial arts class. I gathered a few things, my CDs, some clothes, my copy of *Being and Time*, and I left without explanation. Because the truth was I didn't know why I was leaving.

Walking up Sorauren towards Dundas Street, to catch the streetcar, I realized I'd stepped into a blizzard but somehow couldn't turn back. I kept going, the whirling wind whipping me forward, then lashing back at me. Stinging with rebuke. As if to say: "What the fuck do you think you're doing?"

When I got to the bus shelter there was no one there. Not a good sign. I waited for about an hour, the shelter shaking and clanging, threatening to collapse on me. My scarf was wrapped all around my head so I could hardly see. The snow kept falling as the wind scattered the world into a cold, white oblivion.

Waiting in the thick of the blizzard, I got a text from my friend Jo, vacationing in sunny Italy. "Why go to Italy in winter?" I had said when she asked me to go with her. But she was intent on taking a trip to her late father's birthplace, no matter the time of year. Surely there were no blizzards in Italy, I was thinking, just as the bus heaved its way towards visibility.

I made it home, though my nose had turned white from frostbite. The next day the streets were littered with devastated trees, wreckage of wood and ice, electrical chaos which left the city in darkness for nine days. I had no heat in my apartment, so I had to sleep in the community centre of the co-op where I lived. My phone kept beeping with texts from Daniel. I turned it off because there was nothing I could say, no reason I could give.

There was no power at the flower shop where I worked either so I didn't have to go in. I spent most of those nine days curled up on a yoga mat in the corner of a large room alongside other temporarily homeless neighbours. Rows and rows of flat mats with sleeping bags strewn across them. Little sleep was had, but at least we were warm.

Then in mid-summer, in the middle of a scorching heat wave, torrential rains heaved down on the city, hard and fast. I was home this time when a sudden, brief night descended on the late afternoon and the rain poured down with slamming rage. Everywhere trees strewn, poles levelled, subway stations flooded, the Don Valley Parkway floating cars like a river and people having to be boated home from the GO Trains.

I was watching all of this on the news when Mother called to make sure I was OK. Her worry was often oppressive. But on that night it was good to hear her voice, light with relief.

Later, I discovered that the giant willow tree in my courtyard had been split in two. The air was hot and sultry, the sky clear by then. I gathered up broken branches from the walkway, put them into a pile by the devastated trunk. The willow tree had been my refuge. From living in the city, information overload, abandoned loves, and an academic life I didn't really want—you name it. "Trees are more important to you than people," my friend Jo liked to say.

As I stared up at the battered tree, I heard my name called out.

Great, it's midnight, I'm in my night clothes, wrestling with loss, and someone sees me.

"Hey Chiara. What a wild night! Were you caught in the storm?" It was Andrew, who lived a few doors down.

"No, but the willow tree was."

"I know, what a mess. That tree must be about 200 years old."

"Well, the wind is promiscuous, indifferent to age, always gets its way."

"Oh, come on, Chiara, give me a break, it's too late for poetry."

"It's never too late for poetry, Andrew. Poetry comes from the night."

"OK, I'm done," he said and started to turn away, but then didn't.

"Kind of like love ... I imagine."

"What are you talking about?" he said, with his back half turned.

"The wind, poetry, love. Are you deaf?"

He looked at me, slightly startled and bemused.

"Alright, Andrew. Don't worry. Stupid men are good to relax with, did you know that?"

He was briefly deflated, then shot back.

"I guess you're so smart you can't even come up with your own insults. You have to use other people's book titles."

He stared at me coldly, then walked off.

I was surprised and as usual, felt a little guilty. Hadn't quite pegged Andrew as a literary type. I don't know why I always do that, fling arrows at men. But then again, if they're always grading our bodies, why can't we grade their minds?

I gathered up more branches, piled them by the devastated tree. I had to work the next day at Leaf and Bloom, a job I took just to buy some time. But, as it turned out, the flowers were a refreshing antidote to the years of Kant and Hegel.

My belongings were still at Daniel's place. I had been putting off seeing him for months. I knew what he would say: that I never gave it a chance, that I never intended to stay. I'd heard it all before, and it was true.

I went into my apartment, the one I was not willing to give up, the contentious object at the heart of the matter. No, definitely not willing to give that up, for the precariousness of a sexual relationship. It was the only place I felt safe when the weather got bad, and it was getting bad a lot, lately.

The television set was still on and my phone was beeping. Text from Daniel. They were not so frequent anymore, but still they came.

I first met Daniel in one of those mile-long bus lines at York University. He was wearing shorts, though it was winter, sporting a burly parka over top and a loose-fitting tuque slapped over his long, shaggy black hair.

"Going swimming?"

He was locked into his phone and didn't hear me. I said it again and then he looked up.

"As a matter of fact, yes."

"Don't they have a pool here on campus?

"They do, but I am actually going to work. I'm a life-guard at a community pool in the Jane/Finch area."

"Ah, thus the swimming trunks."

"Ya, well, I hate getting changed."

"I see, and the potential for frostbite is evidently not a deterrent for that convenience."

"No, I guess not."

"You just like guarding other peoples' lives, but not your own."

He shrugged, then smirked.

I was immediately smitten by his languid, green eyes, one looking straight at me, the other slanting away, wandering off into a distance. He was carrying a copy of William Gibson's *Pattern Recognition*. I was not a fan of science fiction. But without even wondering why, I bought a copy immediately. Maybe it was that black shaggy hair, all in disarray, and the haphazard way he had put himself together. That's what I was always looking for in men, depth and whimsy, the opposite of what they seemed to be.

At least that is what I thought at the time, but later, after we got together, the inevitable repeated itself.

"I hate it when you do that," Daniel used to say. "Just roll your eyes back, every time, after we've made love."

"Well, I wouldn't describe it that way."

"Like you're gone, already gone, back to that apartment of yours, or who knows where."

"You always look like that, like you're elsewhere. It's kind of what I first really liked about you."

15

"It's not the same thing. That's just my look. You're actively leaving."

I'm not sure where I go, though he was right, I was always leaving, no matter how much I wanted the person, initially. I just can't stay. Every time I envision the future, I am on my own, some exotic place, by the sea, always by the sea. Sometimes I'd be painting. Big large canvasses with wild strokes of thick red and black paint and the sea calm. I needed the sea to be calm.

It was always easy before. I would just lose interest, feel no obligation or commitment. As for any pain I might be causing, collateral damage, the price of sex, I figured. Or maybe even some sense of payback, or freedom I felt entitled to.

But Daniel found his way past that, without even trying. It was uncanny, almost unbearable. It was clear I had to leave, almost as soon I moved in. I couldn't say exactly what it was, or why it hadn't hit me before. Maybe it was just waking up to that face of his every morning, a face that seemed to throw my world into disarray. I knew I had a problem; I'd known it for a while.

The first time the *Thing* started to happen I was walking along the Danforth. It was late Spring, 2013, around the time I began dating Daniel. I had just been to the Big Carrot to pick up some groceries. I was walking down the pathway on the west side of Withrow Park, when I saw the road kill, a flattened and bloody cat. Someone must have picked it up off the road and thrown it on the edge of the park. It's not like I'd never seen a dead cat before. But I started heaving, like I couldn't breathe, then everything went black inside my head. I heard crashing noises, saw somebody tumbling down stairs. Then I was back staring at the dead cat, a tabby. Could it be George, the neighbour's cat? I wondered. I ran as fast as I could all the way home. To my great relief George was snoozing on my front mat. I didn't wake him. I just sat in the courtyard until the panic subsided. I had no idea what had just happened. A neighbour stopped to chat with me, probably noticing that I looked a little stunned.

I loved that about the co-op. There was always someone around. Maybe I shouldn't call that love. The lush courtyards, the charming sunrooms overlooking them, were a comfort to me, but a solitary kind of comfort. I liked the idea that there were always people around, children playing, cats and dogs scampering, adults having tea or dining together. But I didn't seem to have the capacity to join.

My parents were never very community oriented either. It's not that they were opposed to it. They were just academics, not particularly fond of socializing, though somehow, they thought I should be. Still, until the *Thing* crashed into our lives, I couldn't really say anything bad about them. They were always loving and kind, and unlike most parents who might scoff at their daughter doing several degrees in philosophy, they were delighted, proud even, of the impracticality. I suppose they assumed I would just go on to teach in some university, as they did. But that was not my interest. I always knew that, though I never told them.

I didn't tell them much. Maybe that's not so unusual. Growing up, I often felt bored or angry, without really knowing why. And though my parents were good to me, I could just as easily imagine being someone else's daughter, having different parents, or not having any at all, somehow being nobody's child, born solo.

I certainly never told them *that*. My father was too gentle to get angry about anything, a soft- spoken historian, fixated on the past, on ancient Greece and Rome. And my mother, a radical feminist from the hippie age, taught

Women's Studies. "Post-feminism miasma," she liked to say, and laugh, her disconcerted, disbelieving laugh.

When I was 10, my parents took me to see a psychiatrist. They thought there was something wrong with me. They weren't sure what. They just thought I should be more active, interested in playing with my peers more. When friends called, I would often decline, preferring to just to stay in and read. You would think that university professors would not find this too strange, but they did. No diagnosis was produced. The psychiatrist thought I was a normal kid. That seemed to appease my parents.

It was sex that eventually got me out, shook the emptiness, cracked the boredom. Not that I went looking for it. It just seemed to always come my way. Took me out of myself, though complicated things immensely, and I often wondered whether it was worth all the trouble. Like the trouble I got into when I first dated Daniel, and was still living with Pat. Operatic, was how my neighbour had called my relationship with Pat. What did I expect from getting involved with a die-hard Catholic who loved Christian rock?

Pat had been in my Theology and Film class, taught by the memorable Malcolm Spicer, who would make everyone drop off their cell phones on his desk at the start of class. Sometimes he would come in and not utter a word, play Stockhausen in the background, then stare at everyone till they were incredibly uncomfortable. He would put some phrase on the board by Carl Jung or Marie-Louise von Franz and then ask us to think about it. Once he brought in a guest lecturer, a Jungian analyst. Can't remember her name. When he introduced the woman to the class, Spicer decided to tell us that it had been an important year for him, that he had just learned how to count, "from zero to one." Not surprisingly, most

18

people dropped out. But Pat stuck it out. Pat, with his retro aviator glasses and his obsession with Kierkegaard. Pat who had gotten thrown out of seminary for listening to gangster rap.

He always sat in front of me in class, looking back with raised eyebrows or quizzical smirks. There was an awkwardness about him that I liked. Though once we actually started having conversations, he drove me crazy with his habit of never finishing sentences. It also irritated me that he made it so obvious that he liked me.

* * *

The *Thing* got more intense after the summer storm, the one that split my willow. I couldn't control its intrusions. An inner storm tearing through my clear blue detachment, like a hurricane. Jo thought I was describing panic attacks. My mother wanted me to see a psychiatrist again. She kept putting the phone number in my bag every time I visited.

"Sweetie, what harm can it do, honestly?"

"He can drug me up, that's what, or put me in a loony bin."

"Do you actually think we would let that happen?"

"I don't know very much these days."

"Why don't you call Daniel?"

"The last thing I need right now is to see his face."

"He has a beautiful face."

I could feel pressure welling up in my throat. But I held it back, like I always did. That's the other thing my parents always thought was weird about me, that I never cried. Even when I was a baby, I was as quiet as the night.

One winter, when I was eight, I broke my arm skating on the pond at High Park. It was bitterly cold as it usually has to be to skate on the pond. Jo and I were bundled up like bears and pretty happy because we had won the lottery for when the pond would freeze over, a game our classmate Nino had started. Each year you could contribute a dollar and take a guess at when the pond would get hard enough to skate on. The winner got the jackpot. Jo and I had contributed 50 cents to the same date that year and were elated to have won. Then wham! Some newbie just learning to skate crashed into me and I went flying across the pond on my left arm, which cracked from the weight of the boy falling on top of me.

I didn't shed a tear even then, not when I fell, not at the hospital, not after. At least, that's the story my parents always tell.

When the episodes became more frequent I caved in to Mother and started seeing someone. I decided to see a psychoanalyst and not a psychiatrist, though. It was going to be talking, not drugs.

Peter Allen seemed wise, a big, burly man, light and airy. He caught everything, every word, every nuance, pulled it in from the scatter, like flying things on a windy beach. The first time I went in he had Chilly Gonzales' piano solo II playing in the waiting room, so he couldn't be that bad, I figured.

But as soon as I began going to therapy an odd thing happened. I started to react to the slightest signs of loss or brokenness. The sheddings from my sharpened pencil, the browning dahlias in my garden, the dead piles of raked leaves in the courtyard, carrot peelings in my sink, could all send me into a mysterious, fleeting state of sadness.

I picked up my things from Daniel's place, finally, and expected some relief. But all I felt was sad. I had a key to his apartment. So I phoned him and asked him not be there when I went over. He was incredibly angry and hurt about that, but he agreed. I couldn't see him. It had been months since I'd left in the middle of the blizzard, without so much as a note. And I hadn't responded to any of his texts or phone calls. So among other things, I was a bit afraid of how he might react. I was pretty sure that Daniel was not crazy like Pat, the opposite, in fact, very level, calm. Still, I couldn't see him.

I had moved out of Pat's place in Little India right after my first date with Daniel. And he didn't just text, he would show up at my apartment unannounced, and pound on my door till I answered. Then he shouted and called me names so that all the neighbours could hear. "Heart of steel, cold bitch, promiscuous slut, betrayer." Someone told me that my name had been spray painted in large black letters on the pillars of the Bloor Viaduct by the Don Valley Parkway, with a big black X painted over it.

That's when I decided I better try talking to Pat. I suggested that we sit in his car and talk. I didn't want him in my apartment. He agreed. At first he continued to rant about the abrupt and unfeeling way that I had broken up with him. Then his voice started to quiver and suddenly his head was in my lap and he was wailing. He wailed like that for a long time. Then he sat upright and seemed to be himself again.

"I'm sorry," he said. "I just can't bear losing you."

"We can still be friends," I said.

"OK," he said, morosely.

But I never saw or heard from him again.

* * *

"What was going on in your life the first time it happened?" Peter Allen asked.

I stared at the huge tree-like plant behind him, humanoid branches reaching out towards me. What is that plant called? I wondered—and I couldn't focus on his question. Then I remembered walking by the park.

"Nothing in particular that stands out. I'd been living with someone, a man. Pat was his name. I had just moved out, back to my own apartment. I was really enjoying living alone, again."

"What did you enjoy about it?"

I was aware of the discomfort of the chair. Big plush leather chairs, but too big for my frame. I jiggled around to find a comfort zone and realized I was bored with his questions.

"I like solitude, more than I like people, generally. In any case, I don't like having to put on a façade for anyone."

"You need a façade even for lovers, for family?"

"Oh, especially for family. My parents always thought I liked solitude too much. Always had to pretend to be more social than I really was. Now there's no one to judge me about that."

"You don't like being judged."

"Of course not. Who does?"

My chest tightened and my whole body seemed to go on alert. I felt like lashing out at him for being an imbecile, but I held back. It was only my second session. I looked at his kind face and realized that I'd never really trusted anyone, not even my parents. I didn't tell him that, though.

Instead I said, "Tell me, do you like being judged?"

"No, but we're not here to discuss my problems. Can you tell me a bit more about what was going on in your life at the time the episodes started?"

"Nothing special comes to mind. It was the end of term and I was going to be graduating with my M.A. that summer."

"In what?"

"Philosophy."

"Wow, that's impressive."

"Is it? If I was a guy you probably wouldn't be saying it was impressive, would you?"

"I don't think that's true. I would think it's pretty impressive for anyone to do graduate work in philosophy in this day and age."

"What do you mean?"

"Well, you know, we're not exactly living in a thinking age. Thinking is becoming an endangered species."

I felt my body relax a bit into the uncomfortable chair. I looked up and realized that I hadn't really been looking at him as we spoke. The kind face again, his gentle voice.

"Well, my parents are pretty happy about my choices. I guess you could say they're old-fashioned thinkers. Though they'd probably have been happier if I had continued with my Ph.D. But at least I'm not still selling coffee at Starbucks, which I did for almost a decade, before I decided to go back to school. They didn't like that too much. Not sure yet how they feel about me selling flowers."

"And why didn't you continue with your Ph.D?"

"Well, because in the end, I always seem to get bored with school, and academic philosophy can be particularly boring and tedious. All that nitpicking about the meaning of words and concepts ... and, I wanted to get away from feeling digitally colonized. Pretty impossible to do that if you stay in the educational system ... and, there had been someone I wanted to work with, but he died just before I graduated."

"That must have been disappointing."

"Yes, it was."

I suddenly realized exactly how disappointed I had been. I had taken several courses with Luke Adelman in the years before he died. Hadn't thought I would continue with philosophy, but then changed my mind, and then had to change it back again, when he died.

"What was so special about this teacher?"

"I don't feel like talking about that."

"OK, what do you want to talk about?"

"Nothing, actually."

"That's OK too, we can just sit here together."

"Well, that won't work for me, since I'm paying you."

"Then I guess you need to find something to talk about."

"Luke Adelman was a Russian Jew. I think I might have a thing for Russian Jews."

* * *

After a month or so of therapy, I did get the urge to contact Daniel. That seemed like a good thing. He didn't deserve my abrupt leaving, my shunning. He hadn't done a thing to deserve that, absolutely nothing. Yet until then, I hadn't been able to feel much about it, except that mysterious, fleeting sadness, the same sadness I felt about the carrot peelings, or the leaves, or the countless other signs of time and change or brokenness. Fleeting like a breeze that passed over me, then dissipated with the air before I could catch it.

> *Dear Daniel,*
> *I know it's taken me a long time. It's because I didn't know what to say, and I couldn't bear to hear your voice or see your face. I need things to be clear and distinct, a Cartesian kind of need, I guess. But it's just an emotional need, not a philosophical one. It's got to be like that or things fall apart on me. I know you'll probably be surprised by this, but that's how things work for me. And I'm afraid of the*

*bad weather. The summer storm destroyed the willow tree
in my courtyard. Some solid thing inside of me went with
it. I don't understand what is happening. But I did finally
take my mother's advice and started seeing someone to
talk about it ... I hope you're OK, and I am sorry.
Chiara*

I pressed "send" and then immediately felt panicky.
Not because of what I'd said, but because he might respond, and also because he might not respond.

The e-mail, short as it was, took everything out of me.
I threw myself on the couch in my sunroom. Lay there
for a couple of hours thinking. I had started to become
more comfortable with just lying on the couch for hours.
It was seeing Margarethe von Trotta's film about Hannah
Arendt that did it, a film, among other important things,
about a woman often seen lying on her couch, smoking
cigarettes and thinking.

Then as I lay there, another remarkable thing happened. I felt a wave of intense longing for Daniel. But
almost immediately, it was overtaken by blackness, the
falling, the crashing noises. This time I saw blood splattered everywhere, some stairs, the bottom of stairs.

I leaped off the couch so quickly I almost put out my
back. I put the kettle on, just to do something ordinary,
something practical. I opened the cupboard and shuffled
through my boxes of teas. I decided on chamomile. When
the kettle whistled I was so startled that I poured water
on the counter instead of in the cup. Some of the scalding
water hit my leg. Good thing I had my jeans on. I sat at my
kitchen table for a while to try and calm down. Then the
phone rang and it was my friend Jo.

Jo's voice was calming though the calm turned to anger
when she suggested that I call Daniel.

"Goddammit, why is everyone always telling me to call Daniel! I just e-mailed him, in any case!"

"Maybe because everyone but you can see that things started to go a bit crazy when you broke up with him."

"You never mentioned that before."

"I guess it just became clear to me right now, that you've been this way since the spring, which is just after you decided to move out."

"I had seen it as the other way around, that being with him was causing something in me that I didn't understand, and I was trying to escape that."

"Well, it seems not to have done the trick."

"It has something to do with his Russian Jewish roots."

"What are you talking about?"

I felt a slight panic. But Jo's voice calmed me down.

"The first time I went over to Daniel's parents' place for dinner I had this strange sense that I'd been there before."

"Oh no, Chiara, not you. Please, don't go all past life on me."

"No, I am not. But I did have a déjà vu moment. The smell of the place, the food, the way his parents moved, the sound of their voices, the Russian accent."

"You know, I never really thought of him that way. Daniel was just Daniel, a being unto himself."

"Daniel Cohen," I say, just to hear myself say it.

"I know. I am not saying I didn't know he was Jewish. I am just saying it seemed irrelevant. He was just such an individual."

"Yeah, he was ... anyhow, I thought you believed in reincarnation, so what's your problem with past lives?"

"I do, but not the New Age version of it. It's a bit much, empties it of meaning for me."

I sensed some patches of clear sky overhead and felt the urge to get out.

"I'm not sure I get what you mean, but I think I need to switch gears. Let's pick this up some other time ... thanks, though, and I'm good for now, don't worry about me."

"Boy, when you're done, you're done. No transitions."

* * *

I really wished I knew what kind of plant that was, extending its broad leafy pods towards me. I liked identifying and naming things. Order and clarity. Peter Allen was wearing a nice denim shirt with black tailored pants that day. His hair was a bit disheveled, like he just got out of the shower and had not bothered to comb it. I was glad he was not a cologne-wearing man. I wouldn't have been able to bear that. All I smelled was the mint tea he was making for himself as I settled into the big uncomfortable chair.

On the wall beside me I saw a brown stone plaque I hadn't noticed before, a quote by William Blake. I leaned in closer. But before I could read it Peter Allen asked me how I was.

"Well, I had an episode just yesterday."

"OK, tell me about it."

"I finally decided to e-mail Daniel, the guy I broke up with about six months ago. I had just sent the e-mail and was feeling a bit nervous about it. Then just out of the blue I had the strangest feeling, this feeling of intense longing. It was ever so fleeting though, and then the crash came, the blackness and this time, blood splattered everywhere."

"That's quite a remarkable reaction to feelings of longing."

"I know, but it still doesn't make any sense."

"Why do you refer to the feeling of longing as strange?"

"I guess because it's not something I ever feel. I never miss people. I am usually just relieved to be away from them ... Well, maybe that's a bit extreme. There are some people I feel comfortable with, like my friend Jo. But even so, I never miss her when she's not around."

"Have you always been this way?"

" I guess I have. My parents brought me to see a psychiatrist when I was a kid because they thought I was too solitary."

"What did he say?"

"He thought I was normal."

"Did you think you were normal?"

"Well, I wasn't unhappy. Though I did feel a vague emptiness or boredom at times. But I occupied myself with reading, which always interested me."

"Relationships at a distance."

"Well, I never quite thought of it that way. But I suppose that's true."

I remembered the first time I realized that longing was completely foreign to me. I had been reading Starhawk's first novel *The Fifth Sacred Thing*. A character was leaving his lover to go in hiding for political reasons. His lover knew that his leaving was necessary and that she might not see him again for a very long time. The account of her attachment and sense of loss was so intense, I had to put the book down, struck suddenly by the description of a feeling I'd never known. How amazing, I had thought, to long for someone that much.

But I didn't tell Peter Allen this. Instead I asked, "Do you believe in witchcraft?"

"Relationships at a distance? Witchcraft? I am not getting the connection."

"I thought this was based on free association."

"Well, yes, you are right. But I would still like to try and understand the nature of the association for you. What would make you leap from relationships to witchcraft."

I was having trouble with the honesty. I was not used to having all my thought processes examined. I looked at the plant lunging toward me, at Peter's kind face.

"It's a phenomenon that fascinates me, how we could have gone from burning thousands of them at the stake, to 400 years later, loving them, for example."

"Do we?"

"Why else would the tales of a boy wizard be one of the bestselling book series of all time?"

"Relationships at a distance." He looked at me with his quizzical eyes. I had never noticed his eyes before. They were very soft and blue. That's where his kindness came from. But still, I wasn't sure I wanted to be there with him.

"Well, magic is about relationship isn't it? Even quantum physics suggests that particles are conscious, interconnected. When they feel you looking at them they change their shape, so you can't pin them down. That means everything is in relationship to everything else, close or distant, like it or not."

It was strange to hear myself say something like that. I realized that I wished I believed it, that everything was interconnected, not just arbitrary, accidental, meaningless, which is what I felt most of the time. That's when I remembered sitting at my power spot in Withrow Park with Daniel one evening, when the wind rose up with a wild flare, our hair flung to the skies as we scurried to gather our things. The clouds darkened. We thought a storm was coming, then everything was still again. But we were up and ready to leave, so we did. "That was a sign," I said, "that we should leave. The wind must be obeyed."

"You, my dear, are an unbeliever with a nostalgia for belief," he said and laughed his deep ecstatic laugh. "In good company, like our friend Pasolini."

I looked up at Peter Allen and caught a look with something like affection in it. That's what I thought I saw. Could that really be it? Not possible. Could his warmth come so easily?

"Does that mean you are changing shape as we speak?" he asked.

* * *

When I got home that night I found my front door wide open, piles of leaves blown in by the wind, up my blue staircase. I was often chastised for never locking my door when I went out. That was not usually what people were concerned about, though, the unwanted things that could get blown in. What is it about the wind that always moves me to mythological planes? Maybe it's the closest thing to the invisible that we have evidence for. My 200-year-old willow tree, split in two.

I swept out the leaves from the stairwell and stepped in to check my e-mails. I hated that I did that, first thing, not just because I was anxiously waiting for a response from Daniel. I did it always, couldn't seem to control it. A goal of mine: to not think e-mails as soon as I got in the door.

Since I graduated I hadn't used Moodle or Turnitin. Then I stopped tweeting and blogging and Face-booking. It was like a big emptiness at first, a big absence, maybe like how it feels when you leave an abusive relationship or like a compulsion that does you no good, yet you can't seem to stop.

Nothing from Daniel. It had been three days since I had written. But then again he had sent at least 10 e-mails and countless texts, none of which I had responded to. Not that I was ready for a response from him. I didn't know what I would say or do if he wanted to see me or talk to me.

I watered the plants, put on a CD by the late Lhasa de Sela. Made myself a cup of mint tea. I sat on my teak green couch in my sunroom, the couch Jo gave me after her father died. Jo had been brought up by her father. Her mother disappeared, no one knows where, when Jo was three years old. Then her father was gone too. She couldn't keep all his furniture, but didn't want to sell it to strangers. She started giving it away to people she knew. Whenever Jo comes over, she sits on her father's couch. Even when we're eating, we sit there with our plates on our laps.

I looked out at the maple trees outside my sunroom. Some of the leaves seemed to be changing colour already, just a little bit. Could that be? Then came a wave, not a breeze, but a large wave of sadness. Were the trees already contemplating their brown, bare days of winter, like I was?

I was lost, no idea where I was heading. I had no passion for anything. I suppose that's why I was able to hold a job serving coffee for so long. It paid the rent, only because I lived in the co-op, it forced me to be around people, which I normally would not otherwise have done, and it gave me time to read. I didn't seem to need much more ... now there was the flower shop, which I was thankful for. Among the plants and flowers, the scent of earth, I seemed to feel respite from vexing questions.

I wished I believed, like Jo, in some version of reincarnation. But I can't quite get around certain obstacles, like the soul. What kind of being would it have to be, to reincarnate? How could traces of embodied memory linger in an invisible being like a soul? What kind of boundaries would a soul have to have in order to retain the unity of a personal history and its memories?

Lhasa de Sela's song "Rising" was playing mournfully in the background. "I got caught in a storm. That's what happened to me," she laments, making me want to believe in a soul. Lhasa de Sela had so much of it, how could it not exist? I felt something welling up inside my throat, but pushed it down. I felt angry. That's why I never cried, I thought. Because I was so fucking angry I could punch a hole in the wall. I got up and grabbed the blue ceramic vase Mother had given me as a house-warming present and smashed it to the floor. I sat back down, distraught and frustrated because I didn't know what was going on. I wasn't angry at Mother. That much I knew. The vase was just the first beautiful, breakable thing I had laid eyes on.

It was the first time I'd ever broken anything. My anger had always been more generalized before, like an irritation with the world as a whole, more like a frustration at not being able to trust anyone or anything, and wishing that I could. Now I wanted to break things, smash them to particles, wreck what's good.

A distant memory surfaced. I was 12 years old, that awkward gangly age, in between times, waiting for things to form. Jo had been over. We had been studying algebra together, a test for the next day. Jo had left just before my parents were due back from work. But on that night neither of my parents came home at the usual time. An hour passed, then two. I had tried phoning their work places. They had left, they had gone. Three hours passed, then another, as I paced the house, waiting like an automaton, or so I thought. But my behaviour said otherwise. By the time my parents got home, I had trashed everything in my bedroom, thrown everything breakable to the floor.

When my parents returned they were frantic, but then went speechless when they saw my room. My mother hugged me tightly, then in silence began cleaning up the mess, as I sat, somewhat stunned, on the edge of my bed

They had been delayed by a motor vehicle accident, stalled on the Don Valley Parkway. I had completely forgotten about that night, till then. Were there other such incidents I'd blocked out? I was beginning to feel as if there were worlds that I'd been a part of, that I could not remember, worlds that were breaking through, like memories from another life. I wished I could believe it. But I did not seem to believe in anything.

That was one of the things that had made my relationship with Pat so fraught with tension. He was such a believer, in love, in God, in truth, in me. When I thought about it I realized that we had spent most of our time together having arguments. Yet, there was something compelling about him. I loved having sex with him, for one thing, and so it continued. I could think he was an idiot for thinking so highly of me, for having a child's view of God, for sentences that were always broken, for sugar in the *frittata* instead of salt, and CDs in his sink. God only knows why he did that. But then he would come close and the smell of him would get under all the doubts and judgments.

Another point for the materialists. The power of chemistry.

I looked at the time and decided to make a run for dance class. I could still make it. Getting out of my head seemed like a good thing. Plié, jeté, contraction, release. Anything to make me stop thinking. I decided to clean the smashed vase later. I turned off the CD player and scrambled to find leotards and tights, threw them into my gym bag and ran out to the courtyard to discover it was raining, a warm gentle rain, autumn rain. I ran back in to get my umbrella, then made my way up to Broadview, across the bridge to the west side of Riverdale Park. It was rush hour and the traffic along the Don Valley Parkway was raucous. I put on my earplugs and continued across the bridge, over to the park, the rain lending a soft misty comfort.

* * *

I loved the cactus room. Before I started working at Leaf and Bloom I hardly knew anything about cacti. In fact, I knew very little about flowers or plants in general. I had been walking by the store one stormy, spring day when lightning cracked open the sky and the thunder startled me off the sidewalk, under cover of Leaf and Bloom's green awning. Blazing yellow forsythia was on display just outside the door. A woman with long, red hair, looking like a hippie, came running out to bring in the display. She smiled at me and invited me to come into the shop but I declined. "Suit yourself," she said, and scurried in for cover with the forsythia in her arms.

At the centre of the window display was a huge, jade plant with feathery white flowering, surrounded by several tall, phallic cacti. Numerous hanging ones too, Medusa-like, in braided variety of thickness and shape, and a tapestry of orange and yellow roses, woven into a trestle of wooden twigs in the background. Then I noticed the hand-painted "Help Wanted" sign in the corner of the window.

The middle of the shop had a huge Norfolk pine with leaves that seemed to be pulling down to the ground as they gently curled up, resisting gravity. At the base was a circular wooden bench covered with pots of red azaleas. The tree was so huge that at first I didn't notice the woman now sitting quietly on a chair, by a counter. I felt so intoxicated by the smell of the place that I almost stumbled over the display of small potted plants laid out on a table beside the tree.

I made my way over to speak to the woman.

"Hey, I guess I changed my mind."

"No problem."

"Actually, I was wanting to inquire about the job."

"Oh, good. Unfortunately, Paolo, the owner, is not here today. But I can set up an appointment for you, if you like."

"Sure, that would great."

Days later, I found Paolo in the cactus room, which I hadn't noticed the first time. A small alcove with glass walls, a miniature green house at the back of the store. I caught him off guard. He was sitting on a bench running his fingers through his hair, looking pensive or sad. As soon as he saw me he stood up and seemed unable to say anything.

"Hi, I'm Chiara Jones. The woman who was here set up an appointment for me."

He kept staring at me without saying anything, looking sort of stunned or bewildered, like someone who couldn't believe what he was seeing. He must have been in his 60s, very fit looking and well put together, all in denim, with a small row of blue beads around his neck. Must have been a heart breaker in his youth. "OK, Chiara, let's go into the other room, so we can have a chat."

He asked a few questions then said, "Wonderful, a philosopher selling flowers, I really like the sound of that. You're hired."

I was surprised. I imagined I would have had to work harder to convince him. But he seemed to make his decision almost immediately, even before he knew about my Starbucks experience. Coffee was far from flowers, I knew, but still, I had figured that was my only relevant qualification.

I started working at Leaf and Bloom shortly after I started seeing Daniel. He also really liked the idea of me working in a flower shop. "Very Heideggerian," he had said, knowing that I still read the damned philosopher, despite his political notoriety.

"Nobody is all good or all bad," I said.

"Well, as the 'great' philosopher himself once admitted, 'He who thinks great thoughts can also make great mistakes,'" he said.

I had been working at the flower shop for almost two years when things got a little strange, or at least, Paolo started to get a little strange. I was sitting on the bench in the cactus room, one day, beside the fountain of Leda and the Swan, surrounded by several golden barrel cacti and numerous thick, succulent rods, bending in fleshy contortions around various aloe vera and pots of wild green stringy *Agave Filifera* and *Senecio Serpens*. I felt so proud for having learned all their names, especially because, when I sat in the cactus room, I almost felt happy, or some state I imagined as happiness.

The cactus room was Jean Pierre's room, a memorial Paolo built for his lover who had died five years earlier. Paolo took over the shop after Jean Pierre's death. Paolo had been an office manager for one of the local newspapers before. Knew nothing about plants or flowers himself. Must have been why he was so empathetic to me when I came in looking for a job. He fell off a cliff when his lover died, he had said. But then he got back up, bruised and battered, gave up his career to throw himself into a world he didn't know at all, a world of floral arrangements, ferns and wisteria, tulips and roses and amazing, scented lavender. He built the room at the back of the store, a world of diversely shaped, water-keepers. The store, although off the beaten track, was doing very well.

Paolo was a dear, no question about that. And smart. The guy could talk about anything, with the most impressive eloquence. His beautifully constructed sentences flowed like breath. And I mean anything. You could bring up what you thought was the most arcane topic, like some book on the history of witchcraft written in the 19th century, or Foucault or Maurice Blanchot or Michel Houellebecq and there he was, right with you. At first, I couldn't believe it. Who was this guy, anyway? From a pre-digital universe, for sure, the way he could focus and discuss things. No outsourcing of memory there. He never used his phone or computer to look up anything. All in that beautiful mind of his.

But he often looked sad, sad and beautiful, like the Erik Satie music he always played. Made me want to die, when he put it on. The Trois gymnopédies were unbearable. I wanted to run away, hide in some cave and leave the world behind. A beauty I couldn't seem to bear. Erik Satie tipped me over the edge, the *Sorrow Beyond Dreams*. I said it out loud, once, the words just came.

"Ah, Peter Handke," Paolo said. "He co-wrote the script for the Wim Wenders film *Wings of Desire*. Did you know that?"

" No, I didn't." I didn't even know where the phrase came from, or that it was the name of a book. The music called it up, like the broken memories that seemed to haunt me then. Some sad thing I knew, yet couldn't know, kept hounding me, like black dogs, lurking around corners. Dogs that loved Erik Satie.

As I sat in the cactus room waiting for customers and ruminating about Paolo, I realized why I loved the space so much. It was a place of reverie, an activity the world no longer had time for. A dying art, like so many other things, usurped and vanished, overtaken by digital algorithm. How was it that the geeks and engineers had taken over the world? I wondered. Was it deliberate? Or were they really just part of a long line of guys cut off from their bodies? It was all moving very fast. But things must have been steering along a certain course for centuries in order to get us here. And why were people either just futurists or neo-Luddites, like my parents? Wasn't there some middle ground? The neo-Luddites were not just against the machine, in any case. They were old-time revolutionary socialists, grandfathers of the union movement. Not just destroyers of machines for its own sake.

But here's the thing that really perplexed me. How on earth did philosophical materialism end up de-materializing the world? A paradox that bothered me, one I hadn't been able to sort out, yet. For the air, the earth, the wind and the sea. I should do it for the elements, try to figure out why the sensuous world was disappearing, why people were submitting, en masse, to living in a frantic, crowded, digital universe. I was lucky enough to remember before it was that way. Maybe I was just a freak of nature, born in the wrong time, far from where I was supposed to be, lost … the bell rang, interrupting my reveries. I rushed to the counter to find a man and his toddler looking at the roses.

"My wife's birthday," he said.

"Ah, well, let me know if I can help you."

"Maybe you can. I am not sure of the colour."

"Sure. When is her actual birthday?"

"October 15th."

"OK, Libra. An air sign. Perhaps something lighter, more delicate, maybe orchids instead of roses."

"Oh, I actually wanted roses. My wife is not into that astrological stuff. She's a scientist."

"Well, despite what some people might think, we are not machines, you know. Why wouldn't we be affected by the celestial bodies?" As soon as I said it I realized I had forgotten where I was. Too much time in the cactus room.

"I'm sorry," I said, before he had a chance to speak. He looked at me quizzically without saying anything. Then he just said, "I'll take a dozen yellow roses. That will be all. Thanks."

I wrapped the flowers with extra care, used the expensive paper reserved for special occasions and tied numerous multicoloured ribbons around the base. I stapled the flap down over the top to protect against the October chill. Then reminded him to cut the stems again before putting them in water. All of which he accepted, seemingly indifferent to my inappropriate retort. Just as he was going out the door, with child in one hand and roses in another, he turned around and said, "I actually kind of agree with you."

I felt immense relief. I didn't want any complaints about my behaviour at the shop. Losing my job at that point would have been a disaster. Not that Paolo would have fired me for just for one such incident. But still, he had taken a chance on me. I didn't want him to regret it.

I noticed that the azaleas needed water. They were so sensitive, wilted so easily when neglected, even for a brief stretch. You have to keep close watch over the azaleas. I learned that pretty quickly. I got such satisfaction from watering the plants, a nurturing activity I had been able to cultivate. It was a good sign, I figured, learning how

39

to keep things alive, something I had not been particularly good at. Always going for the kill, cutting things short, abandoning them before they got too demanding or complicated. But I could stay with the plants, tend to them, make sure they didn't die.

The door opened and the bell rang, again. "Hi, Chiara."

It was Paolo, who was supposed to be away in Montreal, visiting some friends that weekend. He had moved to Toronto around the same time as my parents, in the early 80s, a few years after the Parti Québécois had come into power. Joined the English exodus to escape Quebec's political turmoil. But there was something else he was wanting to escape, something to do with a break in his social circle, something he only ever vaguely alluded to.

"I thought you were in Montreal," I said.

"Something came up. I am going at the end of October, instead. So I've come in to see if you could work that weekend as well."

"OK, but what weekend is that?"

"It's the weekend of the 30th, I think."

"Oh, actually, the 30th is my birthday. I have some plans for that weekend."

I could see the colour leaving his face. He ran his fingers slowly through his hair, like he always did, and then decided to just sit down on the chair by the counter, as if he had become faint.

"Are you OK? Are you not feeling well?"

He didn't say anything, didn't respond at all, like he had tuned me out or just couldn't hear. I tried again, a little more forcefully, "Paolo, are you ill?"

That seemed to break his trance.

"No, Chiara, I am fine," he said, the paleness seemingly turning to sadness.

"So your birthday is on the 30th," he repeated, as if to make sure he had heard me correctly.

"Yes, ... and oh, by the way, I should tell you, I just got into this thing with a customer about astrology. I think ..."

He cut me off, which is something Paolo never does. Along with his other great qualities, he was a fantastic listener. "About that weekend, don't worry. I'll get Helen to cover it."

Then he seemed to regain his composure and lighten up a bit. Just before he left, he turned and shouted out, "By the way, you look great today. Love that frizzy kink of yours and that peasant top."

I looked down at what I was wearing, which I didn't often give much thought to. My hair, which I normally wear tied back, was down. There was something off about the exchange. I enjoyed the compliment, though. The great thing about compliments from Paolo is that you can believe them, because you know he's obviously not trying to hook up with you.

* * *

After I smashed the vase I decided to take therapy more seriously. I started to go every week instead of every other week, and tried to be more honest, tried to stop viewing it is a some kind of game I might be able to win.

"Well, how are you today?" Peter Allen asked in his predictably soft voice.

"I don't know. I don't know what's happening to me. My mental processes seem to be out of control. It's strange. I've always taken pride in my coolness, my detachment. But things just seem to be erupting in me that don't make any sense. A few days ago I got so angry I smashed a vase my mother had given me as a housewarming gift."

He didn't interrupt me. He let me keep going. That felt unusual. People rarely seem to listen so attentively. It's was a bit disarming. But under the circumstances, I figured it was a good thing, so I kept talking.

"I thought I was OK, content with how things were going in my life, relieved to be done with school, working at the flower shop. Though not everybody thinks so, like my friend Jo. She doesn't think that working in a flower shop will be enough for me. But she's wrong. It's really the only stable thing in my life, right now. And the owner, Paolo, is a gem. That's a good thing for me, to be around men like that, because I'm generally pretty cynical, don't expect much."

"Why are you so cynical about men?"

"Ever try being a woman?" I realized that my indignant tone was not going to get me anywhere, so I switched gears.

"It's not that I don't like being physically desired, but I hate being objectified or idealized. It so often feels like you can't really find yourself in that twisted jumble of male fantasy, insecurity and superficiality. It feels like a trap and then I have to escape. I'm always on the run, at least that's the complaint I get. And these days, with such easy access to a pornified world of sex videos, cam-girls and silicone dolls you can program to talk sports and cars with you, well, they don't have to make much of an effort, do they?"

"You sound somewhat different today. Has something changed?"

"Well, yes, the vase, the smashing of the vase."

"What was going on just before you smashed the vase?'

"I can't remember exactly ... I was thinking of Lhasa de Sela, I think, a singer I loved, who died of breast cancer at 37 ... a thought just went through my head."

"What is the thought?"

"Step into the sea ... A strange voice, not one I recognize ... see, this is why I'm here. It seems I am going a little bit crazy."

"No, you're not. You have a very strong ego. You won't go crazy."

"Well, that's reassuring," I said, without believing it. But if Peter Allen was convinced, that was something. After a bit of a pause he spoke again.

"The psyche or soul or whatever you want to call it is a mysterious thing, driven toward the good, I happen to believe. Maybe you need to learn how to trust what you know."

"Well, you're absolutely right, there. I don't trust a damn thing. If there is no ultimate reason for being here, then it doesn't matter what we do, does it? What can you trust in a world crowded out by constant chatter and information? A world that's massacred wisdom and abolished truth. Is this really a price to pay for some delusion of immortality? Singularity is what those fucking technocrats deserve. They can have it. But I don't want it. I want my carbon-based, fleshy, imperfect, insecure, ignorant humanity. That's what I want."

"Well, I think we are starting to get somewhere," he said, quietly, but firmly, unfazed by my word storm.

* * *

It was late afternoon by the time I got home, a golden stream of sun still lighting the front room. I sat to consider what had just happened. I felt giddy and weightless from the rant. Until the vase incident, I'd often felt a slightly detached, generalized kind of anger about things I couldn't always articulate. In fact, I rarely even acknowledged it, except when it would intrude, on its own, as if it was some independent entity.

I decided to make some pasta, moved over to the kitchen and started chopping vegetables. Suddenly the apartment turned darker than evening and loud, crashing noises came from the top floor, or maybe the roof. I looked out the sunroom and realized that it was raining, the hardest rain I'd ever heard, harder even than the mid-summer storm. I ran upstairs to find that one of the windows in my bedroom had been flung open, and the force of the wind had knocked down a lamp from a nearby book shelf.

I tried to slam the window shut. It took all the strength I had, but it just flung open again. The wind was fierce and cold. I tried one more time, but I became unsteady and fell backwards, hitting my head against the book shelf. I lay there for a while, shocked, listening to the howling roar. Then I considered that the window could get torn off its hinges and decided to move away, sat on the edge of the bed. There was a bit of blood trickling down the side of my face. I pulled a Kleenex from the box on my dresser and held it to the side of my head. I wasn't quite sure what to do, so I just sat there watching as the ferocious wind tore through everything, including my bedroom. I waited, holding the tissue to the side of my head. I had the urge to call Mother, but my phone was downstairs and I seemed unable to move, afraid to move. I could feel the wind's force from across the room. It had knocked everything off the book shelf. What would it do next? I watched and listened for about 15 minutes. Finally, the rain stopped and the wind abated, without remorse.

Later I heard that it was the remnants of a hurricane from somewhere off the U.S Atlantic coast. Power lines had been torn down and people had to scramble to school auditoriums and churches until the power was restored. The cold and the dark set in for five days before they could return to deal with the devastation. I got the tail end of that destruction. There was no loss of light, no permanent damage. Though it contributed to my unsettled state.

But what came later, in mid-December, that was the stormy *Thing* that finally broke me. In the end Jo was right. It did have something to do with Daniel, though not with my leaving him, but with my meeting him. That's when the boundaries of things began to flutter, and a subterranean world of events I didn't know existed started to rumble.

* * *

After our initial, chance encounter in the York University bus-line in the middle of winter, I didn't run into Daniel again until the following spring. I had just written my last exam and was sitting under the willow by York Lanes drinking a latte, enjoying the relief. The lilacs were wafting and the magnolias bursting their pink suspense. There was a light warm breeze, a poignant softness and the tinge of endings. I would not miss having to travel up to York, though, nor the bus exhaust I was trying to deny as I was having my parting moment, or the crowds and frequent rapes happening on campus, the labour disputes and that goddamn shopping mall. I was happy to be leaving that landscape behind.

As I sat on the bench, besotted and confused by the scent of lilacs, gazing at a light array of moving clouds, I felt a gaze upon me. He was at quite a distance, down by a bench at the side of the pond. I didn't know how long he'd been there when our gazes met. I didn't recognize him without his hat and parka. When he saw that I hadn't recognized him, he came closer and then his slightly stigmatized, blue green eyes gave him away.

"The smart-ass lady from the bus line," he said.

"Ah, the winter swimmer, immune to frostbite. I see you know when to keep your legs covered."

On that day he was wearing brown cords and a denim jacket, his hair tied back in a bun. Underneath, a white shirt with a thin black, leather tie.

"And where are you off to today looking so buff?"

"I am going to the movies."

"I see. A date?"

I couldn't believe I had asked that.

"No, taking my mother out for her birthday."

I found it incredibly endearing that he would get all dressed up to take his mother out.

"There's a Pasolini retrospective at the TIFF. My mother loves Italian cinema. Do you know Pasolini?"

"No, not really. I mean I've heard of him."

"*Teorema* is playing on Saturday. It's one of my favourites. Would you like to go? You really should be familiar with Pasolini."

His confidence was disarming. I scrambled for a few seconds not knowing how to respond.

Then I said, "How can you presume to know what I should or shouldn't be familiar with?"

"I guess you seem like a sophisticated intellectual type."

"Oh, and what does a sophisticated intellectual look like?"

"Oh, you know, black curly hair with glasses, or maybe like you're here because you want to be and not just because your parents want you to be, or because you think it might improve your job prospects."

"Well, an intellectual maybe, sophisticated, no, whatever that means. And yes, I was here because I wanted to be. Now I am leaving because I want to leave."

"And what are you going to do now?"

"Look for a job, I guess."

"What kind of a job?"

"I don't know. With an M.A. in Philosophy, I figure my options are wide open."

He laughed, but didn't say much else. I was aware that I was trying to avoid the question. But he didn't press the issue. He just waited, then finally looked straight at me, his eyes keeping the question open.

"OK, let's do Pasolini," I said, even though I was still living with Pat at the time, and wondering how I was going to manage that.

"What's the movie about?"

"Well ... I guess it's about how, sometimes, someone can just walk into your life, out of the blue, and turn it upside down, or right side up, depending on where you're at."

* * *

I met him at the theatre. He was wearing the same thin black leather tie, with a light blue shirt this time and black denim pants, his hair loose and dishevelled, curling down almost to his shoulders, slicked back, different glasses, not the wire rimmed ones, but black rectangular frames. I saw him in the distance, walking towards me along King St. I hadn't had a chance to catch his gait before. You could tell he was a swimmer.

I had been so entranced observing him that I was a bit tongue-tied. He asked me a couple of questions. I felt a slight relief that we had to tend to buying tickets and finding seats. I was struck by the pitch in his voice, can't say quite what it was, like he was in a constant state of subtle ecstasy, the opposite of me, I suppose, which is why it struck a chord, a hidden chord, one I wasn't really aware of yet. My body responded with fear.

47

Teorema was a bit shocking, even many years after its making. Daniel's description had not prepared me for the silence of the mysterious stranger, who walked in and out of a family's life, leaving trauma, beauty and wreckage in his wake. I had never seen a movie quite like it, though the conversation we had afterwards was quite unsatisfying. It was our first real conversation. So there was that to contend with. But I found Daniel aloof about the spiritual element of the encounters, like he didn't care to talk about that part of it. He just kept saying that Pasolini was an atheist and that the characters had just made whatever they wanted out of the encounter. They took what they needed and maybe in some cases that was to go crazy, or to leave the world altogether. Then he announced that he had to go. So we finished our coffee at the TIFF canteen and parted ways.

I didn't hear from him for several months, and was a little peeved. I'd made the dramatic move out of Pat's place, back to my own apartment, thinking something was going to happen, and then it didn't. Had almost given up expecting it, when in the middle of a scorching heat wave he called.

"Hey, how goes it?

"I'm OK, I'm working now, in a flower shop."

"Wow, didn't expect that, you in a flower shop."

"I know, everyone seems to say that, but I'm good with it."

"So listen, I was wondering if you wanted to go for a ride to the country. I have some friends who live out in Havelock. We can go swimming in some natural bodies of water, if you like that kind of thing."

I was a bit taken aback, but I agreed. We made our plans and off we went, on the Saturday morning. It was about a two-hour ride. He concentrated on the driving and didn't talk much. But when we arrived he became wildly

entertaining, with his quick wit and endearing respon-
siveness. I watched him carefully, since I still didn't know
him very well at all. He was different with Jack and Cindy,
childhood friends, who knew the ins and outs of his hu-
morous slant on things. It brought out his confidence and
playfulness. He seemed pleased to be able to show himself to me, though I was more quiet than usual, not knowing any of them. Daniel engaged mostly with his friends,
though he remained attentive, making sure, always, that
I didn't feel left out.

It was a sweltering day and the heat slowed us down
considerably. All we could do was swim. We spent the
day throwing ourselves into various rivers and quarries,
three rivers and one quarry, to be exact. But the best was
our night swim.

We were lounging about after dinner, satiated from
food and drink, and all talked out, when Daniel leaped
up with his desire for one more swim. It was about ten
o'clock and Cindy didn't seem too keen, but Jack went for
it and so did I. We were all, to varying degrees, stoned and
drunk, and so it was not the wisest idea, since we had to
take the car to the closest river. But we did it.

The moon was a tender sliver and the sky teeming
with stars as we got out of the car and tried to find the
riverbank in the dark. Jack seemed less enthusiastic than
he had been, as if the idea of swimming in the night was
more appealing than actually doing it. But Daniel acted
like he knew the river with his eyes closed, contours his
body knew by heart. I followed him, without fear as he
led me to the water's edge. He jumped in and disappeared
into the night waters. I jumped in after him. He swam so
fast, it was hard to keep up. But then he slowed down to
make sure I was behind him. We looked over to the bank
and Jack was still standing on it. Daniel started cracking

jokes. I was laughing so hard I started swallowing water. I told him to stop, that I couldn't laugh and swim at the same time. We waited a while longer for Jack to join us, but then he shouted out that he changed his mind, that he wasn't coming in.

Daniel asked if I could see the tree further down the river, a large branch that had broken off and fallen across the river from one bank to another. I couldn't see it clearly, but I said yes. Then he challenged me to race him to the branch. He beat me, of course. But when we got to the tree we were able to hang on to the branch and rest. He looked at me and smiled, though it was dark and I couldn't be sure. My feelings must surely have been obscuring my sight as well, a rare feeling of joy.

When we got back, Jack was a bit sheepish at having been too afraid to go in. Then Daniel piped in,

"Hey man, we needed someone to stay on the bank to make sure we could see our way back."

"OK, I get it. You two, fish, me, guard dog"—and we all laughed, the sultry night sweeping over us us, as we moved towards the car to change out of our wet clothes. Daniel stood at the rear of the car and I near the front. When he took off his bathing suit he glanced at me briefly and I could see his lean muscular legs and chest. I felt his nakedness in the dark. First erotic stirrings.

On our drive home the next morning Daniel brought up our last conversation, which I had forgotten. Ruminating about men always seemed like a pointless exercise to me. Because what you're thinking about is usually never where they're at. I know they're not from Mars, but maybe the South Pole, I figure.

"You were right, you know," he said. I turned to look at him. "About Pasolini. *Teorema*."

"Oh my goodness. You're still back there."

"The stranger is like a Sun god, a pagan god. I was resisting your interpretation because at the time I was thinking 'Christ-like' and he didn't seem at all like a sacrificial lamb. He moved them erotically. That didn't seem spiritual to me, in the ordinary sense."

"Well, that's interesting, but I don't think I'm prepared for this conversation right now."

"OK, we don't have to have it now if you don't want to."

"I'm not adamantly opposed to it ... but is that why you never called me, because of that disagreement?"

"I did call you. What do you think we're doing here right now?"

"Well, you waited a pretty long time. Did you just call so you could tell me I was right?"

"No, it's because it was something about you that made me have this realization, not the argument you were making. Something else, but I'm not quite sure what."

"Oh." Then I really didn't know what to say. I waited, let the silence be, looked out the window at the wheat fields, golden against the clear morning sky. A few wisps of cloud followed us along. In the distance some cows were grazing, lined up in a row, beside a white wooden fence. Daniel waited a while then said, "I didn't call you because I didn't think you were interested."

"Oh, then you changed your mind."

"No, I just decided to risk that maybe I was wrong, about you being interested, not about Pasolini."

I knew he was fishing for something, but I couldn't give it to him. I stayed fixated on the passing wheat fields, the animals, the cloud formations.

"It's a spectacular morning," I found myself saying, and then just as I said it some storm clouds appeared out of the blue as if to taunt me or break my weather trance.

"Listen, I'm not just looking to hook up, you know," he said.

I waited a while and then said, "Well, I must say, that's refreshing, but did it ever occur to you that maybe I was?"

He turned to look at me and I caught a glint of excitement in his eyes, his soft, languid, green eyes.

OK, I've done it, I thought. I've managed not to offend this man. I am pleased.

* * *

The first time I had sex with Daniel I cried. I know I said I never cry, or at least that's what I was always told, and that is pretty much what I also remember. But on that night I did, quite inexplicably. I suppose that was the beginning of the break, though it came somehow from beneath the *Thing*, from beneath the shattering, the blood, the broken glass, from underneath everything, everything I knew and everything I didn't know, at the same time.

I guess it's also pretty relevant to say at this point that I'm a sucker for good taste in music, probably rely on it too heavily to judge people. Before living with Pat, I lived for a while with a long-haired, Rastafarian guy called Giri. He had dreadlocks down to his waist and would knock over everything in my small apartment whenever he flipped them back. He stood me up for our first date, so I'd written him off. But then he insisted on meeting me just one more time to explain. And while I had no intention of taking him seriously, no matter what his explanation, I changed my mind when he showed up wearing a Clash T-shirt, even though the reason he had stood me up was because he had spent the night in jail, had punched somebody at a bar. A Rastafarian who liked punk rock. I couldn't pass that up.

When I was walking over to Daniel's apartment that night, I could feel tightness in my body. I had never been to his place before, but that was not usually the kind of thing that created physical stress for me. Even so, I felt good, confident, curious about the green-eyed man who swam like a fish. It was mid-August, summer light was waning, but it was hot and warm.

He had cooked dinner for me, pasta Bolognese, with salad. Pretty good for a non-Italian, I thought. And it was all going pretty smoothly, until I heard him put on Laura Marling, and then everything went kind of strange, like I was in an alternate state of consciousness or something, or like the external world had suddenly become remote, a distant din. I knew I had to keep trying to converse, but I wasn't sure if words would come out. It was like a great silence was waiting to overtake me and I wasn't sure if I could resist. I tried.

"Hey, you like Laura Marling," I said. "I don't know too many people who've even heard of her."

"Oh, she's pretty big in the British folk scene."

OK, it was working, uttering the words seemed to bring me back.

"Ya, she's great," he said. "I love her. Because of her I got into Joni Mitchell, big time. She just kept getting compared to her, so I decided to buy some Joni CDs, and it was exquisite time travel. I always knew she was a major Canadian icon but I had never really listened to her."

"Ya, the exact same thing happened to me," I said, though I still couldn't really connect to the conversation. Instead I started to get angry and felt a strong urge to be nasty to him. The intruder had taken over, the one who wanted to tear at men, make them hurt, make them cry. But it was so clear that my feelings were completely inappropriate to the situation that I was able to control them.

I didn't say anything for a while, just drank some more wine, too much wine.

"You know, about *Teorema*, I think it doesn't matter whether the stranger is divine or not. Maybe it's just that love can destroy you if you don't have a strong enough container for it, you know, like a strong enough ego, or a mythology of some sort. Look at what happened to Anna Karenina ... in *Teorema* the only person who is somehow not destroyed by the power of the stranger is the peasant woman who returns to her spiritual roots. She is positively transformed."

"You talk about fictional characters like they're real people."

"Well, maybe that's Pasolini's point. We no longer have a sense of the mythological and we will be lost without it."

"OK," he says. "I love that, but I gotta say, speaking of spirituality, that come Friday night, I am reluctant to work hard at anything, even thinking and feeling. It's just my Jewish roots, I guess, my Sabbath, my 24 hours of complete down time. That includes heavy discussions."

He was silent for a few seconds while I was still trying to figure out how to respond.

"Oh ... but that doesn't exclude making love."

So it was, that I threw myself into his proposition, as if into a lake, swimming far from shore, where black dogs waited. But I always used sex that way, to escape from actually having to relate to men, and because it was easy. It was a subject you could be sure to engage them in. But on that night, it was a mistake, because I could feel my edges blurring even before we got to the bedroom, because I was trying to escape myself, and because I was too drunk to stop the passion. And though I felt immensely attracted to Daniel, I could tell something very strange was happening.

The scent of him, so powerful, seemed to crack an amour I didn't even know I had. Then just as I was coming, I felt his hand on my face, which was covered with tears, streaming down, uncontrollably, like an ancient grief from some world I hadn't known existed.

Daniel's tenderness afterwards was completely unexpected. I was disoriented and shocked, didn't know what had happened. I wanted to leave, but he insisted I stay. He wrapped me in his red quilted comforter and lay silently beside me, inching closer with calculated slowness as if afraid to trigger me further in some way. He was affectionate and sweet, and as I saw his face, so close, for the first time, he seemed ancient and familiar.

Then he did a remarkable thing. He went into the living room and put on Johnny Flynn's "The Water." I began to cry in earnest. He didn't ask any questions, didn't try to appease me with words or try to make sense of the thing for me. He just stayed with it. Even though I was in a state of humiliation and fear, I kept right on crying, like the "hard rain that was gonna fall."

"I guess I fucked up your 24 hours of down time," I said, when I finally calmed down.

"Well, it wasn't exactly hard labour for me," he said, "so I wouldn't worry about it, if I were you."

Daniel Cohen was in a category all his own. I knew that much, though I was pretty sure I wouldn't be seeing him again.

I was in my thirties then, and though I hadn't made much money, I lived with men, because that's what they seemed to want, at least from me. And it was *Half the Perfect World*, for a while. But after that first sexual encounter with Daniel, things changed. I became disconnected from the self I thought I knew, becoming someone I didn't recognize. So when Daniel called me later that week to invite me to a Sabbath dinner at his parents' place, I was reluctant. I did not feel in good form. I did not know what would happen. The green-eyed fish man was disarming. But the sound of his voice, clear as fresh water and with that hint of ecstasy, pulled me, again.

"I think a Sabbath dinner might be exactly what you need, Chiara."

"Why do you say that?"

"I'm not exactly sure, just a hunch, and maybe, what you said about Pasolini."

I agreed to meet him at the Castle Frank station, where he said he would pick me up at 7:30 pm.

It was a a warm August evening, everything lush and beautiful, no real signs of autumn yet, except for the sun, closer to set, darkness on the horizon.

The Cohen home in Rosedale was like none other I'd ever been to. Not because of its wealth, but because of its warmth. That is the only way I could describe it. Original artworks hanging on all the walls, exquisite, antique furniture. Exotic Persian rugs everywhere. On one mantel filled with family photos I caught sight of Daniel as a young boy, dressed in short pants and cowboy boots, his long black hair falling over his eyes in that dishevelled way of his.

His parents welcomed me wholeheartedly, even though they had never met me before. His mother charming and gracious, her black hair slightly tinged with grey, tied up in a freestyle bun, almost bohemian looking. His father, more traditional, businesslike, with the same green eyes as Daniel, was courteous and kind. They spoke with a thick Russian accent, which for some strange reason felt comforting. Their English was impeccable. They had come in the early nineties, after the fall of the Soviet Union. They were originally going to try Montreal as they had family there. But then decided on Toronto because of the French/English problem in Quebec. They wanted to leave political problems behind.

When we sat down to dinner his mother placed candles into candlesticks and lit them. His father began to chant Hebrew words, like a blessing or grace. This took me away. But my reverie broke when wine was poured into some silver goblets and we toasted to the joy of being together. Daniel's mother cut up some braided sweet bread which we ate slowly and meditatively as if treasuring every mouthful. The rest of the meal consisted of chicken soup, a mandarin and beet salad served with roasted apricot chicken, and apple crumble for dessert, made from apples picked from their own apple tree.

The conversation was easy and warm, from politics to careers, to families and personal history. Both his parents asked me about my philosophical background with keen interest. Then we sat in the living room and Daniel's father put on what sounded like Jewish liturgical music and the conversation turned to more spiritual matters, with almost the same ease, for a while.

"Chiara is a pagan," Daniel piped up at a certain point, when his father got a bit preachy.

"Oh," he said, taken aback. Then he said, "No matter the mythology, it's all veil. It's the heart you give to it that matters."

The trance broke. I had never called myself a pagan and wondered why Daniel would perceive me that way. His father's response made me think of Heidegger, who had said that even technology was like a veil. But I didn't want to bring that up, because of the whole Nazi association. So I said nothing and then abruptly felt that I had to leave. Daniel offered to take me home, and I agreed that he should let me off at Castle Frank Station again. In the car he was sweet and attentive, asking me if I had had an

OK time, to which I tried to respond with appreciation. Then just as we approached the subway he said, "So did you want to talk about what happened the last time we were together?"

"No," I said instantaneously.

"OK," he said and dropped it equally as fast. He just touched my hand, lightly, when I was getting out of the car and didn't even try to kiss me, which at that moment felt just right. But in the subway I experienced regret. I wanted to have sex with Daniel again but was feeling that I had screwed things up. At the same time I was worried about what might happen if I did sleep with him again.

It was 11 pm and the subway seemed crowded for that hour. I was holding on to a pole, thinking contradictory thoughts, when I noticed that the people across from me seemed blurry. I rubbed my eyes to no effect. I could hardly make out the faces. I felt dizzy and was having difficulty breathing. I tried to focus on what I had been thinking about but couldn't remember. I had to remember, if I could not recover my train of thought, my mind would tumble off a cliff. I saw images of men in white coats forcefully restraining me. I leaped out of the subway onto the platform, sat on a bench. It was Broadview station instead of Chester where I usually get off. I walked out to the street, Riverdale Park illuminated by the city to the east. The cityscape, bright and concrete, anchored me. I walked briskly, focusing on every step. By the time I got home I felt almost normal and remembered what I had been thinking about. But the urgency was gone.

The months that followed seem, now, like an intense, erotic blur. Daniel was nervous, not quite sure what he was getting into, but he didn't let me go. While I, overwhelmed with feelings that were decidedly foreign, tried to appear even more detached than usual. I feigned indifference while feeling overtaken by lust. I felt desperate to escape, either away from him or into him, I couldn't really tell. But soon I lost the power to decide. I could think of nothing else, his lean, athletic body, his gait, the way he moved, the slight hairs on his chest, his lips, that disarming, ecstatic pitch in his voice.

We would agree to meet for dinner, but then gave ourselves over to lust, wherever we were: back alleys of restaurants, bathrooms, back seat of his car, his front porch. Once we walked in High Park and as soon as we were on the slope of Spring Road he grabbed my hand and pulled me into a wooded area, pinned me against a tree, ripped up my skirt and pounded me till he came. That's the first time I remember liking the aggression of the sexual act. If I have to break, I thought, then let it be this way.

This went on for a while, until we stopped going out, and just holed up in his apartment, without bothering to go through the motions of dating. That's when it started to get difficult. He wanted me to stay over. It's not that I didn't want to. It was what I usually did, start having sex with some man, then go home less and less, and then half-heartedly move in.

"Come on, Chiara, I miss talking to you. I want to see your face in the morning."

"Oh really, is that what we do, talk?"

"Well, if you lived here, we could fit in the talking, because I love talking to you as much as I love, you know, the other stuff."

I eventually succumbed, against my better judgment, but not against my body, which seemed to want to break, seemed to want the danger.

What Daniel didn't know, what I didn't know, was that something was surfacing. I had to work extra hard to keep cool, to stay level-headed, detached. That had never been a problem for me before. It was my general state of being. I was indifferent, most of the time, or bored, or inexplicably angry, but it had never been difficult to hold myself together.

At the time, the *Thing* seemed completely arbitrary and inexplicable, and each time it intruded I had to retreat in order to find equilibrium. So I knew it was a mistake to "move in" with Daniel at that point, but the pull of him was so strong. It felt like I was giving in to some craving to be broken or a terror to be faced.

But once I moved in, I lost cohesion. At first the passion seemed like a kind of escape, but then it stopped working. My thoughts kept racing towards the cliff. Then I'd catch myself and pull back.

Leaf and Bloom saved me then. There, among the flowers and the plants, the precipice seemed far. Paolo also had a calming effect, as if he was from a world I knew, or had always known. When he talked to me in his casual, affectionate way, I had the glimmer of what it felt like to belong to the world, as if I had arrived somewhere I was supposed to be. The sensation was foreign to me. I confused it with sexual attraction. I convinced myself that I should try to seduce Paolo, even though he was, at least, 30 years older. I figured it was a way to escape Daniel and to get away from the *Thing* stirring inside of me.

I started wearing my hair down all the time when I went in to work, because Paolo complimented me when I did. I wore clothes I might wear to a bar instead of my usual nondescript jeans and T-shirt. But he seemed to catch on pretty quickly, and set me straight right away. It was a quiet Friday morning in January when he pulled me over to the cactus room and sat me down.

"OK, Chiara, I'm gay, you know that, don't you, so what are you doing? And besides, I could be your father."

I was embarrassed, but relieved, that I could count on him to be direct. That's when I told him what was going on with Daniel and about the psychological intrusions I was experiencing. I hadn't told anyone in such detail yet, not even my parents or Jo. I saw him go pale as he sometimes did, when we were talking, like he knew something he wasn't saying, or was afraid. But as always, he shifted back to his warm and affectionate demeanour.

"Chiara, sweetheart, if it isn't good for you, then leave. I don't know you that well, but I can tell that you haven't been quite yourself, lately. Don't worry about Daniel. He seems like a solid guy. He'll survive."

His words were sure and unwavering. I seemed to be able to feel that he truly had my best interests at heart. This had always been difficult for me to believe, even with my own parents. And with men, they just lie to themselves, so you can't trust what they say, even when they think they're telling you the truth. That's how it always seemed to me. But Paolo had the ability to make me believe what he said, without even trying.

* * *

I looked at Peter Allen's attentive face and felt like I wanted to go over and slap him. I didn't tell him this, though. I stayed silent for about ten minutes. That's when I started thinking that I would just be wasting my money if I didn't talk. But I was at a loss for words. I felt like I should tell him about the urge to hit him, but somehow I couldn't. In the past my aggression always took verbal forms but now it was getting more physical.

"I'm going to a cabin in the woods this weekend with my friend, Jo." Peter Allen didn't answer. He just nodded. I tried again, "The owner of the cabin just died, so it's going to be sad to be there without him." This time he answered.

"Oh, did you know him well?"

"Yes, Dave was my soul mate." He lights up. Interested.

"Too bad he was a 95-year-old gay guy," I said. He chuckled. I knew I was avoiding what was going on. It kept wanting to slip away into the oblivion it came from, the urge to hit, to wreck, to destroy. Then I said it.

"I have violent urges. I'm wanting to hit you right now, for no particular reason at all, or just because you're kind and attentive. I want to destroy that look of consideration on your face."

"Is that always the case?"

"No, sometimes I'm completely impressed by how kind and attentive you can be."

"What do you think of when you think of attentiveness or kindness?"

Then I felt myself starting to shiver as if the room temperature had abruptly dropped some 40 degrees. There was a red wool blanket on the couch. Peter Allen pointed to it and suggested I cover myself with it, which I did.

"You can lie down if you wish," he said. But I didn't. I continued fussing with the blanket trying to wrap it around me. Once I had it strapped around my shoulders, the shivering started to subside and his name popped into my head.

"Daniel."

"Yes, what about Daniel?"

"That's who I think about when I think about attentiveness."

"Is that upsetting to you in some way?"

"I guess it is, since I totally destroyed that one, didn't I?"

"I'm assuming that means you haven't heard back from him?"

"Well, it's almost two months, so I think I'm done with that."

"But your body, it seems to say otherwise."

I had to admit, what Peter Allen said was true, though the thought was unbearable, like every cell in my body was blue, like I'd just been born or only just died. I changed the subject, sort of.

"Dave, my soul mate who just died, was an avid environmentalist. He donated the whole of his property to the Conservation Society. No matter who buys the property now, they are not allowed to develop it. Everything has to stay the same, in perpetuity, except for the changes caused by nature itself."

"Why is this so important to you?"

I had stopped shivering, so I took off the blanket and faced Peter Allen directly.

"Because mankind cannot be trusted, and I don't mean that in a generic sense."

The weekend at the cabin was difficult, as expected.

Dave's absence from the landscape tugged at our hearts, as if his gnome-like presence had always been the true magic of the place. "No matter what's going on in your life, when you sit by this river, everything is OK," he used say about the view of the Credit River from our cabin.

There were three rental cabins on the property, besides the one that Dave lived in. Ours was known as the "river cabin" because of its frontal view of the river. When you sat on the deck, you became part of the flow, as if the river's currents were running right through you.

We kept expecting Dave to pop by with his reliable cheer and good will, and his genuine curiosity about you. I suspect that everyone who stayed at the cabins probably wanted to claim him as their soul mate. That's because he seemed to want to mate with every soul he met. Like Lhasa de Sela, when she sang, as if everyone was her lover.

It was my birthday that weekend, so we tried to be festive, despite the air of sadness. Jo cooked dinner for us and then brought out a sumptuous lemon cake, which we ate on the deck, after it had gotten dark, with the stars overhead and the river flowing through us.

The day after was All Hallows' Eve, the witches' new year, which Jo could not let pass without a ceremony, this one more fitting to the mood we were in. Or, maybe, that is just what new year means, birth and death, side by side.

Jo gathered piles of fallen leaves, the remnants of dead flowers, lots of goldenrod, stems of the red phlox that grew outside Dave's cabin and threw them all onto the cabin deck. She spread out one of those scarves she wraps around her head and laid out the dead foliage on the scarf. She put a candle in the centre and photographs of people she knew who had died. There was one of her grandfather and Dave as students at the University of Toronto. They were standing in front of Hart House, Jo's grandfather, tall, lanky, and Dave, reaching only to his shoulder, his arm wrapped around her grandfather's waist. They had the wide-open grins of those just starting out, the long line of life still ahead of them. There was also a photograph of Roddy, a fiddle player from the Cameron Family Singers, who had also died, earlier that year. He had been a friend of Jo's father, who pretty much lived at the Cameron House when he was alive. Sometimes Jo and I went with him to the Saturday matinee, to listen to old-time country and hang with the local cowboys. There was a guy in the band who made cowboy boots for a living, and every spring there would be a show of his boots: boots that were like canvases, boots too beautiful to wear, boots definitely too expensive to own. But all the same, I always loved to go look at them, and the guy who made them, he was pretty nice to look at too, as beautiful as his boots.

I had no photographs to contribute, so Jo suggested I just I write down the names of ancestors or other people who had died, that I wanted to remember. Of course, I put down Lhasa de Sela, but I had no sense of ancestors at all. It was as if before my parents there had been no one. I knew that couldn't be so, but that is how it felt. My grandparents had died before I was born, or so I was told, and neither of my parents had any siblings. But I liked the idea of honouring ancestors, even if it felt like some great unknown territory.

At the last minute I thought of Luke Adelman, my philosophy teacher who had just died, and I put his name down. Jo formed a thin circle of leaves around us, lit the candle, called to the elements and to the power of Hecate and conducted the ceremony, which I loved participating in, but from which, as always, I felt a kind of detachment.

Jo knows I'm an agnostic, but that doesn't usually bother her. Though we did get into a tiff that weekend, the same one we've been getting into for over 20 years. Late one night, after we had been drinking pretty heavily, she blurted out that she was tired of always having to be the one who called all the time to initiate contact, the one who somehow kept the relationship going, who suggested things to do, like that weekend away, for example.

"Come on Jo, how can you say that? We've had a lifetime together."

"Yes, and it's always been this way. It's been a burden feeling like I'm the one who has to keep you connected to the world or you'll just disappear."

"I suppose I could disappear. I don't particularly like walking this earth. Though I don't even know exactly why. Like I could take it or leave it."

"Ya, except that lately, you seem a lot more like you could leave it."

"Well, I've been dealing with 'things' lately, you know that. I guess it's making my need for solitude even greater than usual."

"I want you to enjoy my company. I want you to spend time with me, because I matter to you, not just because I happen to call."

Then she started crying. Blurting out "the mother wound," she ran into the dark woods without a flashlight. I ran out after her and found her on the hillside by Dave's house, the stars scattering the night sky and illuminating the field of goldenrod. I sat down beside her and put my arms around her.

"Jo, you gotta know me by now. I don't mean you any harm. Quite frankly, I don't know what I'd do without you. You've always been my only true friend."

"That sounds like you're talking about the past. What about now?"

I felt momentarily confused.

"Well, you know that I've always been emotionally challenged. But lately, I don't know what the fuck has been going on. I'm doing my best, Jo, please don't get angry with me now."

She didn't say anything for a while, then just nudged in a bit closer. We could hear the flowing mantra of the river in the distance, and everything did seem OK, just then, but only for a little while.

* * *

After the failed seduction, my relationship with Paolo changed for the better. I stopped seeing him as just my boss. We started going out for drinks at Allen's every time we worked together. And I never seemed to tire of his company. I had never experienced that kind of enjoyment in social interaction before. Friendships had always been difficult for me, and with a man, pretty much impossible. Paolo was handsome and gorgeous and smart, and it was pure pleasure to be able to enjoy him without any looming sexual tension.

But one night, after a few drinks, he asked me some strange questions. Like if my parents had ever talked to me about my birth and whether we were living in Toronto or Montreal when I was born. He kept running his fingers through his hair the way he did when he was nervous or agitated. Then he abruptly changed the subject and asked if I'd ever heard of the Red Brigades. "Vaguely," I said. "One of those seventies terrorist groups, right?"

"Yes," he said, and then seemed to be stumped as to where to go with the conversation, which is not something I'd ever seen happen to Paolo.

"I had a friend in Montreal who was involved with them," he said.

"Montreal? I thought it was an Italian group. You don't mean the FLQ?"

"No, but I knew people involved with them as well."

"OK, I knew you were too good to be true. You're a fucking terrorist! Is that what you're trying to tell me?"

"No, but that group of friends I had in Montreal were mostly Italians. Some of them moved back to Italy and became involved with radical politics."

"And you?"

"I guess I was always the voice of reason, but by that time our social circle had completely fragmented and I was too far away to have any sway. But in any case, that was a different time, and even terrorism was different then."

"I'm not sure what you're getting at."

"Well, take the Red Brigades, they were fuelled by a sense of injustice and by positive political ideals that they felt couldn't be realized in any other way. Even the FLQ had legitimate grievances."

"Are you fucking trying to justify terrorism! Paolo, now you're scaring me."

"No, I always argued against violence when I was a part of those circles. All I'm saying is that what's going on now with groups like ISIL or ISIS or whatever you want to call them is a very different kind of beast."

"Well, I refuse to taint an Egyptian Goddess by calling them ISIS, for one thing, and what do you mean?"

"I just think that current terrorism is motivated by revenge and lust for killing. There's a big difference between loving death and loving justice. The darkest and most base part of human nature is out of control. And the West, with its denial of culpability, has become a danger to itself and others."

"Well, now you've just defined insanity."

"Yes, maybe that's what it amounts to, a kind of madness, without any real ideals for truly bettering the world. That's the difference I'm trying to get at between then and now."

I didn't like what Paolo was suggesting that night. Terror was terror as far as I was concerned, no room for fine distinctions. But because it was Paolo, it got me thinking. I could tell that what he was saying was coming from something he had wrestled with, something he had been through.

I called Mother that night. She was so happy to hear from me. Like everyone else, she too, often complained that I never called. I knew that I had been born in Montreal, but I asked again about why they had decided to move. She gave me the usual line.

"You know that, honey. It was the political situation, and your father had gotten a post-doctoral fellowship here at the University of Toronto. So that gave us the push to make the move, which we had been wanting to do."

"Did you know people that had been in involved with the FLQ?"

"No! Why are you asking me that?"

"Why did you call me Chiara?"

"Chiara, bella, what kind of a question is that? Because we loved the name. Because we wanted clarity for you, lucidity of being, what can I say? Why is this an issue now?"

"Just curious."

I let it drop but didn't feel satisfied, so I called Jo, who was also happy to hear from me, until I immediately started talking about Paolo.

"What is it with you and this guy?"

"Nothing!"

"Well, he seems to have a strange hold on you."

"No, he doesn't. He's just really interesting, thought provoking. You simply don't want me having relationships with anyone else."

"That's bullshit and you know it. Who was the one pressuring you to call Daniel?"

"Well, a lot of good that did. Let's not do this. I just wanted your feedback on something that has been bothering me. Does it always have to be about us?"

"No, it doesn't. I don't know why we're always bickering lately. You just seem a lot touchier than usual."

"I could say the same about you."

"Well, yes, I have to admit that's true."

"You want to go to the Cameron House tomorrow night and listen to some mountain music?"

"Sure, let's do that, let's get a dose of paradise, that's what we need."

The days that followed had a strange anticipatory edge to them. I felt like a dog who could sense a storm coming, but had nowhere to flee. The Cameron House was fun, as usual, but the whole night a part of me kept wanting to run, far away, leave everything behind, go somewhere where nobody knew me, start again, a different life, a completely different life. But I was getting used to my wild thoughts, used to them enough not to follow through. Fleeing was something I knew well, but I had the distinct sense that wasn't going to work anymore, that I needed to stop and face the *Thing,* head on.

It was a Friday, when I usually see Peter Allen in the mornings. I decided to speak more explicitly about the intrusions, the flight of stairs, always, a body tumbling down, broken glass, blood. Peter Allen tried to approach it from the point of view of some trauma I was remembering, something I had repressed that was resurfacing. But it was nothing like that as far as I could tell. None of the images resonated with any memories I had access to, or experiences I had known. He kept asking for more detail in hopes of unlocking the thing, but nothing came, nothing except the panic of uncertainty, of realities beyond my control. I left his office frustrated and hopeless, wondering why my world was cracking in ways I could not make sense of.

I made my way to Leaf and Bloom for my afternoon shift. Helen was working mornings. She informed me that a big batch of Christmas cacti had come in and asked me to organize some of them for a window display and put the rest of them in the cactus room.

"What's up?" she said, "You look kind of gloomy"

"Not my favourite time of year, I guess."

"I get it, it's not my favourite time either, though Paolo loves it, so you may have to put up with his cheerfulness. He phoned to ask when you were in, so I think he may be dropping by today."

When Paolo arrived I was setting out the Christmas cacti in the window display. He looked grim and anxious. I felt frightened, thinking something terrible had happened. But then he just took my hand and led me away from the window. He had a small suitcase which he put down by the cash register.

"I am going to lock the door for a while and put up the 'Closed' sign because I need to talk to you about something."

He put up the sign and came back, picked up the small suitcase again and took my hand.

"Are you off on a trip?" I said, jokingly, trying to lighten the mood.

"No," he said, "the contents of this case are for you. I may be overstepping some boundary here, since I have no idea what your parents have or have not told you. But you're not a child anymore, and you have become my friend, so I feel I have a right to let you know. At first I wasn't sure of what I suspected, but when you told me your birth date, I knew my suspicions were true."

I felt blurry eyed for a while, and dizzy, like I was going to fall over. That's when he took my hand again and led me to the cactus room. He sat me down on the bench and pulled over a chair to sit across from me, suitcase still in hand.

"I hope I'm doing the right thing, Chiara. I hope it will help, in the end, to sort out what's been happening to you lately. Though I have to admit, I'm not entirely sure about that, so I'm taking a risk. But you have to know that I'm doing it out of concern. I've become extremely fond of you, and I would not want to do anything that would harm you."

I felt my thoughts hurtling themselves towards the cliff, as if I was about to fall off the edge, the edge of sanity. Paolo's hand tightened its grip on mine, helping me stay present. Then he let go and pulled the small suitcase on to his lap and opened it. It was brimming with letters, in a handwriting that seemed vaguely familiar. There were also several notebooks and what looked like a diary.

"I want you to take these home and read them," he said. "I think it's time that you knew what happened and why."

TANGLED UP
IN BLUE

*C*ARO PAOLO,
　How far they seem now, those years of youth and yearning, when you entered our lives with your flaming beauty and easy eloquence, and threw us all into disarray. At least that is how it seems to me, now, 25 years later.

　You probably concluded that I disappeared from your life because of what I came to know about you. But it wasn't that way, not really, not entirely. I had been strategizing my disappearance for years. Then, it was forced upon me by circumstance, circumstances I didn't feel I could talk about at the time. Everything was about escape, then. The lies and the truths, all tangled up in blue.

　I knew that at some point, I would have to find you and tell you what happened, though I didn't think it would take this long. Then by a strange twist of fate, I heard about your mother's death, in the most accidental way, here in Rome. It was then I decided to write.

　And without knowing why, I felt compelled to read a story I had loved, long ago, and discovered that I had hidden you in its pages. There it was, the photograph Ricardo had taken of you, that weekend at Titiana's cabin in the Laurentians.

　In the photograph you are leaning against a pine tree, graceful, eyes vivid, your head slightly tilted forward in expectation, confident of your beauty. Occasionally I would long to see that photograph, to be reminded of that "first love" I had for you. But I could never find it, could not remember that I had filed you away for decades, in Peter Handke's Sorrow Beyond Dreams.

For a very long time this story has been fractured, the pieces in scattered directions, across continents, flashes of black and falling things, the stairs, the blood, the blue and the red of something far away. But now, finally, it is different. Finally I can piece it together.

So here it is, Paolo. This re-remembering is for you, and also for my niece, Chiara, whose abandonment was fallout, from this twisting tale of blue. I understand that you know where she is, and I am hoping that this story will find its way to both of you, somehow.

* * *

We started our transatlantic crossing from the port of Naples and ended up in the neighbourhood of Notre-Dame-de-Grâce, in Montreal. We descended from our hilltop hermitage, built in the Middle Ages and set ourselves to sea. At the time, Volturino was a village like many others in the south of Italy, populated by illiterate, destitute peasants desperate to feed their families. America pulled with the dream of abundance and misery pushed with its dark tide.

I remember the night of arrival, the way you always remember the hands of fate. It was a dark, rainy night, storm-shattered sky, as we huddled into Zio Matteo's car waiting for us at the Montreal train station. I was only three years old and had just spent nine days at sea, not knowing where we were going or why. I had a pack of cookies I was bringing for my cousin Ottavio, whom I had never met. That's all I knew, that I was going to meet a cousin. What disappointment to find him sleeping when we arrived. I peered into his room. He was huddled under blankets, oblivious to the arrival of his seafaring cousin. Ottavio was a few years older than me. Micola wasn't born yet, nor was Ricardo.

Those early years were a kind of blur. I had been plucked from a warm and sunny place and dropped into a strange, cold hinterland, oblivious to what I had lost. I gave myself up to blissful days of running through snowdrifts and creating white worlds of igloos and snowmen, tobogganing on Mount Royal and skating on Beaver Lake. This was the only happiness I remember from my childhood in Montreal, the happiness of winters. Summers seemed more fraught with sadness, as if only then, I got a glimmer of what I had left behind.

Though winter had its dangers, too. A few years after we arrived, a massive blizzard submerged the neighbourhood under walls of snow that seemed to reach the rooftops and winds that tore away our electricity. I had to skip school while we took refuge at Uncle Pasquale's, who still had lights and heat. We stayed with them for a week. Micola was just three years old and not yet in school.

We moved around a lot, then. At first living with Zio Matteo's family and then with various other relatives for brief periods of time, until we could finally afford our own apartment on Melrose Avenue. The previous tenants of the Melrose apartment seemed to have left their life behind them. The place was already furnished with maple antiques, including a piano in an alcove past the hallway entrance.

As a child I spent my time reading, though my father hated my nose always buried in the books. But I was never one for obedience. It's not that my father didn't want Micola and me to be educated, but he was afraid of losing us to worlds he could never know. And I always fought with him, especially when he tried to defend Mussolini. He was too ignorant to really know what had gone on. He remembered only that the Germans had stolen his accordion and that the mothers of the village always scurried to hide their young daughters when the Germans came. But my father was intrigued by Mussolini, impressed by him.

"*U sap tu che quill accis u jenere. Imagin che curagg a fa ques.* (He killed his own son-in law, you know. Imagine what it takes to do that)," he'd say, as if this was a sign of great courage. But I had no patience for his political ramblings.

His other great obsession was Jesus Christ. I was a little more versed on this topic, but still, I didn't have what he was looking for, some kind of confirmation for his opinions, something to appease his gnawing sense of ignorance.

"Maybe Jesus was just some powerful person in his village, you know, someone people looked up to? Then everyone just decided to make him the son of God, because that's what they wanted, that's what they needed? Ever think of that," he would say, in his crass dialect.

I always looked at him blankly at those times, when he seemed to forget that I was the daughter and he was my father, with his sad eyes and a look from some faraway past, unknown to me, then.

But Micola, she always loved our father, with his shambling beauty and pain. When he sang she always cried. She was under his spell. All I saw was his ignorance and his need to control us. I did not want to understand him or to love him. I just wanted to get away from the whole dark, peasant thing, the constant misery and despair. I just wanted to get free. Micola just wanted to sing.

Sometimes she would say that it was the sea that made her want to sing. It moved her with its great depth, "a depth that only singing could reach," she would say. Only now can I see the strange foreshadowing, because then she had never been to Italy and had never been to the sea.

I was sitting at the kitchen table, my zia Rosa was making breakfast for us. Ottavio was there. We were still living with them at the time on Old Orchard Street. My mother had gotten a job at a textile factory and my father was lugging crates for Canada Dry. Zia Rosa was buttering our toast, burnt toast for Ottavio. He always wanted it that way. That's when it escaped from her, one of those lamenting, Neapolitan songs our father sometimes sang. Until then we hardly knew Micola had a voice, because she was so quiet.

I was always wanting to impress Ottavio, make him like me. But he was brash and tough, always trying to get me to do bad stuff, like help him gather cigarette butts from the street so he could smoke them, or cross the train tracks to go to school so we could avoid going through the dank, pissy, Melrose tunnel. I was watching him, waiting for my toast, when the song came through Micola like a lament or a plea. Ottavio burst out laughing. But my aunt stopped what she was doing to look up and listen.

"Micola, *ma chi si?* (Who are you?)" she said with utter amazement and with a look of pleasure that made Micola somewhat nervous. She always felt uncomfortable with people's gaze. She never liked being looked at. It made her want to disappear, she'd say. But she kept singing until Ottavio stopped her by wrestling me to the ground and Zia had to split us up. That was Ottavio. Even at 13 he had no time for pleasure or beauty, just battle.

My father was overjoyed by Micola's sudden burst into song. After a brief stint at Canada Dry he started to work in construction. This was much more demanding. He came home dirty and exhausted, his thick black hair dishevelled, covered in concrete dust. He would wash up, get himself a glass of his homemade wine and play his accordion.

"Micola, *viene qua, candamo un po insiemme*," he'd say. She'd rush over, full of excitement. Before she started singing he rarely talked to her, or to any of us, really. Preoccupied with other things, more important things, like work and money. Always money, money, money, a constant preoccupation, because there was so little of it at the time.

In the summers, after dinner, we sat on the large balcony of our Melrose apartment and my father would teach Micola the latest songs by Italian pop singers, like Gianni Morandi, Mina, Pepino di Capri. He played the accordion and she sang. It was so easy, the easiest thing she'd ever done, she said, singing with my father, the songs of his time, his country, his heart. She couldn't believe her luck. It seemed to make everything else disappear. All the things that were difficult and hard, the violence and the ignorance, the poverty and social isolation, all the things that later tore us apart. She pushed them all away with singing. For Micola singing cleared the dark, chased away the family demons, for a while.

That's just the way things were then, at least in our clan. The men would try to drink away their frustrations and insecurities and then wreak havoc on the women and children. My father was no different. His arguments with my mother often flared up into violent outbursts. When she was very young, Micola would hide in her room, stay in her closet until it subsided, then pretend it hadn't happened, stay away from my mother for a while, so she wouldn't see her bruised and bloodied face. Maybe she stayed away from me too, so I wouldn't have to see how upset she really was. I went to school, buried myself in my books, played music on my portable record player in my room, and Micola sang herself to sleep. Singing became her medicine.

But as soon as I was old enough, I fought back. The first time was when I was 12 years old and Micola was 10. She was sitting at the kitchen table doing her homework. I was on the phone talking to a friend, when we heard the crashing of broken dishes and screaming. I ran to the kitchen to see my father chasing my mother with a plate in hand to throw at her. Micola was immobilized when I stormed in and grabbed the plate from him. "You fucking bastard," I screamed, and shoved him away from my mother. He took a swipe at me and missed, then tried to kick me, but hit the wall instead. I ran over to my friend, Titiana, who lived just down the street. Micola sat in her dark closet, singing quietly to herself. Things calmed down. The next day, it was like nothing happened, except that my father limped for about a week. No one said anything about it. If anyone asked he said he had twisted his ankle at work.

We were always afraid, always living under the threat of his temper and outbursts. Micola thought I was fearless because I stood up to him. But that didn't mean I wasn't afraid. My anger was just greater than my fear. I had to fight him off. I couldn't allow it, not for myself, and fatefully, not for others. That's how I learned to act in the face of terror.

Micola was more delicate, a remote creature from some other world, always looking for the sidelines. Yet, as she grew older, she had a strange way of drawing attention to herself, even though it was the last thing she wanted. We all knew this, so at school we never left her alone, had our eyes on her, always drawing a kind of invisible circle around her beyond which others were not allowed to cross, except for Ottavio and Ricardo and later, of course, Paolo. We banded around her like bodyguards, as if foreseeing a future, as if trying to forestall an inevitable fate.

In her teens, Micola's love for singing became her own, not just a way to be close to our father. Her repertoire expanded to include songs by Joni Mitchell and Judy Collins, Leonard Cohen, Nick Drake. She loved Nick Drake. She was becoming less interested in the songs of the world my father left behind, and more interested in her own world, the world of the sixties and seventies, counterculture and the folk revival. She taught herself to play the piano left behind by the previous tenants. It was as if her fingers had been made for it, her body finding its home. She played and sang, usually during the day, on lunch hours and after school, when our father was still at work. Then she seemed happy, a stolen happiness, tinged with a sense of imminent danger, because she knew our father would not approve.

Though it was the sixties when we moved to the Melrose apartment, Micola and I did not have much involvement with the spirit of the time, except through music, which we listened to it with our transistor radios, mostly in our rooms, and on our front porch, where we also played our records on my small, blue, portable record player. We spent a good deal of time on that porch, listening to music and dreaming of escape. At least I was dreaming of escape, and Micola mostly listened to my plans, my strategies.

In Grade Ten, Tom Brooks, who sat next to Micola in English class, asked her to the school dance. She was boy shy, but I knew she liked Tom Brooks. He had introduced her to the music of Joni Mitchell. He knew a lot about pop music and had seen many of the musicians she loved in concert. She wanted to go so badly. I pleaded and pleaded with my father to let her go, but he refused. No reason, just because people would think we were whores, if they found out about it. That's what it was to be a whore in our clan, simply to be in the company of the opposite sex without parental supervision. If ever I was late coming home from school: "*Dove sei state, putane*? (Where have you been, you slut?)" If some guy called me on the phone and my father happened to answer. "*Chi ca date u numero, putane*? (Who gave him the number, you whore?)"

Somehow he seemed to restrain his verbal abuse when it came to Micola. She was the Madonna, I was the whore. Though by then I'd hardened myself against him, didn't care what he said. I was already in CEGEP, but I went to the dance anyway, crawled out my bedroom window, after my father had fallen asleep, while watching television. Micola stayed home, dejected and afraid, afraid for me.

Our teenage years were the worst, with the old-world values of our peasant household colliding with flower power and free love. Luckily, we were allowed to go over to Zio Matteo's house after school, where cousins, Ottavio and Ricardo were always plotting revolution in the basement. The Vietnam War, the Chinese Cultural Revolution, Quebec nationalism, the FLQ, and then of course, the 1970 October crisis, which had us all in a panic, especially Ottavio. He had attended some demonstration supporting the FLQ, so when the War Measures Act was declared, he was terrified.

"Stay home," he kept saying. "Don't go anywhere. They can arrest you for anything without a warrant."

"Come on, Ottavio, what have we done that could ever get us arrested," I once said in disbelief. "We're not even allowed go a movie on a Sunday afternoon. They're going to have to come to our house and get us."

"This is no joke, Francesca," he shouted. "Don't you get it? They can come to your house and get you. I have two friends that have already been detained and interrogated. They can arrest you just because you know me, and because I know them."

83

I guess it was true, I didn't really get it. I knew that the French were angry that the English had all the power, but I didn't know much more. Our parents were illiterate. There was no reading of newspapers at our house. We never talked about anything. It was still stories about Mussolini, as if we were still living in 1944. The fact that we were caught in the middle of a crisis between the French and the English seemed irrelevant to our parents. And our mother thought the world was always a dangerous place, anyhow, even when the military was not out roaming the streets, looking for members of the FLQ and its sympathizers.

Everything was in bits and pieces. The kidnapping of politicians, the reasons why, Ottavio's involvement, his friends being arrested. It was alarming. I just didn't know how to put it all together. Yet still, somehow, I thought it would all work out. I had no reasons for my optimism and had no idea what was really going on.

But then, when Pierre Laporte's body was found murdered in the trunk of Paul Rose's car, I started paying attention. Serious attention. The shock of it all was a political awakening for me. After that, those meetings at my cousins' house stopped being just a social thing. I was determined to educate myself. I was tired of always feeling so ignorant.

The meetings continued, for years, long after the October Crisis ended. Often Ottavio invited friends from various leftist organizations he was involved with. Sometimes they would give talks or presentations on workers' rights, class consciousness, and the insidious draw of consumerism. But other times, though not often, it was just the four of us, speaking in our crass village dialect, laughing and mocking our southern Italian roots.

By that time I was in university, and Ottavio had started to treat me like a kind of protégé. He was always giving me books he thought I should read, like *White Niggers of America,* so I could understand the Quebec situation better. And then, what would become formative for me, *The Communist Manifesto* and *The Wretched of the Earth* by Frantz Fanon. That's how I came to understand something really important, that we weren't inferior, we were just oppressed. That we belonged to an important class of people, one with a historical mission. That changed everything for me. Because though I had always tried hard to repress it, I was convinced that we were inferior and that I, more specifically, was also stupid and ugly. But the *Communist Manifesto* changed that. Yes, there it was, the truth I had been looking for, that history was the history of class struggle. It seemed so obvious, so clear, the clarity of youth, without any of the ambiguity that experience inevitably brings. What did ugliness matter in the face of class struggle?

Micola was always less vocal than I was at those basement gatherings. She couldn't muster up any political fervour. It's not that she didn't care about what was happening in the world. I think it just felt very far away from her, far from the day-to-day problems of her own life.

"Forget about her, she's got her head in the clouds," Ottavio would say about Micola, but not in a mean way, just to explain the difference between us.

Then one day, Ricardo brought his new friend, Paolo, to our rec room political salon. Peter was there too that day, Peter Cormier, a guy Ottavio had met at a demonstration he had been involved in, at Sir George Williams University. Something that turned violent, computers being throw out the ninth-floor windows, people arrested and detained. This was even before the October Crisis. But Ottavio had managed to get away then, too. He seemed to have a knack for that.

When Ricardo walked into the rec room, we all went silent.

Then Ricardo said, "Hey, this is Paolo, he's cool."

"Ya, I bet he is," Ottavio said, immediately suspicious. But Paolo was, and always would be, indifferent to Ottavio's arrogance, sweeping into our motley crew of would-be revolutionaries and repressed artists like an intellectual hurricane.

No matter what the discussion, politics, philosophy, music, film, Paolo always knew more than we did. And he spoke with such eloquence that he struck us dumb. Always completely casual, too, without a tinge of condescension. I couldn't believe that someone who lived in Westmount could be so earthy, so easy to be around. Neighbouring Westmount was where the rich lived. That's where the FLQ had planted a lot of their bombs. That's all I knew about it. Then, like an Adonis coming down from some Olympic mountain, he descended into our midst.

Ottavio reacted with such vehemence to Paolo's presence that it created a rift between him and his brother, Ricardo.

"Stop bringing that bourgeois asshole to our meetings," Ottavio shouted, one afternoon when Paolo happened not to come.

"Well, he's hardly an asshole and you bloody well know it. You're just fucking jealous, aren't you? You can't keep up with him. That's your problem."

"Keep up with what? You think I want to speak like that! What does he know about the workers' struggle. You think that pretty language of his will help our cause. It's useless, bourgeois indulgence. I thought you knew better than that, Ricardo."

But Ricardo was already under Paolo's spell, in ways we had no knowledge of at the time. They became inseparable, and Ottavio's rants against Paolo went in one ear and out the other.

"He's an infiltrator, Ricardo, can't you see? It's so obvious, why are you so blind?" he said on another occasion.

"That's ridiculous. You're the one that's blind. He's on our side, he's educated. He knows things we don't know. He can help us with analysis."

"Analyzing what? You have no idea what you're talking about! Have you heard what he says about the separatists?"

"Well, he's got a point, though, doesn't he? Maybe it's the only way the French will get their due. They are the majority in this province, after all. Why should the English have all the power?"

"Yes, but do they need to be a separate country for that?"

"Maybe they do. Maybe they do."

It was the fall of 1975. The Parti Québécois was mobilizing towards its first victory, and everyone was anxious. Yet we had in our midst an Anglo guy from Westmount who was a passionate defender of the separatists. Ottavio didn't know what to make of that. He was already confused about the whole French/English thing. He had been somewhat supportive of the FLQ, before the kidnappings and the murder of Laporte, but later, I understood it was more because of their leftist political leanings than their plan for separation. He couldn't really see how a separate Quebec could be good for us working-class Italians. He was all about workers uniting, not separating.

Paolo's views on the separatists just made Ottavio more suspicious. Though, in the end, I think Ricardo was right. Before Paolo showed up, Ottavio was the kingpin, the leader of our cell. He felt threatened by Paolo's intellectual virtuosity. He wasn't used to being challenged that way, and certainly not by an Anglo guy from Westmount. He was furious. But he was forced to put up with Paolo, because it was clear from the start Ricardo was not going to give him up.

Micola and I were happy for that, at first. Paolo seemed to walk into our lives like a charm, with an elegance that was the antithesis of our crude peasant ways. Even physically, he towered over us with his height and beauty, full of a confidence that was unimaginable to me. I understood why Ottavio was having difficulty with him, because I too, though thrilled at the sight of him, was always pushed to an extreme of self-contempt.

I was never one to put much emphasis on appearance. But whenever I saw him, I couldn't help hating myself, wishing I was somebody else, somebody else entirely, wishing I'd been born into a different world. Yet, at the same time, I wanted to be right there, wherever he was, like a drug I had to have, a drug that then left me full of despair and longing for something that was clearly out of my reach.

Once, we went to Chalet Bar-B-Q after school instead of Ottavio's basement. It was Ricardo's birthday. We wanted to do something festive. Of course Paolo came. He was all decked out in a white shirt and black bell-bottoms, and those delicate, turquoise beads he always wore around his neck. My heart skipped a beat when he sat right next to me and put a welcoming arm around my shoulders. Because we were sitting so close, I could hardly say anything the whole time we were there, even though the conversation was lighter than usual. Until the end, that is. Just before we were leaving, somehow, the subject of the oil embargo came up. And Ottavio started talking about the Yom Kippur War, which I didn't know anything about. There were lots of things I didn't know anything about.

"What's the Yom Kippur War?" I heard myself say. No one responded, at first. Enough silence to drown myself in my feeling of stupidity. Why did I have to ask? Wasn't I smart enough to at least hide my ignorance?

"Don't feel bad, Francesca. Not everyone follows politics the way Ottavio does. Maybe, it's not for you."

But it was for me. I wanted to know what was going on in the world. It's just that there was too much to know, too much to piece together. Then, as if hearing my thoughts, Paolo said:

"The Yom Kippur War was an Arab/Israeli conflict which resulted in an oil embargo affecting a number of European allies, including the U.S. and Canada. It was retaliation for the military support of Israel."

"Oh, OK," I said. "And thanks."

"No problem, Francesca." He put his arm around me again and drew me closer. I didn't want him to let go of me, but he did.

"Francesca, I understand your situation more than you think."

I wasn't sure what situation he was referring to. But still, my heart skipped again.

At those times, his kindness and consideration made me think that maybe he liked me. Then I would notice that it was just the way he was with everyone. Deflation. I wanted his kindness and consideration all to myself. I thought that it could prove me wrong, that I wasn't really stupid and ugly, that maybe I had a chance to get free, free from the morass of violence and ignorance I had been born into. He filled me with hope and despair, all at the same time.

Politics aside, music became the great unifier. Paolo seemed to have figured that out, pretty fast, the solution to the friction he was causing, which clearly he was aware of.

The first time it was tickets to see Sean Phillips. We all liked him but Micola was ecstatic. Then he hit the jackpot when he got us free tickets to the Rolling Thunder Revue at The Forum. Ottavio and I were both fanatical Dylan fans. We never knew how he got those tickets and we didn't care. We were thrilled to be going.

But there was the problem of how to get Micola and me out for the night. This was an ongoing issue with our parents, even though we were in our early twenties and attending the west end university, then known as Loyola College. Getting us to a party or a concert was a major enterprise. But I was always determined to make it happen. Micola, on the other hand, was resigned to her solitude, even happy with it, most of the time. But she wasn't going to miss a Dylan concert.

At the time of the Rolling Thunder Revue I had a ready alibi. I was working at a youth hostel on campus and often worked evening shifts, which meant I had to be out at night. My father wouldn't stop me from going to work, and he certainly couldn't call me a whore for that.

"*Pa*, I can't make dinner on Friday. I have to work."

He was lying on the couch in our rec room watching the *Dean Martin Show*. He loved those Italian, American crooners. I'm sure that in some secret part of him he thought he could have that kind of fame and fortune. If they could do it, why not him?

"*Pa*, can you hear me?"

"*T send, t send.* (I hear you, I hear you). *Dice a Micola ch fa iese.* (Micola will do it.)"

I didn't want to complicate things by saying Micola was going out too. So that time, I left it for her to deal with.

She was planning to speak to our sympathetic neighbour, Juanita, who often hired us to babysit. Juanita would be Micola's alibi, saying that she had been asked to babysit. That's how we both got out on the night of the Rolling Thunder Revue. That's how we got to see Dylan and Joni and Joan Baez.

But the guilt would always wreck us, especially Micola. It was like we were escapees from a prison, terrified of being caught. I could never really enjoy anything, in the end. And on that particular night, as I watched that skinny angel with his painted face and the incomparable Joan Baez sing songs that cracked open my heart, I started to feel something else inside of me, a dark thing growing. The small figures in the distance suddenly became illusive, and coming close was an approaching dread, an inexplicable dread. It had something to do with Micola and music. I could see how happy she was that night, as if the music was joining her to the world, a world which she normally felt indifferent to, didn't want to be a part of. That was the difference between Micola and me. She was always trying to escape from the world. I was trying to escape into it.

But in her teens she grew into a dark-haired, green-eyed beauty, and could no longer stay invisible. And on that night, I saw something else, something different, a life she wished she could live.

Though the growing dread was in her too, I could feel it. Side by side, the desiring heart and the shattering thing. She walked as silently as she could, afraid to disturb the balance that kept them apart. She wanted to keep them apart.

Before Paolo came into our midst Micola sang only with my father, or secretly, on her own, at the piano in the entrance alcove of our apartment. I knew she loved singing, but didn't encourage her. Because I saw that it was an impossible thing, that my father would never allow it. Though he might have imagined fame and fortune for himself, such a life for a woman could never be anything but scandalous, in our clan.

One day, much to Ottavio's consternation, Paolo showed up at our political salon with his guitar.

"Hey, why don't we skip the politics for today and have some fun?"

It was after the concert. He must have noticed something too, since he'd never brought a musical instrument before. He started playing and singing "Four Strong Winds". Micola hesitated for a while, then started to softly sing along. Peter Cormier was there that day too, and so was Jack Stein, a Montreal Maoist, who talked incessantly and never listened, always spouting his Mao-think like an automaton. But Ottavio liked him, so there he was, the first time my sister ever sang for anyone outside our family.

When Paolo heard Micola's voice he urged her to choose another song that she might want to sing and he would play it. She looked conflicted and afraid, I remember, glancing over at me and Ottavio, as if to get approval. But we were still a little disoriented, that Paolo would just show up with that guitar and sabotage our political meetings with song.

Then she did it, she broke out singing Joni Mitchell's "Woman of Heart and Mind", a capella at first, and then Paolo caught up with her with the guitar.

Her beauty, suddenly, a thing of radiance, none of us could deny.

"You've got amazing talent," Paolo said afterwards.

"Really?" she said.

"Are you kidding me? Hasn't anyone ever told you that?"

"Not really. Well, my father loves my singing," she said. "He's a singer too. Just family weddings and things. Nothing professional."

"Well, you could be a professional, no doubt about that," Paolo said, with his usual confidence.

Micola was thrilled to hear that. No one had ever said anything like that to her. We remained silent as Paolo went on and on about her talent. Micola kept glancing over at us. I could see her wanting us to say what we all knew. "Yes, yes, it is true, you have a special gift. You have to use it. You have no choice."

Ottavio repeated his usual refrain. "Yeah well, she also has a special talent for keeping her head in the clouds. So don't make it worse with your pipe dreams."

"It can't happen," I said. "So leave it alone."

I knew we were right not to let Micola know about her beauty and her talent, because it would only lead to trouble, trouble of the sort she wouldn't be able to handle, because she would never be able to defy our father. Paolo kept pressing the issue. To an outsider, it would have seemed incomprehensible not to encourage her gift. So Paolo did, and Micola eventually heard him. Her passion rose up briefly, against the Forbidding, against a peasant mentality that felt it had to shackle and contain a woman's beauty and talent, a mentality that would never allow its free expression, except for the purposes of a marital match.

But beauty has its own magical powers which sometimes cannot be stopped. I understood that so clearly, one evening, when Ricardo brought Paolo to those yearly dances celebrating the patron saint of Volturino, which our parents always dragged us to.

They always made us go, hoping that some interested *paesano* might pick one of us out and make the waited marriage proposal. My general brashness and constant tone of indignation towards Italian machismo could hardly have been alluring. But Micola was another story. People flocked around her as she cringed and imagined her escape. She didn't seem at all interested in relating to people. Music was the only thing that interested her.

At the dance I was wearing my navy blue bell-bottom pantsuit and a gold chain belt Micola had given me for my 21st birthday. My hair was cropped short, boyish and hard-edged. An incongruous sight, I thought myself to be, a female impersonator of some sort, with that gentle sway of crepe fabric against my skin, low-cut neckline and dangly earrings. It was not an ostentatious outfit. Except for the low neckline, it was not even particularly feminine. Yet I felt like an impostor, on those occasions when I would much rather not have been there, indignant at having to adorn myself, just for show, just for appearances, so others wouldn't talk, wouldn't get the wrong idea about the Benvenuto daughters.

I saw Paolo instantly from across the hall, shy, though strident and elegant. Ricardo had a strange look in his eyes, as if maybe he knew something he wasn't saying. Paolo greeted my parents first, and then he came over to Micola and me. I wanted to laugh or cry, not sure which.

"Francesca, you know Paolo. I dragged him here. I knew you'd need some support," Ricardo said, rather sardonically, and then he chuckled.

Paolo looked at me directly, gently, and then, with the most remarkable confidence I'd ever encountered, and with the same ease as he might have remarked on my hair or my shoes, he said it, almost in a whisper.

"Saddest eyes I've ever seen."

I turned away, abruptly, feeling violated and confused. He smiled and touched me lightly on the shoulder as if he'd instantly realized the intrusiveness and liberty of his remark.

I was always jealous of the attention Paolo paid Micola, especially since that day he had gotten her to sing. I felt I had nothing to offer, nothing that could make me interesting to him. Then that comment, it just seemed to feed into that feeling of hopelessness. I was a sad hopeless case.

The first song they played that night was Mina's "La Stanza e un Cielo." It still reminds me of Paolo, that pained moment, when he saw something I didn't even know was there. It also reminds me of his eyes, not sad, but wide, open and soft, a clear blue sky of warmth. And I feel now, at the thought of him, as I did then, and always would, a peculiar mixture of joy and dread. The dread increased that night as he moved to greet Micola. I saw suddenly how her long, black curls framed a beauty which I hated. Glancing at her sleek, red, satin dress, showing her voluptuous breasts, her shy smile and delicate elegance, I could hardly believe she was my sister. I thought of Helen of Troy and of how beauty had a power that could be dangerous and destructive, how it could take hold of people in a way that was beyond their control, how it could devastate, betray, tear things apart, create wars. In that moment I hated Micola. The power of her beauty tormented me, even though I couldn't really blame her for it. It was nothing she'd done to call attention to herself that way. She was in fact not very comfortable with her beauty, always awkward with it.

But in spite of their medieval attitudes about girls and women, our parents seemed to like to flaunt Micola's beauty, use it like a treasure to mitigate their sense of poverty and ignorance. It was as if she was expected to adorn herself in order to prove their worth, but in the same way as they might display some piece of furniture, like the plastic-covered couches in their unused "living" rooms, symbol of their new-found status. But beneath the shiny façade of their new "American" life, there always lurked a breaking force, a psychic wound which never seemed to heal, festering its constant expectation of catastrophe. Like a dark vortex, the past, with its gruelling labour and constant struggle for survival, sucked up everything in its wake. But then there was Micola. As miserable as we are, they must have thought, we can still produce beauty.

Though I tried hard not to show it, I was always acutely aware of our strangeness. I began to feel it most when I first learned to read. I would go home at night eager to be guided in the mysterious world that was opening up to me and find my parents hesitant. But I persisted, and my father, finally, began to make some effort. "*Jann a qua*, Francesca," he would say, and call me over to sit at the dining room table with him. He would sit by my side and listen to me read, making like he could judge whether I was pronouncing things correctly or not. But he was rarely much help. I always ended up correcting him.

Many years later, I was sitting in a car with my friend, Titiana. We were in our teens. She was driving me home and made some reference to buying some magazines for her father. Suddenly I broke down into an inconsolable wailing. She didn't know what was going on. I suspect she thought I was losing my mind, just like my mother always said I would, because I read too much. There was a woman in her village to whom this had happened, she was fond of telling me.

But Micola did not seem bothered by these strange things about us, like the fact that our parents couldn't read. She remained enamoured with our father and followed him around as an adolescent almost as much as she had when she was a small child, dancing to the rhythms of his operatic outpourings. That is how I can remember that my father must have been happy, once, about our transatlantic crossing, because in those early years he always sang.

Perhaps there was something in Micola's nature which corresponded with my father's. He was never diminished in her eyes, never less than he should have been, despite his shambling ignorance and illiteracy.

Much to my irritation and pleasure, Ricardo seemed to bring Paolo everywhere in those days, even to our extended family dinners. The constant chatter which he could not understand. Stories about their hardships, tales which they now found amusing, which they told for entertainment.

"Do you remember how we all used to sit around the table eating from one small pot of polenta?"

And they would laugh.

"Or the time Lorenzo and I were left at the *campania* alone, and instead of watching over the sheep, we sneaked over to the cat eater's farm and stole a couple of chickens. But Vince, he was the toughest. Once he dared to sell a bushel of olives which belonged to his parents so we could buy some booze. That night he went around saying goodbye to all his friends because he knew he was as good as dead."

These are the stories they found amusing, seemingly removed from the strain of poverty which they told, because though "America" had tied them to the misery of the factory, it had given them an abundance they never dreamed possible. They never stopped marvelling at how different their lives were, different from when they slept with their donkeys and cows, and when eating a meal of stale bread, softened with hot water and olive oil, was a question of survival and not just an expression of some peculiar nostalgia.

Though Paolo seemed delighted to be in our midst, I was utterly embarrassed. I hated Ricardo for bringing him there. I could have killed him, were it not for the thrill, twisted in with the fear, fear that some conversation would break out into a fight, that someone would scream, fart, laugh too loud, eat with their hands or start singing and dancing in the middle of eating. Crude, unrefined, that is what I felt, that everything about us was crude and unrefined.

Ricardo knew this. I thought he was deliberately trying to torture me by bringing Paolo to those family dinners.

* * *

A few months after we had all been to the Rolling Thunder Revue, we were in the rec room. By then Paolo always brought his guitar, which changed the whole experience of our gatherings. There was still politics, but some singing too. Amazingly, though it was obvious that Ottavio did not like the power Paolo had to command things, to make things go his way, he stopped complaining, he let things change, he let things shift. Maybe he knew about Paolo and Ricardo in a way that I did not, at the time.

Micola had just finished singing a version of Joni's "Rainy Night House."

"I read somewhere that 'Rainy Night House' is about Leonard Cohen," Paolo said to Micola. She hadn't known that, and was a bit stunned as she had always felt kind of in love with the person Joni was describing in "Rainy Night House."

"That's my kind of man," she once said to me.

Then I noticed tears streaming down Paolo's face.

"What's going on?" I asked.

"I'm sorry. It's her voice." He ran his fingers through his thick black hair, then wiped his face with some napkins. "Listen, there's a coffee house downtown called the Yellow Door. They have open mike there every Friday night. I really think Micola should go sing there."

For a moment I imagined Micola as a different person, unrestrained by the peasant mores of the world we came from, the person she might have been if she had been born into a world that applauded and encouraged her musical talents. But my reverie was interrupted by Ottavio.

"Back off, Paolo. You don't know what you're getting into."

"What could possibly be the problem?"

"Your ignorance, evidently."

"What are you talking about."

"Look. Her father won't even let her visit Titiana at night. You think he's going to let her sing at a bar?"

That's one of the things I loved about Ottavio. He understood our situation, one difficult to explain to anyone else, who wasn't southern Italian or peasant stock, living in an urban setting, in the age of counter culture and free love. It made no difference that we were in our twenties and could, if we truly wanted, make our own choices. It would mean being completely ostracized and shunned by the *paisani* community, if not killed by our father.

"It's not a bar and she's twenty-two years old. She can do what she wants, can't she?"

"Well, you're obviously not southern Italian."

"What? What does that mean?"

"It's hard to explain."

I was silent for a while. It took incredible effort before I could speak.

"Paolo, he's right. You shouldn't get involved in this. It can't happen."

Then, with a voice from a faraway place, a voice from someone I almost didn't recognize.

"I want to do it. I am going to do it. I'll say that I'm babysitting, like when we went to the concerts. Juanita will help. She understands our situation."

I could see the danger growing, but Micola's passion was too strong to stop.

That's why we went ahead with the plan, resisting what we knew. It was the injustice of it all. It didn't seem fair that a parent should have the power to prevent one's happiness. Somehow I convinced myself that once my father understood how much joy singing brought Micola, he would change, he would let her go, he would let her be free. I convinced myself of this lie in order to mitigate the fear of catastrophe.

In the weeks preceding her debut at the coffee house, Micola started to behave strangely. We usually cooked dinner together, which we had been doing since our early teens. My mother got home at 6 pm from the textile factory and my father would go out drinking with his buddies, often just showing up in time for dinner. I liked spending that time with Micola. I was a serious girl, but she could make me laugh, especially with her imitation of our village dialect, which we both spoke, but in a rough kind of way, all mixed up with Anglo.

"Get off that piano, girl, or we'll never get this pasta and *faciul* ready in time. You know how *sfacchnet* Mom is when she gets home." Sfachhnet is a word impossible to translate, something like beat or broken with exhaustion. "And Dad, *scurdatenn*, forget about it, he's always *ancazatt*, always angry, for some reason or other."

One day we were at Ottavio's after school. When I said, "Come on Micola, we have to get going to start dinner," she shrugged her shoulders and said, "You go, I'll be there shortly." But she never came. She showed up just before my parents did, went up to her room and came down to eat dinner. When I asked about it later, she made like she had an essay to work on and had no time to talk. This was unusual for Micola. I was the defiant one. She was always the one cautioning me to be more careful, tip-toeing around, trying to be as obedient as possible, so as not to provoke our father. Because even if I did something to incur his wrath, she would have to witness it. She would have to bear it. But the prospect of singing in public seemed to unleash in her a hidden strength, like she was mobilizing for war, mobilizing for unmentionable consequences. It made me very uneasy, as if I was suddenly weak, helpless, like she had taken my strength. Or maybe I just let her have it, for a brief period, because I knew she would need it.

* * *

Whenever Paolo and Ottavio argued about politics, it was always a scene. Paolo, ever cool, would try to talk Ottavio down, but it never worked. I knew it wouldn't work, not coming from a privileged kid from Westmount. Ottavio would just fly into a rage. He was never going to take anything Paolo said seriously. After what happened to Salvatore Allende in Chile, there was no going back as far as Ottavio was concerned. The workers and peasants had to arm themselves if they were going to get their social-ist revolution. It was the only way. The capitalist powers would never allow it to happen democratically. That was the lesson of Chile, everyone knew that, Ottavio would say with exasperation.

But no, Paolo always argued, no! That was not the lesson. The lesson was a failure of co-operation, the failure to convince the various factions to support the socialist cause, that more work had to be done to resolve the various forms of dissent. What is the point of replacing one violent dictatorship with another, he would say. Of course, I understood where Paolo were coming from. I had always hated the idea of a dictatorship of the proletariat. How could dictatorship ever be a good thing, I thought, but never said. Because these were semantic subtleties that would never have been tolerated in those political circles, in those days.

For most people, identity is formed from a variety of personal experiences. But for Ottavio, it seems almost to have been only one thing: the loss of his uncle Antonio in a construction accident in the spring of '68. What he was before, and what he might have become after, was erased by its impact, erased by his single-minded will to avenge that tragedy.

I saw it clearly, though I couldn't name it at the time, a subtle change in his body posture. A new brittleness entered it, a more precise swing to his gait, a firmer, less transparent look in his eyes, and a growing intolerance for ambiguity, subtlety or nuance.

I can say these things, now, of course, because I know what those changes led to. I can also see why those qualities would have drawn me to him. They were the opposite of the shabby chaos I knew, the ignorance and illiteracy of our parents, the constant anxiety about money because our father drank it away into oblivion, and then the predictable violence.

Just before Antonio's funeral we had all gathered at Ottavio's place, bringing food, as was the custom. Everyone was shocked by Antonio's sudden death. Zia Yolanda, hysterical with anxiety at how she was going to bring up two boys in their teens and two not yet ten? Only Ottavio seemed composed and without emotion, for the most part, except for one particular occasion. We were eating with my father and Giuseppe San D'Angelo, Ottavio's father. Ottavio had gone with him earlier in the day to buy the coffin, because Zia Yolanda was a mess. There had been an argument about which coffin to buy. We ate for some time in silence. Then Giuseppe remarked that the coffin was plain. No one answered. We continued to eat, barely glancing at each other, in silence, not uncommon to me, since silence was the norm at our house, but the San D'Angelo home had always been full of lively discussion.

After some time Giuseppe looked straight at Ottavio and said, "*Ma p che? Dimm p che!* (Why, tell me why). Antonio deserves better. He was no shepherd, you know."

Despite his humble origins, Antonio San D'Angelo had a pride and confidence one couldn't help but notice, all the more because it was so rare among our village clan. He had made the most of his meagre resources, including his Grade Five education. Had it not been for his dark, stocky, southern physicality, he might have been mistaken for a university-educated northerner. He was articulate and mentally disciplined, speaking a "proper" Florentine Italian as easily as he spoke our village dialect, a self-taught worker who stood out in our mostly illiterate clan.

But what stood out to me most about him was his attitude towards his work. He talked about his work in construction as if it was a labour essential to society. He didn't view himself as some lowly, manual worker. I feel almost certain now that with Uncle Antonio's death, the enclave of villagers from Volturino that had settled in the area of Notre-Dame-de-Grâce had lost the small bit of hope and self-respect which he seemed to inspire in them.

Giuseppe continued with his complaint about the coffin.

"He's my brother. I don't want people to think I'm too cheap to give him a decent burial."

Ottavio took a couple of deep breaths, not looking up at his father, continuing to eat. Suddenly, unexpectedly, he got up, picked up the plate of pasta in front of him and threw it at his father.

"Then you pay for it, you fucking bastard, you pay for the fucking coffin. Zia Yolando has four kids to bring up. Who's going to pay for that? You?"

Ottavio had always been outspoken and direct, but I had never known him to be violent. He didn't possess any of the pretentiousness which seemed to characterize some of the community's newly prosperous members, like the Monacos, who lived across the street from us on Melrose Avenue. Tony Monaco had made it big as a contractor and never stopped bragging about all the property he owned around town. He was always inviting people over to show off his gaudy, baroque furniture and huge cheesy paintings of Volturino and the surrounding landscape. Micola and I always snickered and complained to ourselves at such times. But Ottavio never mocked or showed contempt for Tony Monaco and the like. He always seemed to have an analysis for it, always showed compassion and understanding for the insecurities of the nouveau riche in our community.

"They came from dirt. They had to cross an ocean just so they could feed their kids. Give them a break," he would say, even if this sometimes contradicted his view that American consumerism was a barrier to class consciousness.

I had been present when uncle Antonio had complained about his working conditions to my father, about the scaffold from which he later fell to his death, along with three other co-workers. He came over one evening to have of glass of wine with my father as he often did. I was clearing the dishes and overheard him speaking, Antonio telling my father that he had spoken to his immediate supervisor about the faulty scaffolding. But nothing had been done. To Ottavio it was clear. It was the dispensability of workers, indifference, negligence which had killed his uncle. This is what tore him apart and pushed him irreversibly and fatally into terror.

My own turn into political radicalism would come later. At the time the main source of torment for me was my friendship with Paolo. I was always looking to be alone with him, though it seemed impossible. My father's vigilance was obsessive, so much so that he couldn't even stand my cousin Ricardo's visits, on those Sunday afternoons, when he came looking for someone to talk to, about his confused sexuality.

Among the family clan Ricardo and I recognized early what we had in common, a kind of natural deviance from the strictures of southern Italian gender codes. We gravitated towards each other, even before we knew why. But even this benign attempt at awkward intimacy made my father suspicious. As if, there too, trouble lurked, as we sat around the kitchen table on Sunday afternoons, casually drinking coffee. Little did he know that Ricardo posed no threat at all. His fantasies were already haunted by the love of boys and men.

But Micola did not seem bothered by our father's vigilance. I, on the other hand, was filled with fury at his expectation that every time we stepped out of his sight we were sexual game for the taking. I was indignant that he seemed to exert his power over us, simply because he could. Torment, robbery, stealing, forbidding everything we wanted to do, except for school and work. I could never fully enjoy the simplest of social pleasures without guilt.

When I turned twelve and the bloody fluids came, he even forbade me to visit Titiana, because she had four brothers. Though I had absolutely no interest in her brothers nor they in me, he deemed these masculine presences a sexual threat. Without concern for the importance of that friendship for me, he simply forbade it.

I worked hard to find ways around these social and moral strictures. My father had the habit of resting, sometimes going to sleep, right after dinner. In the summers he would lie on a lawn chair on the front porch. I would wait until I could see for certain that he was asleep, and then, like someone trying to sneak past a sleeping guard dog, I would silently step by him. But always with a fear for my life.

Sometimes he would wake up and ask about my absence. Since both Micola and my mother were always concerned with averting his violent outbursts, they implicated themselves in my sins of disobedience by lying. I was either reading in my room, which I often did, or babysitting for some neighbour. This lying worked, most of the time. But sometimes it didn't, like the time I went around with that patch over my eye for two weeks. I didn't accidentally bang into a locker door. But I couldn't say it, then, not because of the shame and embarrassment of having to admit my father had slapped me around. But because of guilt, a guilt I didn't really understand, like I came from a bad breed or something. I saw my parents' lack of education, their enslavement to tradition, their archaic customs and superstitions as a sign of some kind of biological inferiority. The violence too, it was all part of it, part of being from a bad lot, and that was something I wanted to hide, especially from Paolo.

* * *

The only thing Micola ever really enjoyed was singing. In high school she was chosen once to play the lead in a production of *La Traviata*. She wanted it so badly. But, of course, our father forbade it. I was there when she asked him. I was sitting at the kitchen table reading the last few chapters of *Gone with the Wind*, I looked up in exasperation and disgust. *"Che voi tu? Stai zitto, putane!* (What do you want? Shut up, you whore.)" He grabbed the book from my hands and began tearing it apart. He hated that I read so much, because being illiterate he had no control over my thoughts.

The odd thing was that my father loved Micola's singing. He would brag about it, embarrass her with his profuse attention. Sometimes he would have his drinking buddies over, playing cards. He would drag her out of her bedroom and order her to sing for them. Micola hated this but she always complied. It is as if the beauty and the pleasure which Micola could give was for the family only. If it escaped into the world, it could breed dishonour and disgrace. That is what came with freedom, for women.

This is why I knew that arranging for Micola to sing at the Yellow Door was a bad idea. We all knew that, except for Paolo. But by then Micola's passion had been unleashed and there was no stopping it.

* * *

Besides song, religion was also important to Micola. She was still devout at that time. Myself, I saw no reason for a grand designer. If he existed he would have to be just. But there was nothing just about life as far as I could see. It was our job, as humans, to create justice. Letting Micola sing at the coffee house seemed like a kind of justice to me. So in the end, despite our apprehension, we all got behind it, come what may.

We met at the Chalet Bar-B-Q on Sherbrooke Street, beforehand, then sat for a while in N.D.G. park. It was late July and warm, the trees green and lush, the breeze soft and summery. We stayed calm for Micola's sake, not speaking of the Forbidding, the Danger.

Though the Youth Hostel had closed in mid-July, as far as my parents were concerned, that's where I was, still working. And Juanita, as she had so many times before, lied for us, in order to get Micola out for the evening.

"Oh sweetie, you're going to nail it," Ottavio finally said, in an uncharacteristic show of affection and support.

"Of course she will," Ricardo said. "Whoever doubted that?"

I could think of nothing to say, so I took Micola's hand and squeezed it, almost as if I was the one going out to sing in public for the first time.

We took the 105 bus to Atwater and St. Catherine, just east of Westmount, an area we rarely ventured to, except for when we went to see Dylan at the Forum. We took another bus, to get to the café on Aylmer Street. We saw its famed yellow door and I could tell that Micola was experiencing some kind of disbelief that she was there. I felt the same, excited and afraid, but somehow happy about our defiance, not quite believing we were pulling it off.

The room was dark and smoky, already crowded. Paolo saw us immediately and came running towards us. My heart skipped a beat, as it often did at the initial sight of him. He had saved us seats at a table near the front of the stage.

Micola had asked to be scheduled near the beginning so that her anxiety wouldn't have time to build. Each person had 15 minutes. There were a couple of people before Micola. One was a comedian, another sang a couple of jazz standards.

Then it was Micola's turn. She hesitated for a couple of seconds when her name was called, as if she was still considering whether to turn back. Then she slowly rose from her chair and walked gracefully up to the stage. She looked out at the audience, silently, once again, as if still considering whether she was going to go through with it. She looked at Paolo, sitting at the piano waiting for her to give him the signal.

Then she broke into song, without any introduction, she entered her own world, a world that loved her, a world that saw her beauty and cherished it, where she was free to be herself, a world with no fears or punishments.

"Black, Black, Black, is the colour of my true love' s hair ..."

I had never heard her sing that song, never even heard her practise it. Just as good as Joan Baez's version, I thought. Couldn't believe it was my sister up there. Then she sang "Diamonds and Rust" and Joni's "Rainy Night House," which I suspected she would, as I knew it was a favourite of hers. Her last song was the shocker that had us all stunned. She ended with a song in Italian, something I had never heard before, something she seemed to have written, her prescient ode to the sea, "Vivere al mare."

I had no idea she was actually writing songs, no one did. That was the mystery of Micola, even then. She inhabited worlds, invisible worlds, where things happened which you couldn't see or know. Only she could tread lightly enough to travel there. The song seemed like an expression of time travel to worlds past and future. She blew us all away. For a few moments we were transported to some wild windy place where, still, she stood.

When she was done, everyone stayed silent, as if not wanting to break the trance, as if hoping for more. She too stood motionless for a few moments, trying to come out of her own disbelief at what had just happened, having no idea what to expect, hate or love. But as soon as she started to move off the stage, the applause roared, and I could see her body relax with relief.

But we, her circle of protection, did not get to her in time. As she stepped down the side stairs of the stage, there was Andy Cohen. "Here I am," was the first thing I heard him say, "your black-haired love." Cool, confident, handsome, and with his black, black hair, he swooped in and put his arm around her waist, as if he already knew her, as if he already owned her.

I expected her to be shaking like a leaf as she often did when she was showered with unwanted attention. But she was beaming, still riding high from her performance. Ricardo, Ottavio and I went over and introduced ourselves, Ottavio with authority, as if commanding Andy to take his hands off Micola, which is exactly what he did. I knew it had already happened, something we couldn't stop. There was a sinking feeling on Micola's face when Andy took his arm away from her waist, as if that arm had been holding her up, as if that arm was the only safety she'd ever really known, despite all our past attempts to encircle her.

"Listen, this beautiful young lady here is mighty talented. But I'm sure you already know that," Andy said, once he let Micola out of his grip, though not out of his sight. He stared at her, even though he was talking to us. Then Micola started to shake and shiver, in a way that only I could recognize. Not because she was afraid of Andy, but because she thought we were going to take it away from her, take away the world that had started to open up, take away the *Thing* that had started to happen.

"Yeah, we do know, that's why we're here," Ottavio said.

"Well, she doesn't belong here, that's for sure. She's too good for this hodgepodge."

"Well, what are you doing here then?"

"Looking for people, just like her, who don't know how good they are. My cousin manages the New Penelope coffee house. I come here scouting talent for him sometimes and get to play a few tunes myself with my jazz trio. I am a trumpet player."

"Are you playing tonight?" Micola asked, in an uncharacteristically forward manner.

"Yes, but we're on last. I hope you can stay that long."

"Maybe not," Micola said, more quietly this time.

I agreed that maybe that would be too late for us, and then Paolo showed up.

"Micola, that was exquisite. It couldn't have gone better. That last song, wow! Is that something you wrote yourself?"

"Yes," she said meekly, her high having left, replaced by familiar trepidation.

"Listen," Andy said to Paolo. "Don't you think she'd be great for The New Penelope? I can get her a gig, maybe a weekly one."

Micola lit up, again. The New Penelope was a holy place for her, where Leonard Cohen and Joni Mitchell also played. Was it possible that she was being included among them by this alluring dark stranger? Disbelief, delight and fear, all at once. I could see it in her eyes as she struggled to contain events that were cracking an old self and calling for a new one.

"Well, I'm with you on that," Paolo said, "but it wasn't exactly easy getting her here, so good luck with that idea."

No one knew what we were contending with at home.

"Not right now. Let her adjust a bit to performing. This is her first time."

"Are you her manager or something?"

"I'm her cousin, and I know her better than you do," Ottavio said, a bit indignant.

Paolo had scurried off to talk to someone else. I looked around but couldn't see him, though I could hear his calming voice in the distance. I seemed to want Paolo there, right then, I didn't know why. Maybe because he knew Andy, and knew enough not to let things get pushed too far.

Then a new, emboldened Micola set the situation straight and we were struck dumb.

"Ottavio, I can do it. I'm ready. I'd be a fool not to take this opportunity." Speaking, I understood then, from another world, a world where she did what she had to do and listened only to divine reason.

Though I knew the risk Micola was taking, I encouraged her attempt at rebellion. It was I who suggested she get a part-time evening job, so she would have a reason to be out at night and then could lie about her shifts. That was one of the few advantages of our parents' illiteracy and scant education. They simply didn't know how things worked outside their small, insular, immigrant world. I had heard a story, once, about a young Italian girl, who finding herself pregnant, had tried to convince her parents that it was due to a science experiment at school.

We knew by then that Paolo had connections, so we spoke to him about our plan and he got Micola an interview at Classics bookstore on St. Catherine street. Micola started working on the days when she didn't have classes, and also some evenings. She was happy, both to have the job, but also to have a plan in place to get her out in the evenings. Andy Cohen had gotten her number from Paolo and was calling her already about singing at the Penelope, but she managed to put him off for a while, telling him she had some personal matters to sort out before she could do it. But he kept calling her anyway, just to talk. She loved the sound of his voice, she told me, sultry and deep, like he could make her do anything. I'd never heard Micola speak like that about anyone. Since she was a teenager boys and men teemed around her while she retreated and went away, leaving them stranded with desire, which she hardly noticed, until Andy Cohen. Then she woke up.

At first, I was jealous, knowing I could never incite such passion in anyone. It seemed unfair, another injustice that plagued me, one that could not be remedied, unfortunately, that some people are just born beautiful and others not. Was it my fault that I was born ugly? No! What could I possibly do about that? Nothing? Resign myself to a life without love? But then there was Paolo, who despite my sense of ugliness, treated me kindly, listened to me, as if I was intelligent and had things to say that he wanted to hear, as if only he saw my worth, a worth I did not even know I had. Then I would think I was wrong, that I was reading him wrong, because though he seemed to have affection for me, it never amounted to anything.

But Micola was another story, embroiled in a passion that completely overtook her, as if she had fallen in love with Andy, after one meeting. There was no turning back, her will was gone.

After her debut at the Yellow Door, Paolo and Micola hijacked our after-school political salons in order to practice for the gig at the Penelope. Ottavio became increasingly disgruntled. But he was outnumbered, because it was obvious, we all loved Paolo. Despite his agitation at how Paolo had completely overturned the intellectual tenor of our former gatherings, he seemed to understand what was happening, the defiance, the erotic force between Micola and Andy. He was not immune to Micola's beauty and talent. He could have stopped it, but he didn't, he let it unfold.

Micola's first night at the Penelope was a formidable success. She looked stunning, wearing a dark green shift she had made herself, bangles on her wrist, her hair loose and wild, framing those sensuous, swarthy features of hers, like a windswept bush. She did a whole set with Andy playing the piano, which I am assuming Paolo arranged. Or maybe they had practiced together. She had stopped telling me things by then. I think she needed to lie to me as well, in order to help her keep her secret life away from my parents. She was working a lot at the bookstore and that had been the plan, hadn't it? My plan, in fact.

She played "Made to Love Magic" by Nick Drake and Violeta Parra's "Gracias a la Vida," a song which, surprisingly, Ottavio loved. At the end, again, she added a few songs in Italian, which she'd obviously written, since I didn't recognize them.

I was speechless at how perfect they seemed to be together on stage. This was only the second time I had seen Andy. He was clearly not just a jazz trumpeter, but a master musician in general. I don't know how often they had practiced, but they seemed like twins, dark sides of each other, wild beauties, joined at the hip, hypnotizing with their erotic trance of song.

When they stood up and looked at each other in the end, I could see them leaving for another planet, a planet of their own. They got a standing ovation, but were oblivious to the fact. They stumbled off stage, as if drunk. When we walked over they were locked in passionate kissing, barely stopped to let us congratulate them.

We had a few drinks, Ricardo, Ottavio and I. Paolo had disappeared, I can't remember where he was. It was past 11 and we really needed to leave. The staying late for work story was not going to be feasible for much longer. We went looking for them again and at first we couldn't find them. Ottavio looked in the back alley. There they were, Micola pinned against a garage door, her shift pulled up over her waist, Andy all over her. We literally had to tear them apart. Micola said she wasn't coming.

"Are you fucking crazy?" I said. "You've lost your fucking mind."

I never lost my cool with Micola. There had never been any reason to.

"Your sister's right," Ottavio said. "Get yourself in order, we're leaving."

She kissed Andy one more time, then came with us.

Ottavio had his father's car that night. We sat in the back seat in silence. Micola was trembling, as if she was some young tree bracing for a hurricane. It was late, later than usual, but I'm sure that is not why she was trembling. I put my hand on her knee hoping to calm her down.

"You were fantastic tonight," I said.

She nodded, but said nothing.

"Don't worry," I said. "I'll say I came to pick you up at the bookstore, because you had to work later than usual. They have no idea what time bookstores close."

Ottavio piped in, "Look, Micola, you don't know anything about this guy, except that he's a good musician. You're putting a lot on the line here. Be careful."

Then Ricardo: "Stop it, all of you. Just let her enjoy her success, would you, instead of filling her with fear."

Still nothing from Micola.

We were approaching Decarie and Sherbrooke Street when she said, "Let me be. I'll work it out."

I said, "Listen, Ottavio, maybe you should let us off at the corner of Melrose. It'll look suspicious if we show up with you and Ricardo."

As we walked down Melrose Avenue towards the house, I had visions of my father on the front porch waiting to hit us. Then I saw the full moon, large and luminous, facing straight at us as we hurried down the street. The moon had a calming effect, putting everything in perspective. Such puny fears in the face of the infinite cosmos. I took Micola's hand and we ran the last stretch.

There was my mother, not my father, waiting on the front porch in her nightgown, her arms flailing about.

"You girls are so fucking lucky that your father fell asleep!" Then in her crass dialect, accused us of being devils, or deviled up, taken over by devils, a phrase difficult to translate. Something like "You're the ones behaving like devils and I will have to pay." She was right about that. Her fear was for herself, if we fraternized with the devil and behaved like whores and sluts.

She shoved us inside with force, then pushed us into our rooms. We felt safe, we had escaped another round of violent dramatics.

Micola became so paralyzed with fear she stopped talking to me, as if lending any reality to what she was doing would put her at greater risk. She was right. She started pretending that she was avoiding me because she was exhausted from working so late.

One night I made her talk to me.

"Look, Micola, you're going to need my help. Let me know what's going on."

"What's going on? What's going on? Can't I have some privacy?" she yelled, then burst into tears.

"Look, you can't do this on your own. It's too dangerous. Dad will kill you if he finds out."

"No he won't. He'll kill you. You know him, he'll blame you."

"Oh, so now you're protecting me."

"I don't know what I'm doing. I just know that I've never felt this way, ever. Andy is like home, like the home I never had. Here, this is a madhouse. I never realized it, till the safety I felt with Andy. That's when I knew I've been living in a state of terror, all my life."

"OK, I get it, but is this going to be possible in our world? Will he marry you?"

"I don't know about that. All I know is that I feel like I'm suffocating when I'm not with him. And having sex is like a mystical experience."

"You're having sex! Already!"

"Aren't you the one that's always promoting free love?"

"I know. I know. I just didn't think you would do it so soon."

One night she came home and when she took off her coat I saw that her blouse was torn at the shoulder and she seemed to have dirt all over her.

"What the fuck happened? What did he do? Did he rape you?"

"Of course not! You know, passion can get violent sometimes."

"No, I don't know that. What is going on, Micola?'

"Nothing, we just went for a walk on the mountain and then we did it. He wanted to have sex, then and there."

"And did you?"

"I always do, I do. Stop trying to convince me otherwise."

"Well tell me, Micola, can he breathe OK, when he's not with you?"

"What are you implying?" She burst out crying.

I saw that her lip was bleeding and that she had scratches all over her shoulder where the shirt was torn.

I decided to talk to Ottavio and he thought we should talk to Paolo about Andy Cohen. As far as Paolo knew Andy was a good guy, a bit of a womanizer, maybe. But he'd never heard anything untoward. They'd gone to the same high school, Westmount High, though they hung with different crowds. Paolo didn't know him very well. His reputation was based mostly on his music. Everybody thought of him as some musical wizard.

Somehow I wasn't convinced, nor was Ottavio. Reading newspapers, houses full of books, money to buy anything you wanted, that's a different breed of people, I thought. What's right and good for them is not the same in our world. We were still contending with a medieval mentality. Ottavio just said, "You can't trust bourgeois values," and left it at that.

Those were difficult times for me and it would get a lot worse. I felt abandoned and alone, like I'd lost my only real ally. Micola and I had a particular dynamic that worked well for both of us. I was the rebel, the rationalizer, the plotter, she was my soul, my heart. Her sensitivity kept me in check. Without her, I was more like Ottavio, detached, angry, maybe even ruthless and uncaring. I would have left the madhouse, as she called it, had it not been for her. It was she who could not bear to hurt our parents, shame them in the eyes of the *paisani,* so I stayed. But then, Micola was leaving, and I was left behind, disoriented, worried and anxious, without a plan. Nothing made much sense without her, as if in defending her all those years, I had been defending myself.

The bookstore job worked for a while. Making money was something our parents would never object to. But my mother started to get suspicious, maybe because Micola had become so jumpy at home, especially every time the phone rang. She would leap up and run to pick up. Luckily, my father spent much of his time in the basement and our bedrooms were upstairs. But it did not escape my mother's traumatized nerves. I would see her watching and shaking her head. I knew she would never say anything to my father, because she did not want hell to break loose.

It took several months before I realized that Micola wasn't working at the bookstore anymore, that she was performing at the New Penelope, and Andy was giving her money, so it would seem like she was still working.

"Now you really are a whore," I shouted. She was so distraught. I immediately regretted saying such a thing and apologized. I realized that I was not angry because of what she was doing, but because she was living her life without me.

"Stop being angry, Francesca. Here, come listen to this. It's amazing," she said, wanting to appease things between us as much as I did. She took a cassette tape out of her bag and put it on our ghetto blaster. It was Italian, but not like any of the schmaltzy pop stuff my father would always play and sing. It was poetic, sombre, deeply moving, almost like an Italian Leonard Cohen.

"Who is that?"

"It's Fabrizio de Andre. Andy gave it to me. See what I mean, he even knows Italian music."

That was impressive. I had to also admit that Andy Cohen was pretty handsome. I could see why Micola had become besotted by her black-haired lover. After that all I could hear coming from Micola's room was Fabrizio de Andre. Years later, I thought that it must have been Fabrizio de Andre that she really fell in love with, and that she had somehow projected him onto Andy.

I lightened up a bit after that. If Andy had given her such a tape, he must have real feelings for Micola, I thought.

Ottavio and I went to see Micola perform at the Penny, again. That was the best thing we thought we could do, just stick around, let things unfold, keep watch. Though Ottavio was distracted that night by the Parti Québécois victory. He wasn't happy about that. He thought it was a distraction. He hated nationalism of any sort, couldn't see how it could ever come to good for the workers' cause. I was confused, I didn't know what to think about it.

One summer I had worked at my mother's textile factory and it was a hellhole. It was a deciding factor in my fight to persuade my parents to let me go to university. But there was no class consciousness in that crop of workers. They laboured, plainly, for the money, so they could help support their families. They had no interest in changing the world. They didn't care that they were exploited or alienated from their labour. They were not even unionized. They didn't want a union. Someone had tried and failed to get the majority support. I understood the point Ottavio always made about North America. Consumerism had taken hold, workers wanted to own their own homes, they wanted comforts, they wanted fridges and televisions, they wanted to buy things like everyone else, they wanted a good life. In my family, the truth was, that no matter how bad it got, it was always better than the back-breaking peasant life they'd left behind. And how could an independent Quebec change that?

But there at the Penelope, I thought for the first time, independent Quebec or not, that maybe Micola could escape, that maybe she could leave behind the economic and social tatters of our peasant backwaters, and make a different life for herself. When I saw them together, on the stage, that night, in late November of 1976, I felt envy, but at the same time excited for Micola, hopeful. The chemistry between those two was unmistakable, free-floating, wild, palpable. They were beautiful, the music was beautiful, Micola's singing, the erotic energy between them, a thing of magic. Even Ottavio seemed briefly transported, away from his political preoccupations.

"Well, I thought he was a jazz musician, but he does seem to be able to play anything, doesn't he?" he said. "Maybe we should just let this go, let it be."

"Easier said than done," I said.

"I know," he said, somewhat solemnly.

It seems now, in retrospect, that Micola knew what was going to happen. She'd always been a collector, collecting just about anything associated with the meaningful moments of her life. Her room was strewn with dried flowers, letters, leaves, records, chip bags, crystal balls, napkins, all symbols of some moment, event or situation.

My mother complained about her room, calling it the garbage bin of Melrose Avenue. She didn't see Micola's sensitivity, her inability to bear the loss of anything, her constant attempt to arrest the passage of time with her array of symbolic objects. And music. Music was the most important. She would play songs over and over again, like a mantra, as she was doing with Fabrizio de Andre.

Even as a child Micola had been this way, easily stuck on things, as easily as things stuck on her, as if there just wasn't enough space between herself and the world.

Then Micola began to clean her room, throwing out garbage bags full of those little items, bits and pieces of herself she had collected for years. She tidied up her records which were usually strewn all over the room, putting everything in some kind of order. She was preparing for something. I thought, at first, that she was preparing to move, maybe throw caution completely to the wind and move in with Andy. But when I asked her she denied that.

"I don't know why," she'd say. "I just feel like I need more order in my life, that it might help me see things more clearly, help me make decisions better."

"Decisions about what?"

"I don't know, Francesca. I don't know. Everything is changing so fast. I just need some clarity."

Things were changing for me too. In the face of Micola's reckless charge into a new life, I felt stranded, shipwrecked.

Our rec room salons had disintegrated, so Ottavio started taking me to political meetings at the university. Through Peter Cormier he had become more interested in Maoism. I wasn't clear at all on the differences between the various revolutionary groups. All I knew was that the Russian Revolution had gone really bad. So at the time, Stalinism was out, and Maoism was in.

One meeting he took me to was on the Loyola campus, in Hingston Hall. We were a little late so the presenter was already speaking with a kind of stilted passion about the spontaneity of the masses, how action had to spring from the people, that this was the only truly revolutionary action, the violent uprising of the masses. This was the only true morality in the face of the legal crimes of the state.

I found myself getting irritated and angry. I believed in the class struggle, Ottavio had convinced me of that, that we had a historical mission. But I hated hearing these people talking about us like that, the masses, the people, the proletariat, pawns in a chess game. Their allegiance felt false, rehearsed, unlived, like they'd never stepped foot in a factory, or known a peasant.

By the end of the discussion I became angry enough to speak. I was surprised to suddenly hear my own voice.

"I like the idea of the spontaneity of the masses," I said, "but what do you do if the masses are not really interested in action, if they just want a better life for themselves and their families? I can't really see any revolutionary action springing from any member of the masses that I know. I think, maybe, they need to be educated first. I think they need someone to lead them, inspire them to action." But not someone like you, I thought, though didn't say.

The presenter was silent for a moment, and then with a shocking fierceness said, "It's you, it's people like you, that are getting in the way of the revolutionary cause. Get this reactionary out of here."

I was stunned. I couldn't say anything. Thankfully, Ottavio stood up, with a force that matched his and said, "So much for listening to the people. You would certainly never make an inspiring, revolutionary leader, you fascist, political hack." Then he grabbed my arm and we walked out.

I had no idea what a Leninist was or a Maoist for that matter. I just said what I was feeling, what I had observed. I was a member of the working class after all, and my parents had also been peasants. That much I knew. I had the right to speak.

"Don't worry, Francesca, you did the right thing by speaking. You showed up their contradictions. Whether they'll understand that or not is another matter."

I felt relieved by his comments. I had expected, some- how, that once we got outside, he was going to yell at me and accuse me of embarrassing him with my ignorance. Instead he told me that I should read more, develop my analysis, that I had good political instincts. That's when he told me that he was thinking of going back to Italy, that the struggle had heated up there. He had connections in the movement and they had asked for his help.

My first thought was: Everyone is leaving me behind, what will I do now? But I didn't say that to Ottavio. I sim- ply expressed my surprise, because though he had always complained about how North American consumerism made class consciousness impossible, it had never oc- curred to me that he would leave.

"When are you going?" I asked.

"I don't know. I'm still thinking about it. Maybe I'll go for a visit next spring or summer and see how that goes."

Just before Christmas I noticed that Micola was look- ing dishevelled and unkempt, that she was not going out to 'work' so frequently anymore. I asked her if she wanted to go Christmas shopping with me, but she said no, that she had stuff to think about. I asked her if something had happened with Andy.

"No, nothing has happened with Andy."

"You don't seem to be going out to 'work' as much," I said with a smirk. "Did you lose your job?"

She burst into tears.

"OK, what's up, Micola?"

"You know, Francesca, I feel that I didn't really exist until I met Andy, that I had no being, that I was immate- rial. How am I supposed to go on without him?"

"Did he break up with you?" I asked, with concern, though I felt relief and hoped it was true.

"No, nothing like that," she said, her face streaked with tears. "I'm just afraid that he will find a reason to leave me, because I'm just not good enough."

"What do you mean, not good enough? You guys look great together."

"Yeah well, looks aren't everything, you know that!"

"Yes, I guess I do."

"Look at us, there's not a newspaper or book in this house except the ones we bring here. Our parents grew up with donkeys and sheep, they can't even write their own names, our furniture is from the Salvation Army. We wouldn't have anything cool to wear if we didn't make it ourselves." Then she burst out crying. "And we're always afraid our father is going to kill us."

"Micola, these are things that have always eaten away at me. But I always thought they didn't bother you. You seemed oblivious, in your own world, even happy at times."

"Like I said, I didn't really exist before."

It was a jab in my heart when she said that, again, like I had been completely inconsequential to her, like everyone had, Ricardo and Ottavio too.

"Ottavio has helped me in this regard," I said. "Politics has helped me to exist, maybe not in the same sense that you're taking about, but it helped me to stop seeing the poverty, ignorance and violence of our family as something personal, but rather to see the personal as political. That's what the feminists say too."

"Yes, you were always better at analyzing things."

"You were always more beautiful. You can't have everything, Micola."

"I never felt beautiful, I always hated myself, and now I hate myself even more, because compared to Andy Cohen, I'm nothing. Look at us, the poverty, the ignorance, the violence," she said, repeating the words I had just used, but with an inconsolable anguish that seemed intractable.

"You're wrong, Micola. You couldn't be more wrong about that. Did you ever think that maybe he doesn't deserve you?"

"Well, that's a joke."

"Stop it, stop it! You're impossible." I was almost shouting at this point. I couldn't bear hearing that self-contempt, which I knew so well, coming from her. No, not from her, not from her.

"You're wrong, Micola," I said again, more calmly. "You're wrong."

And though she didn't seem to be taking in what I was saying at the time, our conversation appeased her. Micola looked better after that. Christmas came and went without drama, but winter set in and blizzards came, those Montreal blizzards, exciting as a child, but immobilizing when older, because we couldn't get out, we were stuck at home, couldn't even go to classes some days. We hated being stuck at home. We would each retreat to our rooms till the weather emergency subsided.

In February I discovered what had been bothering Micola. It was one of those stay at home blizzard days. I knocked on Micola's bedroom door to see if she wanted to help start dinner. She was still in her pajamas, her eyes red from crying.

"What the hell is going on, Micola? This guy is bad for you. You're always a mess."

"I think I'm pregnant," she said, with a voice that seemed distant, lost in some zone, one of her faraway places. I sat down on the edge of her bed, but didn't say anything. I knew something was wrong, but somehow, that had not crossed my mind.

"Are you sure? Does Andy know?"

"No, of course not. I am not entirely sure yet. But how can I tell him this?"

"You're making it sound like it's something you did to him, as if he wasn't a part of it. How the hell did it happen anyway? Weren't you taking precautions?"

"Yes, we were. The condom broke a couple of times. It just happened. But the last time it happened, somehow I knew, I could feel it."

Well, if anyone could feel conception, Micola could, so I trusted her on that.

"So he's aware this could be a possibility?"

"I suppose," she said meekly.

"You have to tell him. That's the first thing to do. Or maybe just wait till you get the test done. Then find out his intentions, where's he at about this."

"I just want to get rid of it and not tell anyone," she said with a little more force.

"Really?" I was skeptical, knowing that Micola would not be capable of killing anything.

"It just seems like the easiest thing to do," she said.

"Easy, for you? I don't think so! If you are in love, maybe Andy will marry you. Get him to propose before you tell Mom and Dad. That will make things easier on that front," I said, without really believing it.

"Or maybe you can try telling them it was a science experiment," I said, wanting to lighten things up.

She looked desperate. She threw herself on to her bed and pulled the covers over her head. I left to prepare the ragù, which is what we usually had for dinner on Thursday evenings. But I could not shake the dark foreboding. I was afraid for Micola and for myself and for my mother too.

When my parents came home I told them that Micola was sick, though I was vague about the malady.

For two weeks Micola hardly ever came out of her room. She did not go to classes or to work. I hovered around the phone just in case Andy called, which he did, several times during the first week. I told him Micola was not feeling well. With him I was more specific, I said that she had the flu. The second week he stopped calling, which I did not take as a good sign. Every day Micola asked whether he had called, a couple of times I lied, so as not to upset her.

My parents were starting to worry about Micola, urging her to go see a doctor, which she refused to do. Finally I said that Micola was depressed, that her illness was mental and that there was nothing the doctor could do about that.

"What the fuck does she have to be depressed about?" my father said, in his angry, crude dialect.

"Really?" I said, looking at him accusingly.

"You girls have everything, we're slaving away to make a better life for you, and what do you do, you get depressed. That's some kind of gratitude."

He did not usually get so crass or angry when it came to Micola. But I suppose he had sensed her withdrawal from him over the preceding months and was angry at her. I never really understood their relationship. I had no affection for my father at the time, and it was hard for me to imagine the bond he and Micola had.

What happened in the following weeks remains a kind of blur, because I put immense effort into forgetting it. I was successful at that, for a long time, mainly by becoming enraged and throwing myself full force into the cause of revolutionary justice. Everything had gone wrong for us, and it relieved my suffering to see a single cause for it all, the injustices endured by Italy's South. Had it not been for that we would not have had to uproot ourselves, our parents would not have had to cling so hard to their archaic values, Micola and I would not have been trapped in the unbridgeable chasm between the backwardness of our parents and the modern world we were living in. We would have been able to speak the same language as our parents instead of fumbling with a dialect that was crude and strange to us. We were all victims of the same problem, my parents included, I came to believe afterwards.

When two weeks passed with Micola barely getting out of bed, I decided that I would speak to Andy Cohen myself. If he phoned again, I would ask to see him. But he didn't phone.

Finally Micola mustered enough energy to do the test. It was positive.

"OK Micola, you can't wait any longer," I said. "This problem is not going away. The longer you wait, the fewer options you will have. I think Andy should know what has happened, and you should know how he feels about it all. If you don't tell him, I will."

"Are you crazy! Don't you dare." It was the first sign of life I'd seen in her in weeks.

"Micola, it has to be done. You have to do it. It's not fair to him either, if you don't tell him."

"OK, OK, tomorrow, I'll tell him tomorrow."

"I can go with you if you like."

"OK, that's a good idea," she said without much energy. She was looking pale and gaunt and hadn't combed her hair in weeks. "He's performing with his jazz trio at a club on Stanley Street tomorrow evening. We could go there."

"How do you know that? You haven't been talking to him."

"He told me a while ago. It was a big deal for him because he'd never played there before."

"Is that really a good place to be talking to him about something like this?"

129

"I told him when he first mentioned it to me that I would try to be there. So he might be expecting me."

"Even after you haven't talked to him for weeks."

"I don't know, Francesca, I don't know. I just don't have the energy to arrange anything else."

"OK, OK, let's do that. You can say you're going back to work and I can say I'm babysitting."

I had classes the next day, but Micola stayed home again, and did not go to school. I was set to graduate with my M.A. in the spring, so I was determined to not let that go, in spite of the trouble that was heading our way.

When I got home I was relieved to see Micola out of her bed clothes, her hair in a ponytail and looking like she was ready for a night out, or a night at work, as far as my parents were concerned. She was wearing her brown bell-bottom cords and the green pullover I had given her for Christmas. Even though she was depressed, pregnant and had not left her bed for two weeks, she still looked beautiful. A marvel, I thought. How did she ever land among our motley cast of peasant characters?

It was March, but still bitterly cold, so we had to bundle ourselves up like snowmen, which I didn't mind, but Micola complained about it all the way to the club. Maybe something else to focus on besides the problem at hand. I let her complain and tried to be as supportive and encouraging as I could be, seeing that she was getting increasingly anxious and tense as we approached the Peel Metro.

We walked down from Sherbrooke Street, then over to Stanley, farther south, closer to Dorchester Street, looking for Roberto's, which turned out to be more like a restaurant than a club. We were both nervous at this point since we were not used to being downtown by ourselves. But we found the place and went in. Someone asked us if we were planning on eating or just here for the music. We said, just the music, so she showed us over to some stools near a bar. We took off our coats, sat and looked around. The show wasn't supposed to start till 8 and it was only 7. Andy did not seem to be there. We ordered a drink and we waited.

"Maybe we should go," Micola said, finally, breaking a along silence.

"No, Micola, you have to do this. We came all the way here in this frigid weather. We're not going anywhere."

The place was filling up but still no Andy.

We went to the washroom, which was downstairs. Micola was in front of me and as she got to the last step, she stopped abruptly and almost tripped. I grabbed her by the shoulder to prevent her from falling. There was a long hall ahead of us. At the end of it, just outside the women's washroom was Andy, with a blonde pinned up against the wall, his hand up her blouse.

I pulled at Micola, indicating that we go back upstairs. She could hardly walk. I took her by the hand and led her back to our bar seats. She was pale, frozen, from cold and shock. I tried to hug her, but she wouldn't have it.

"Just let me be, Francesca. Don't say anything, just don't say anything."

"OK, OK, let's just finish our drinks and you can figure out what you want to do."

About 15 minutes passed, we saw Andy finally coming through the downstairs door, without the girl. He walked towards the bar, though I was sure he hadn't seen us. As he approached, Micola completely surprised me. She called out to him with a cheery voice, as if nothing had happened, as if she was delighted to see him. He turned towards us, looked right at us, but somehow above us, as if he had never seen us before in his life. Then without a word, just walked toward the stage.

My heart was breaking for Micola. I didn't know what to do or say. We continued to sit in silence. I think she still kept hoping that Andy might come back and say something, explain himself. But he never did. We saw the girl come and join Andy near the stage. She was tall and elegant, wearing expensive jewellery. She had an air of confidence about her, like no one could ever knock her over, the way Micola was being knocked over, right then and there.

"I guess he doesn't have to put out money to spend time with her," Micola said, finally.

I put my arm around her. "Let's go, Micola, he never deserved you." Though I understood her sentiments, the depth of her insecurity.

We couldn't go home yet since we were both supposed to be "working." We headed toward Atwater along St. Catherine's, not knowing where we were going. It had gotten even colder and I could barely feel my hands and feet when we got to the Alexis Nihon Plaza. Micola had stopped complaining about the cold and had not said a word until we got to the cafeteria beside the movie theatre in the Plaza, where we decided to stop and have a coffee.

That was probably the last full conversation I ever had with Micola.

"Maybe he was angry with me for not taking his calls for the last few weeks," she said, though not quite believing.

"Maybe he saw us on the stairs and felt shame and embarrassment about us catching him in the act, is more like it."

"Really, but that wouldn't cause him to walk right by as if he didn't even know me." When she said this she burst into tears. "How could this be? I can't believe it. This is not possible."

"I don't know, Micola, I don't know … You have only known him for a few months. You can't truly get to know someone in that short period of time."

"I knew him, I knew him. This is not possible. Maybe he didn't see us at the bar."

"Micola, you called out to him. He looked straight at us."

"Maybe he was high?"

"On what?"

"He told me he does heroin sometimes."

"Oh my god, he's a heroin addict."

"I didn't say that," she yelled.

She would have been willing to forgive his sexual betrayal, I could tell. But that he had walked right by her as if she didn't exist was killing her.

We went on like that for about an hour, Micola obsessing on the possible reasons for Andy's behaviour, going round in circles, getting nowhere, and wondering whether she should tell him about the pregnancy or not. She hadn't decided what to do by the time we left the cafeteria to head home. But after what happened later that night, she let it all go, Andy, music, everything.

As we trudged down Melrose Avenue we decided that she would go in first and that I would wait a while in the Melrose tunnel, so it wouldn't seem like we had been together. When I walked in they were all standing by the entrance to the basement. Micola had blurted out the fact of her pregnancy. She hadn't planned to. I don't know what was said when she arrived that changed her mind. But as soon as I approached them, with my coat barely off, my father slapped me hard across the face and started yelling at me and kicking me.

"You whore, you fucking whore. *U sapiv ch tu arruvnev.* (I knew you would ruin her. I knew it)."

"What the fuck are you taking about?" I screamed back.

"Look what you've done, you've ruined her, you've ruined this family."

My mother and Micola started crying, helplessly. But when my father did not stop hitting me and kicking me. Micola started screaming and yelling.

"Stop it! Stop it! It's not her. She didn't do anything. She didn't do anything. It's me. I am the one who had sex. Yes, I had sex! It was me! Not Francesca! Leave her alone," she shouted as she tried pulling him off me. Then she shoved him, a small shove, not a big one, just to show her anger, her frustration. But he stumbled, perhaps because he didn't expect that from Micola, he stumbled and fell down the basement stairs. My mother started screaming and wailing, cursing the devil, as if she knew all along this had been his plan. Micola froze into shocked silence, the silence she would live in for decades. I ran down the stairs to find my father's body splayed across the floor. The glass table on which he had hit his head was smashed. He was covered in blood and bits of glass. I tried calling out to him. "*Pa, Pa.*" But no answer came. I rushed back upstairs to call an ambulance. They came immediately and took him to the hospital. But they could not save him. That is how my father really died, not from a heart attack, as the story went, what we told, at the time, but as a result of a family dispute, a domestic spat gone wrong, terribly wrong.

Those months that followed were some of the darkest of my life, and it hadn't really been a rose garden before, nor has it been since. We were all dazed, not knowing what to do with ourselves. But one thing was certain for my mother, no one was to know what happened. The police reported it as an accident, and heart attack is what we told anyone else that asked, especially the *paisani*. We were ruined enough, my mother said, the devil in our midst. We would not make it worse by having the community know about it.

"*Prie p nui.* (Pray for us)," was her mantra, to family and to friends, as we went through the funeral proceedings of burying our father. But after that, we all seemed to go our separate ways. My mother was lost in her grief and disoriented, as if she didn't quite know how to be in the world, without fear, without the constant threat of violence.

Micola retreated completely into herself. She ate, she went to her medical appointments, but she dropped out of school, no longer socialized, hardly left her room. The rosy glow of her complexion began to fade, her eyes caved in to an unknown place. Sometimes when I came home from school, she was still in bed. I often pulled her out by force, making her help me with the *pasta e fagioli*.

The child was due in late October and was to be given up for adoption. It was early summer when my mother proposed we all move back to Italy after the birth. Micola was indifferent to the idea, as she was to everything at that point. At first, I couldn't bear the thought of leaving Paolo behind. He became ever more important to me that summer, as if he held the only hope for kindness and beauty that I could imagine, as if I was torn between a growing rage and a flimsy hope for love. Paolo was that love, and I could not let it go, no matter how thin the thread felt, at times, no matter how unfit I felt to be loved by someone like him. But that was the way it was, he always made me feel good about myself, in a way no one else did, but at the same time, bad and inferior, and even more so after the tragic events of that winter. My desire to see him was always desperate. I think Ricardo was starting to pick up on it and tried to tell me about him, on a couple of occasions. But then somehow he didn't. Perhaps he thought I was already dealing with enough.

Then, of course, it happened on its own, that weekend at Titiana's cottage in the Laurentians, a few months before we left. Micola was holed up in her room, six months pregnant and did not come. I, lost and desolate, jumped at the opportunity of spending a weekend with Paolo. But as it turned out, it was the last time I would ever see him.

Springsteen was playing on the ghetto blaster.

"Babe, babe, babe, I swear, I'd drive all night just to buy you some shoes and to taste your tender touch."

Paolo and Ricardo were sitting at the table playing cards, and I was debating with myself about whether I should take acid or not. I had never done it before and was afraid of losing control.

When the card playing ended, we went out to light the coals for the barbecue. It was Saturday evening and everyone was still scattered about doing their own thing. Paolo and I decided to start dinner while Ricardo went for a swim. Because I was so unaccustomed to being alone with him, I was nervous. As we crouched down fiddling with the coals, our arms brushed ever so slightly. I lost my balance for a second and almost fell. He grabbed me by the arm, looked me straight in the eyes, with a sympathetic yet anxious expression. He looked as if he was about to tell me something, something he was finding very difficult to say. It was a look I had never seen before. It left me feeling estranged from him, which I hated. Sometimes when he looked at me, his eyes seemed to slide into mine, other times, they were distant and far.

I was bothered that whole evening by that strange look. I'm sure it was a factor in my finally deciding to take the acid. I needed a different perspective, I needed some way into the truth or maybe just a way to break free.

It was late evening. We had already eaten and everyone was high or in a slumber. I was in complete control, or so I thought, except for the smell of pine which seemed to permeate everything. We were sitting around except for Paolo. He was leaning against the pine tree beside the cabin, with the sexiest smile I'd ever seen. Ricardo took that photo of him, the one I recently found again. I don't know how I ended up with it. I was swooning with his beauty when I seemed to fall off an edge, an edge of what I can't say, some edge in myself.

Everyone got into the car to go into St. Jerome to get some beer. I stayed behind to clean up a bit, which I never managed to do. Instead I drifted down to the lake and fell into it backwards. An abrupt melting of all the edges, as if the matter, shape and colour of things had suddenly lost all boundaries, and the matter, shape and colour of myself, too, faded into the lake. I scrambled desperately to hold on to something personal, something firmly mine. Then I became full to the brim with longing for Paolo. As quickly as it rose, it fell away into the perception I so often had, of my inability to reach him, of the Forbidding. I seemed to fall off the edge of the world, for I don't know how long. It seemed like a timeless period until I heard his strong, firm voice call me from the distance.

"Francesca, Francesca, you fool, come back, come back!"

At first the voice was faint. Then it gradually grew louder, until I found Paolo sitting beside me, holding my hand.

"You take my hand and I'm suddenly in a bad movie. It goes on and on. And why am I fascinated?"

I laughed at his reference to the Margaret Atwood poem, as the soft blue of Paolo's eyes and the firmness in his voice brought me back. He continued to hold my hand as he walked me to the cabin. The ghetto blaster was blaring and everyone was sitting around the picnic table drinking beers. But all I could do was crash.

When I awoke in the small one-room cabin, everything about the night before was a blur. Someone's feet were hanging down from the upper bunk and Titiana was sprawled out next to me. I noticed that the bunk Paolo and Ricardo had been sleeping in was empty. I got up, fumbled with the coffee and sat at the kitchen table which was in the same room as the two bunk beds. With the heat and angle of the sun streaming in through the window, I realized it was not morning, that it had probably been morning when I went to bed. Then it came back to me, Paolo's voice, the pull of his voice. I was convinced that what he had done had been an act of love. I put down my coffee on the worn table and ran out, looking for him. I was flying higher than the night before, as I ran through the meadow behind the cabin, filled to the brim with love. The meadow led far afield to a well-trodden path into the woods. I knew Paolo liked going for walks there. I ran in the blazing afternoon sun, ready to find him, to meet him in that soft, faraway place which at that moment felt close, closer than I'd ever known it to be, moving outward through my skin and bodily movements, reaching out, as if I was leaping over the forbidding chasm, which kept him on the far side of my love.

I heard shuffling sounds from behind a pine tree, like the one Paolo had been leaning against the night before when Ricardo snapped his photo. I approached quietly, as I moved slowly behind the tree, our eyes met once again, in a way they never had before. Hard. Blue and penetrating, as Ricardo was crouched at his feet with Paolo's cock in his mouth.

I felt like such a fool.

Paolo came running after me. Breathless, excited. He grabbed me by the shoulders with such aggression, I thought he was going to hit me. He shook me and shook me, as if he thought he could shake it all out of me, the sight I had witnessed. He had not wanted me to know. His look was piercing and angry. He was threatening me, warning me not to speak what I had seen. Without words. And then, as he stood there, trembling with fear and anger, he suddenly softened. His eyes watery and his grip on me loosened. He fell back against a nearby tree. After some time, he reached out, tenderly, towards me, tears flowing visibly.

"Francesca, Francesca, please listen … I love you."

These words I had been waiting so long to hear, now incomprehensible, gibberish, a foreign language, as if the sense of the words had just left me. I ran back towards the lake, shouting at him as I left, "Leave me alone! Don't you dare come, don't you dare come." And he didn't.

He tried to approach me a couple of times as we were packing up to leave.

"There are different kinds of love, you know, Francesca," he said, while I was taking the sheets off the bunks. He tried to touch my arm as he said it. But I swatted him off like a bug.

"Leave me alone," I said again, emphatically.

On the drive home I made sure I went in Titiana's car instead of Ricardo's.

It is my cruelty now which I find unbearable. Desperation, flight. The inverse of love. That is all I was capable of, then. Without the fantasy of Paolo, the reality of him, everything became impossible. After my father's death, he was my only tie to life, a fine red thread. When that was cut, all I had was rage.

139

Persuaded by Ottavio's letters, who was then in Rome, in the throws of revolutionary fervour, I finally told my mother that I agreed with her.

"*Ma, arraggiun. Iamcenn a L'italie.*" (Ma, you're right, let's go back to Italy). "*E meglie p tutt quant.*" (It's best for everyone).

"*Minu mali, t si arruolat,*" she said. (Thank god, you've come to your senses).

"We have to wait, though, for the baby to be born. We already made the arrangement with Paolo's friends to adopt."

"*E che so stupido.*" (You think I'm stupid)? "We wait," she said in English.

* * *

When my mother first mentioned it, it had seemed impossible that we could leave Canada. I had been born in Volturino, but I'd never been back, and Micola was a Montrealer, who had never set foot on Italian soil. But everyone was leaving Quebec then, after the Parti Québécois had come to power, so why not us, and why not move back to Italy? I began to see that returning to the homeland could be a solution, for my mother, especially, but also for Micola and me. This much I had in common with my mother, the desire to escape. She wanted to forget what happened in Canada, the whole tragic mess, everything. She damned "America" with its lure of money growing on trees. She wanted the old misery back again. That she knew she could handle. But the *Thing* that happened to us in "America" turned out to be a deal with the devil, as far as she was concerned. She wanted her old life.

My idea of escape was, of course, very different from hers. Though I didn't know it at the time, what I was trying to escape was something internal, a kind of personal demonology, which I ended up acting out in the "years of lead," as they refer to them in Italy. Ottavio had gone back to Rome that summer and decided not to return to Montreal. You might have guessed why. The politics. In Italy he found the battle he so desperately needed to fight. And as always, for me, Ottavio was a pull, and so I followed.

* * *

I'm sure it won't surprise Paolo how Ottavio and I ended up. Yet, I am ashamed to admit that somehow I bought into the idea that personal and emotional life was some kind of petit bourgeois luxury, that poetry and philosophy, too, were indulgences of the rich.

I couldn't have been more wrong. Still, when everything broke, and all was lost, it seemed easy to cast everything aside, in favour of a political cause.

Ottavio was my inspiration then. He had always been my informal teacher. Taught me things I needed to know, knowledge I couldn't easily find elsewhere.

"Why do you think we're here, Francesca?" he had asked, just before he returned to Italy.

"What do you mean?"

"Why do think our parents had to cross an ocean just to find work?"

"The dream of money growing on trees, I guess."

"No, it wasn't just the dream of an easy life. They felt they had to. They couldn't survive. They couldn't feed their kids. They had no choice. That's because the North had such contempt for us Southerners, they simply didn't bother to deal with any of our problems. They left us in the grip of a feudal system that broke our backs, then gave us nothing. And when the landlords weren't breaking our backs, it was the *Camorra* terrorizing us. What choice did they have, Francesca? Tell me, what choice did they have? Our parents were illiterate, they didn't even know their own history. They knew only the misery and the poverty they were trying to leave behind. We inherited that ignorance, but we have the chance to break free of it, to call reality as we see it, to make some real changes."

I listened, I took it in. It was just after my father died. Ottavio knew my mother wanted to return to Italy, so he was planting the seed.

And after all that happened to us in Canada I needed a simple explanation for the *Thing* that had killed my father, wrecked my sister, and left my mother and me carrying the baggage. The economic and political reasons we were ejected from our native land to begin with, became the origin story for me.

Throughout the spring and summer of 1977 Ottavio sent me letters reporting on the political situation in Italy.

The fires of discontent are raging, he wrote. The conditions are ripe for revolutionary change. It's happening here, Francesca. You need to come.

The postwar years had been difficult for everyone in Italy, he told me, but it was particularly bad for agrarian southerners. The Italian economic boom of the 50s and 60s never reached the South, where there was no money to pay the taxes or rent on your small plot of land, which often had to get paid in produce, leaving less than subsistence for the family to live on. Whole families toiled, from sunrise to sundown, children among them, lives of hard and heavy labour, only to just barely survive, if you were lucky and the harvest was good. These were the stories we had grown up with, but not knowing their social or political context.

I remembered that my own grandfather, Salvatore Benvenuto, had left Italy in 1926, as an illegal, along with six other men, moving secretly, from freight car to freight car, carted from country to country, in hiding, across Europe. Then on a ship to Cuba, where he stayed for a month, waiting for passage to New York. When he finally got to New York, he worked illegally for three years on the railroad, living with an uncle who was a landed immigrant.

But even after three years of illegal labour in New York City, though he was able to return to Italy with enough money to buy his own plot of land, his son and daughter faced the same predicament in the 1950s. That small plot of land was not able to yield enough wealth to keep his children in Italy. They too had to leave family and friends, and the village they had been rooted in for centuries, in order to find work, across the sea.

Though not everyone left, Ottavio told me, not all the destitute peasants of the rural south made that great leap to another continent. Some left family and friends behind to work in the industrialized cities of the North, Genoa, Turin, Milan. During the 50s and 60s, Italy's developing north was eating up its countryside, replacing it with industrial sprawls.

The peasants who arrived in the Northern cities, hoping to reap some of the economic benefits of the industrializing north, landed in a concrete jungle of indecent housing, poor transportation, and no health care or services to help them adjust to their situation. Transplanted out of the earthiness of a centuries old agricultural and religious life, into the severity of an industrial one, they were isolated and disoriented. But no one cared, least of all the barons of capital.

Ottavio's letters helped me to piece together the collective history of the South, with that of our personal past. When our Montreal life imploded, and we all wanted to escape, Ottavio's call to action became timely. Though returning to Volturino with my mother and Micola was only a provisional plan for me. They didn't know it, but I was headed for Rome, to meet up with Ottavio, to address an old and ancient wound, whose logic I came to understood only later, much later.

* * *

When we first arrived in Volturino I was enchanted with its oldness. As a child I'd had recurring dreams of strange, exotic, hilly landscapes, with a quality of familiarity, yet clearly, unknown to me. There it was, the landscape of my dreams, Apulia. Volturino was on the tip of the highest mountain in the area, a place where the wind never stopped blowing, and the people who lived there were known to have heads full of wind. It was so far up, people rarely ventured there, at least if they could avoid it, a place where Micola would clearly have been at home, even before the silence, even before the tragedy. But by then Micola had withdrawn completely into herself and no longer spoke. She was gone. I had become accustomed to it. There was no protest when we told her we were returning to Italy. She gave up the child too, without protest, asked only that she be called Chiara. If before the birth she was simply silent, after she became hermetically sealed.

After staying in Volturino for a couple of weeks, I started to feel the same sense of restriction and suffocation that I felt in the Italian community in Montreal. Though it was worse in Volturino. Television had reached there by then, but aside from that, there was no other pastime, except gossip. Old people sat like vultures, watching, listening, imagining their tales to tell. And there were many tales being told about us.

"*Ma p che n sonn spusat quisti duie?* (Why are these two not married)?" I heard one old lady ask another when Micola and I were walking by their stoop on our way to the village piazza.

"*Hai sntuto ch u padr s ie cis, ch a figlia faciv a puttan, cantav dnt i barr, e po avut nu figl.*" (I heard that the father killed himself, because the daughter was a whore, went around singing in bars and then she had a child).

"*E mo u figl ando sta?*" (Where is the child now)?

"*E ch ne sacc?*" (How do I know)?

Micola was tuned out and didn't hear anything, but I couldn't bear it. I went over to them and said, in English, "It's none of your fucking business. Chew on that for a while, why don't you, if you have nothing else to do?"

They both just folded their arms across their chest in unison, as if rehearsed. As I walked away I heard one of them mutter, "*Sonne mal aducato pure.*" (Bad mannered too).

Living in a village where everyone spoke the same archaic dialect I had grown up with had a comforting effect at first. Though I soon realized that the attitudes and values, the almost biological pessimism of the people around me were more than I could handle. How could such a stunningly beautiful landscape contain such misery? Small encrustations of failed attempts at survival, in the middle of great, open expanses of poppied fields, sunflowered hills, vineyards and rivers, olive groves and lemon-scented air, wild cactus pears and roads lined with oleander. Beauty and misery, side by side.

The only thing that fired me up, then, that made me want to live, despite all that had happened, was joining the struggle. It was the Fall of 1977. Italy was on fire, it needed me. I decided to leave for Rome. My mother tried to stop me, of course.

"*Pche ti nada ie? Mo sim arruvat.*" (We just got here. Why do you have to leave)?

"*E che ei fa qua?*" (What am I supposed to do here)?

"*Avvard a soret.*" (You can watch your sister).

"Oh, great," I said in English, this time. "That is a perfect pastime."

She knew she wasn't going to get anywhere with me, then. So she let it go. With my father gone, briefly, I seemed to have no fears. The sadness was buried deep. A whole new life seemed finally within reach.

Rome is a crazy, bustling and magnificent city. Cars, scooters and people buzzing every which way, narrow cobblestone alleyways opening unsuspectingly into wide, grand piazzas with fountains that take your breath away. A modern world lodged in an ancient one. I knew immediately that this was a place I could stay. Even if my standard Italian was less than adequate, I was determined to learn. For the first time in my life, I felt as if I had arrived where I was supposed to be.

Ottavio was already involved with the political scene, so that would make integration into a social circle easier, I imagined, as I waited for him at Piazza Mattei in the old Jewish Ghetto. My bus had arrived early so I went to a café on Via Arenula. Surprisingly, everyone seemed to be standing around the counter drinking their coffee, even though all the tables were empty. I must have looked a bit perplexed, as a short bald man with very thick eyebrows nudged me and said, "*I tavoli sono per i turisti.*" (The tables are for the tourists). He rubbed his fingers together, indicating money, which I assumed meant you had to

146

pay more if you wanted to sit, which I certainly did not. I drank the coffee as quickly as I could, standing with everyone else. Then I left.

It was still early so I took a walk along the Tiber River. Maybe everyone feels this way about the Tiber, like they've been there before, perhaps in a dream, or had lived a life along its banks in another century and were somehow returning. Certain currents of the past must be biological, I thought, and experiences remain like phantom outlines, in our cells, in our bones, or in a smell or a certain light, as it falls at a particular moment, on a particular landscape. Was this partly what drew me back into the political turmoil of Italy at that time, a kind of cellular commitment to something that was working itself out in the landscape of my origins, a pent-up rage that I was unleashing, for my ancestors?

When Ottavio arrived I was sitting on the stoop of one of the kiosks in Piazza Mattei. I was staring at the Fontana delle Tartarughe and didn't notice the tall, well-dressed, clean-cut man coming towards me. In fact, not until he stopped right in front of me with a questioning look on his face did I recognize him. Then I yelled out, "Ottavio, Oh my god, is that you?" He hushed me with a look of panic.

"That's not my name anymore," he said emphatically. "Don't ever call me that again."

I looked around and there just seemed to be a few tourists taking pictures of the fountain.

"There's nobody here," I said.

"And how would you know who is who? You only just got here."

"OK, OK, Ottavio. It's not my fault. You could have told me what was going down. How am I supposed to know you've changed your name?"

"You're right. I was careless. I didn't inform you properly before coming here to meet you."

"So what should I call you now, anyhow?"

"Now, I am Raffaello Cordoni, a bank teller."

He certainly looked like a bank teller. His long, curly, black locks were gone, so was his beard, the jeans and worn T-shirts. Instead a suit, and clean-shaven. Because his face had always been covered with so much hair, I had never realized how good looking he was. He kissed me, finally, on both cheeks.

"OK," he said. "You can stay with us, me and Teresa, for a while. We're supposed to be married. She works as a travel agent. But it's a very small apartment, so you will have to find your own place as soon as possible. You can sleep on the couch till you get settled."

"I want to take courses at the university," I said.

"Well, that may prove difficult at this time. You can try enrolling but I don't know if you'll manage. The University of Rome is almost always shut down these days."

"Shut down?"

"It's been shut down due to demonstrations and riots. There are a couple of other groups besides the one I am involved with. *Lotta Continua* and *Autonomia*. They have been doing a lot of agitating ... I think trying to take some courses is a good approach for you, though. But you're going to have to get a job too. I might be able to help you with that. I know someone who owns a bookstore near Termini station."

I started working at the bookstore almost immediately. It was a crowded, dusty old place, run by a tall, dishevelled guy called Vittorio, who looked a bit like Ottavio used to look. His warmth and friendliness went a long way for me at that time, especially after I got my own apartment in the neighbourhood of Trastevere. Ottavio had to help me with the rent, at first, but he did not seem to mind.

Vittorio spoke English too, with his beautiful Roman accent, which was a great relief.

"Very unusual for immigrants to come back," he said to me one day.

"Not really. They miss their homeland, some come back," I said, trying to avoid any discussion as to why I really came back.

"Yes, but not your generation."

"True, not usually." I hesitated, then added, "My father died and my mother wanted to go back to her village in Apulia, so my sister and I decided to come with her."

"Ah, a southerner, so many left. The Northerners, not so much."

I understood, finally, that he was not prying, just trying to get into some kind of political discussion with me.

"What do you mean?" I asked, giving him the leeway to do so.

"Well, the peasants in the rural areas of the North, like Tuscany and Umbria, for example, were just as poor, just as destitute as those from the South. But they did not flee their native land in such great numbers."

"Oh, I didn't know that. Why?"

"Because, in the North there was greater socialist and communist organization. Local governments helped the peasants organize workers' cooperatives and trade unions. This helped them mobilize against the landlords. It gave them hope, a sense of power. But the southern peasants, that's a different story. They were abandoned by everyone, had no recourse against the landlords who took all the fruits of their labour and left them to starve. So they were more susceptible to the pull of the 'American dream'."

I was immediately enamoured with Vittorio. How different he sounded from those arrogant, armchair revolutionaries I had met in Montreal, who babbled their ideological jargon without any compassion or emotion.

"Helpful to know, Vittorio. Our generation, we simply weren't aware of why we had been transplanted. Our parents told their stories of poverty and misfortune, but we didn't want to hear them. Old world attitudes we wanted to escape, that's how we felt."

"Yes, but here you are. Something must have changed." At this point, I wondered if he knew why I was there. Perhaps Ottavio had spoken to him about me. I wasn't sure, didn't even know if he knew his true identity, so I kept it vague.

"Things did change. I changed. Raffaello was instructive in that. He helped me to become class conscious."

"Good," he said, and gave me his wide, charismatic Roman smile.

For a time it felt like I had landed in paradise. I was smitten with the sense of history, the sculptures, the fountains around every corner, the rhythms and sounds of my mother tongue. But like most romances, it was brief, soon giving way to the dirt and noise, the pollution and overcrowdedness, the rage, discontent and brutality erupting everywhere in Italy, in those "years of lead."

I did, eventually, manage to enroll at the university, though Ottavio was right, it was not easy. At first, every time I showed up, the crowds of protesters were so large I could not get access to the building where I was supposed to register. "*Assai classe non si fanno.* (Many classes are not taking place)," one of the protesters told me. "*I pofessorri anno pauro di presentarsi.* (The professors are afraid to show up)." I soon discovered why.

On a cold, December afternoon, when I arrived at the university to make my fifth attempt to access the registrar's building, I heard random shots being fired somewhere in the crowd. Within minutes an ambulance pulled up right beside me and I was ordered to move out of the way. The paramedics swept through the crowd very aggressively, making it clear no one was going to stop them. They returned with a middle-aged man on a stretcher, arm in a sling, face and chest covered in blood.

"He's not dead," I heard someone say, "but he deserves to be."

"Who is that?" I asked the person beside me, a young boy, no more than 17, wearing a red bandana, and an over-sized knapsack hanging on his shoulder. What's he got in there? I suddenly wondered.

"It's Ricardo Capuano, a history professor, a right-wing, fascist pig," is what I think he said, in Italian.

"*Che ha fato*? (What did he do?)" I asked.

Again, my translation. "He tried to fail a student because of his political views. The student came back after class with a gun and shot him."

I am in over my head, I thought. The universities had supposedly opened their doors to the less privileged, but was I ever going to get in, and did I really want to be there?

When I told Ottavio what had happened later that night, he hardly reacted at all to the professor being shot. He just went on about how, in Italian universities, rebellion was a whole different ball game, how it was not just a 60s phenomenon, that it was an ideological war that had been going on for over a decade.

"Professors are helping to steer student discontent along revolutionary lines," he said, "linking it up with the workers' struggle. They call them *cattivi maestri*, but they are the true theoretical leaders of the class struggle."

"OK, OK," I said. "But to show up to class and shoot a professor you disagree with. Is this the kind of revolutionary justice we're aiming for?"

"You have a lot more to learn," he said, and then just changed the subject.

That night I started to worry that maybe I wasn't cut out for the class struggle. Or had Ottavio changed? I had always trusted him, always been able to count on him. He had gone through a noticeable change when his uncle died in that construction accident in Montreal. Still, he was Ottavio, my cousin, my family, a familiar. Now he was Raffaello Cordoni, and starting to sound, just a little, like those friends of his I hated, those insufferable, ideological automatons. But I decided I couldn't afford to be worried, brushed aside my concerns and focused instead on the daunting task of registering for a course at the university.

It occurred to me, finally, that if I showed up very early in the morning, I might be able to avoid the demonstrators. It worked. That's the day I met Alfredo Negri, one of those *cattivi maestri*. I was sitting on a bench outside the registrar's office when he walked by, a handsome, middle-aged man with an unruly tangle of curly grey hair. "*Nesuno e arrivato*? (No one has arrived?)"

"*Angora no*." (Not yet).

He asked what course I was trying to register for. When I told him I wasn't sure yet, he immediately encouraged me to take the course he was going to be teaching, "The Philosophy of Political Action."

"That sounds great!" I said, in English, then tried to switch back to Italian.

"*Va bene, va bene*, I understand," he said. "I know little bit English."

"Oh," I said, surprised, and as always, relieved, whenever someone could speak English.

We had a brief conversation about where I was from and what brought me to Italy. Because of what Ottavio had said to me about the role of professors in Italian radicalism, I decided to be open about my interest in revolutionary politics. At this point he sat down beside me, and said, "For sure, you must take my course. *E perfetto per te.* (It's perfect for you)."

"Yes, I think so too," I said.

We continued to converse for a while longer, in my broken Italian and his broken English. The chemistry was clear.

When he got up to leave, he said, "You are very courageous."

Alfredo's course managed to go ahead without too many incidents. It was scheduled in the early morning, which was helpful, as there were always fewer protesters at that time. Still, one morning a tall, gaunt, young man with shaven head showed up and started chanting "History will kill you! History will kill you!" in the middle of the lecture. Alfredo simply ignored him at first, then politely asked him to leave. When he didn't stop his chanting, several other students stood up and simultaneously started walking over toward the man, at which point he pulled some rotten apples out of a bag and threw them in Alfredo's direction, then ran out of the classroom. Another time, a gang of four or five guys came in near the end of the class and dumped some cans of red paint all over the floor and then fled without saying a word. At least it wasn't a gun, I thought.

From the beginning I was drawn to Alfredo Negri. There was something about the way he moved, his gait, the rhythm of his speech. I was certain I had known him in some other context. Yet I couldn't imagine where. Maybe the familiarity had something to do with the fact that he came from the same region of Italy as I did, I thought at times. I had experienced something similar when I first visited Volturino; the rhythms of people's speech, the way people moved, resonated with some deep archaic memory, something I knew but could not say, something about our collective roots in that particular patch of earth.

Alfredo was also drawn to me. He noticed my self-consciousness with the Italian language and took it upon himself to help me, but with a level of care that puzzled me. I was a Canadian, from Montreal. Did he have some connection to Montreal? I wondered. But when I asked him, he said "no," with a curtness that told me I should not question further on the matter.

I later learned that Alfredo had been a child prodigy who impressed his fellow villagers from a young age. In a time and place where even a grade school education was a luxury most could not afford, Alfredo was sent to the University of Naples through the efforts of the local priest, who helped him secure a scholarship for the poor. The priest had been a bit of a leftist himself, and saw in Alfredo's intelligence a voice of hope for the destitute villagers.

Alfredo got a law degree from the University of Naples in 1945, studied political economy at the University of Rome, and became a professor in the 1950s. When I met him, he was an ideologue and advocate for the extreme left response to the failure of both the socialists and the communists to change anything in favour of the South, or the industrial working class of the North. He had been a member of the communist party in the late forties and fifties but left, as many did, when it became clear that both the socialists and the communists had abandoned all revolutionary impulse in favour of increasing their own power.

There were many extreme left-wing groups in Italy at the time, but the *Brigate Rosse* had a reputation for being the most organized and committed to action. Some criticized their Marxist/Leninist top-down emphasis on the leadership of the party in mobilizing and organizing the masses. But I knew that the fatalism and resignation I had experienced in my own family and in the people of Volturino would not spontaneously overcome itself. It was too old, too strong, too deep. People needed to be educated and encouraged to hope for dignity and life beyond mere survival, when they had never known it.

Ottavio had advised me to just lie low for a while, to get used to the city and focus on improving my Italian. But under the sway of Alfredo Negri's charisma and my earthy sense of connection to him, I let go of my reservations and joined the class struggle wholeheartedly.

* * *

The Brigate Rosse were organized into a series of columns, based mostly in the industrialized north. But around the time that I met Alfredo, one was being formed in Rome. The original founders of the Brigades, Renato Curcio and Alfredo Franceschini, were in jail. And Margherita Cagol, Renato Curcio's partner, had been gunned down in a rescue operation of a kidnap victim. Mario Moretti became the leader and came temporarily to Rome to form a column. The columns were made up of regulars and irregulars. Regulars referred to those individual members who, like Ottavio, lived undercover, using false names and identities as they engaged in subversive activities. The irregulars, like myself, were those who, having less suspicious pasts, lived and worked as ourselves, according to our actual identities and regular jobs, while secretly aiding the organization in a variety of different ways. Alfredo Negri was not a member himself, though he was in contact with Curcio and Franceschini, who set up my initial meeting with Mario Moretti.

At first, I was simply asked to distribute flyers and propaganda, at the university, at demonstrations, a few times at factories. I continued to attend my course, worked at the bookstore near Termini station with Vittorio. After a few weeks I started getting instructions in the mail. One note informed me that someone was to arrive at my apartment on a certain day, at a certain time. They were to hand me a bag that looked like groceries. I was to store the bag in my apartment until I received further instruction. The bag was full of explosives. Someone came to get them a week later.

On another occasion someone came to my apartment and left a knapsack which I was also instructed to store. This time the note told me to deliver the knapsack to someone at a café near Piazza del Popolo. The person was described in great detail and I was given a code word that they would repeat, which was "history". It was February 10th. I remember the day well. It was cold and blustery and I wasn't dressed properly, unlike the man who met me, who was bearing a black parka with the hood practically covering his face. He had a red scarf sloppily strung around his neck and wore brown gloves, which he took off when he sat down to have a coffee. He did not pull down his hood, which I thought was strange, as it only made him more conspicuous. He stayed for about 15 minutes, had a coffee, said very little. Then just before he stood up, he leaned over to my side to take the knapsack, and whispered the word "history".

The knapsack contained explosives, I knew that much. I wondered about their intended use. No one ever me told anything about that, which made me feel quite anxious. I wandered over to a nearby kiosk and bought a scarf and gloves and went walking in the Villa Borghese gardens, which were nearby. I walked for hours before I made my way back to my apartment in Trastevere. When I turned on the television later that night, there they were. Images of people being ordered off a bus near Piazza del Popolo. The men were masked as they forced people off the bus, before they turned it upside down and set it on fire. Over and over, images of the flaming bus and panicked people screaming and running in all directions. I turned off the television and tried calling Ottavio, but couldn't reach him. He was getting increasingly difficult to get hold of as he sank deeper into his clandestine identity. I called Vittorio at the bookstore, who simply said, "The rage of the under-classes is long and deep in Italy."

"But why this bus, why these people?" I asked.

"I don't know. Sometimes it's just random, Francesca. If it's Autonomia, they're just into the spontaneous illegality of the masses for its own sake. They organize 'political shopping', take food from supermarkets without paying, occupy unrented apartments. They're against the whole capitalist concept of work. They think people should just be paid a standard wage without—"

He was going to continue, but I stopped him.

"I don't think this was Autonomia," I blurted out, though knowing I shouldn't be talking about it.

"Well, I don't know, Francesca. I can't confirm or negate that."

"OK, OK, I have to go," I said, brusquely, before I had time to leak anything I would regret.

Then things got somewhat easier. A meeting of the irregulars was called, which took place in the back room of the bookstore where I worked. That's when I realized that Vittorio was also an irregular.

He smiled that gorgeous smile of his when he saw me, then me gave an affectionate hug.

"I sort of suspected, but you know how careful we have to be," he said, as we waited for others to show.

"I'm so relieved, Vitto, I have been feeling very anxious and isolated lately."

"*Va bene*, Francesca, I'm relieved too. But you have to be careful. There is no room for vulnerability in this work."

People were trickling in, so we discontinued our conversation.

A tall, bearded, heavyset man with a huge scar over his left eye stood before us, someone I'd never seen before. He gathered us together and started talking.

"The violence is escalating, but we are not responsible for it," he said. "But it is good for us that professors and students are afraid to show up for class, that contractors are afraid to clean the slogans painted all over the walls of the university, that people are afraid to get on buses. Our aim is to destroy the bourgeois state and get justice for the people, build a fighting party for the people. This chaos and upheaval serves us well, it destabilizes the state, makes it vulnerable, which is what we want."

He talked like that for about an hour, then ended his ideological pep talk by mentioning a massive demonstration which was going to take place on the Saturday. "Make sure you attend," he said. He was about to leave when I raised my hand to ask a question. I hadn't intended to, but having Vittorio beside me, somehow, bolstered my courage.

"Is it possible to know more about the intended consequences of the specific actions we are instructed to take? It causes a lot of anxiety not knowing," I said, in my broken Italian.

"Absolutely not. It is safer for everyone if actions are broken down into seemingly unrelated tasks. That way they are harder to trace and attribute to anyone in particular."

"OK, thanks," I said, his reasoning seeming to make sense to me at the time.

When the meeting was over, Vittorio and I opened the bookstore for a few more hours, then decided to go home.

"I never asked where you live?" he said, as he was locking the door.

"Over in Trastevere."

"Ah, just across the river from me. I am in the old Jewish Ghetto."

"Great, we should meet and go walking along the Tiber sometime. I love doing that."

"Sure, Francesca, anytime," he said, though with a tone of reluctance that left me disappointed.

Almost every night the news showed images of streets filled with tear gas, crowds throwing rocks, Molotov cocktails and firing pistols, buses and trams being hijacked and overturned, drivers forced out of their cars, vehicles set ablaze, kneecappings, professors, journalists, politicians, industrialists, kidnapped, threatened and sometimes killed. The country was being terrorized, all in the name of destroying the capitalist regime.

I watched and I worried, wondering if this was indeed the only way to get "justice for the people."

No one seemed to be talking about what a just society would actually look like, after all this destruction, how it would be put in place. Did the proletariat really want to be dictators? I was confused, uncertain, but I carried on, not knowing what else to do.

Shortly thereafter, I was entrusted to buy two train tickets to Milan, then meet someone I didn't know at Piazza del Gesù and give them to him. A few days later,

I had to pick up a car at the corner of Via del Portico d'Ottavia and Via Arenula, then to drop it off in front of the National Museum of Art, near Termini station.

Finally, what would become the last act of my brief and fateful involvement with the Red Brigades, I was instructed to buy four aviator caps. Operation Fritz as it came to be known. As usual, at the time, I had no idea why I was being asked to buy the caps. I simply headed to the Trastevere flea market that took place every Sunday, as instructed. A brisk, sunny morning in early March, I wandered through the crowds of shoppers and tacky parade of junk, searching for the kiosk with a sign that said *cappelli per tutti,* (hats for all). Obscured by the crowds, at first I couldn't see. Then I caught sight of it, at the end of the market corridor, just before the Trastevere train station.

A tall, lanky woman, with blond, shoulder length hair and glassy, blue eyes looked at me, then said, "*Poso aiutarla*?" (Can I help you?)

I gave her my code word *pilota*. She smiled, bent down to look under her counter, pulled out the caps and put them in a bag.

"*Quando*?" (How much)?

"*Vent mille lire.*" (Twenty thousand lire).

I gave her the money and made my way to Piazza Farnese, where I passed them on to a tall, young, corporate-looking man, dressed in a suit and tie.

And that was it, the last of my missions, the one I shall never forget, the one for which I paid with 14 years of my life.

The aviator caps, referred to a week later on television, were worn by the four individuals who kidnapped Aldo Moro, the president of Italy.

The men were hanging around the former bar Olivetti at the corner of Via Fani and Via Stresa, posing as Alitalia pilots, waiting for a ride to the airport. Moro was being escorted to his daily mass at the church of Santa Chiara, along Via Fani, a route he apparently never varied. He was in his car with his long-time driver Domenico Ricci, followed by another escort vehicle with four bodyguards. In front of them was a Fiat 128 with false diplomatic licence plates, driven by Mario Moretti. Moretti stopped abruptly causing Moro's car to collide with his, which then caused Moro's car to collide with his bodyguard's car. Mario Moretti stepped out of his car. That must have been the signal. In those brief moments of collision and commotion, the firing started. The four Alitalia pilots, wearing their aviator caps, took guns out of large black bags and started shooting. They were not trying to kill Moro. In the storm of fire from three automatic weapons and three semi-automatic pistols the driver and the bodyguards were shot dead. In the midst of the carnage, Moro was dragged to a BR car and taken away. The *brigatisti* had equipped their getaway cars with sirens so they could freely escape in the morning rush hour.

Pedestrians and witnesses remained with the horror, bullet shells and glass littering the street, blood everywhere. One of the *brigatisti* had left behind his cap and the President's newspaper blew in the wind, landing on the bodies. Beside one of the bodies was a false mustache and an unused cartridge.

Vittorio had a small television set at the back of the store. We were together when we heard the news. My legs gave way and I had to sit down. I couldn't say anything, I couldn't move.

Vittorio started screaming, "What have they done? What have they done? This is a terrible mistake. This will never move the cause forward. We're finished. This is the end." He sat down, seeming exhausted and defeated. "Killing five police officers, what were they thinking? Those police officers are southerners, the police come mostly from the poor southern regions. They want to liberate the people, these are the people, they are killing the people. This will not go over well, this will not go over well."

"Why Aldo Moro?" I asked, tentatively, afraid to show that I barely knew who he was. I knew he was the President, but not much more.

"I don't know for sure, Francesca. I am obviously not privy to the planning and strategizing at the top. Moro had managed to get all the political factions to form a governing coalition. The socialists, the communists and the *Democrazia Cristiana* were going to join forces. Moro had managed the impossible feat of getting them all to rise above their constant bickering and try governing together. This would have stabilized and increased the power of the state, obviously not something desirable for us. There is also the fact that the US was very opposed to the coalition. They made it pretty clear they did not want communists having any power in the Italian government. So there's also that to consider."

Without intending to, I blurted it out. "Vittorio, I bought those aviator caps. I didn't know what they were for. But I did it, I bought them." He didn't respond at first, almost as if he hadn't registered what I'd said. Then in a calmer tone, finally, he spoke.

"Don't worry, Francesca, a very slim connection. They can't possibly trace that back to you."

I tried to be appeased by those words, but my nervous system was on high alert. For weeks I watched and listened, glued to the television set, as was everyone else in the country at that time. Ottavio was unavailable, and for all I knew he could have been one of the gunmen.

I relied on Vittorio for comfort and reassurance, which he provided without question. Though he was pretty frantic himself, which made me think he might have been involved in the operation, in some way he wasn't saying. But I did not ask about that. Though after several weeks of unmitigated worry and anxiety about my impending fate, I did ask for something else.

We were sitting in the backroom of the store having beers, after hours, listening to the news. The BR had sent out a communiqué saying they wanted to negotiate with the *Democrazia Cristiana*, suggesting they would consider releasing Moro in exchange for the release of 13 political prisoners, among them Curcio and Franceschino. Supported by the Communists, the DC were not budging. They were refusing to negotiate with the terrorists. It seemed inevitable that Moro would be killed, if the prisoner exchange did not happen.

I walked away from the television set and into the storefront area. I couldn't bear to listen anymore. I saw my future laid out before me, a barren stretch of loneliness, a grey prison of regret, a whirlpool of sadness swallowing me whole. That's when I did it.

I went back into the meeting room, looked at Vittorio sprawled out on the couch, his thick head of black hair, his bearded face and swarthy lips, his slender, muscular frame.

"Turn off that television set," I said.

"Why? You're already up, turn it off yourself, if you want it off." I turned it off, walked over to him, straddled myself on his lap and started kissing him.

"Oh! Oh! *Che fai*?" he said, as he pushed me off. "I'm sorry, Francesca, but what are you doing?"

"Vittorio, I don't want to go to jail without ever having had sex."

"You've never had sex?" he said, surprised, and with the barest glint of delight starting to show on his face.

"No, I am 26 and I've never had sex."

He gave me that charming, inviting smile of his. "Look, Francesca, it's not that I don't find you attractive. But Raffaello, he's a friend. He asked me to look out for you. I wouldn't be looking out for you if I started taking advantage, would I?"

"It's not taking advantage if I'm the one who's asking."

"Well, you have a point there." He hesitated for a few seconds, then pulled me back on to his lap and started brushing my hair away from my face in an affectionate manner. Looked at me very intently. Then he took off an elastic band which he had around his wrist, and tied my hair back with it. "I want to see that face of yours. You're always trying to hide it."

"Am I?"

"Yes, you are," he said, as he leaned in and kissed me, languorously at first, then with increasing ferocity, as if all the fear and anxiety we had been carrying was discharging itself in the kiss, as if the kiss could help us disappear from the world, as if we had found our freedom, our flight through kissing.

We let our bliss give us the temporary illusion of safety. The leaden years pressing their weight against us.

* * *

On May 9th, 1978, Moro's body was found in the back of a red Renault, parked on Via Caetani. Visions of Montreal's October crisis flashed before me. Only now I was directly implicated. All hope of escaping the guilt and consequences of my actions dissipated, and I could no longer sleep.

After the assassination, Ottavio told me that he had been among those who had strongly opposed the kidnapping of Aldo Moro. But the hardliners had won out. He was devastated by what had happened, felt it was the beginning of the end for the BR. But still, he could not abandon the cause. Though after hearing about my involvement with the Moro affair, Ottavio insisted that I stop all participation in irregular activities for the BR. Vittorio urged the same. I listened.

In the summer of 1978, demonstrations were banned because of escalating violence from all sides. In defiance of the ban a protest was set to take place at Piazza Navona. Ottavio suggested that we all go together, he and Teresa, his pretend wife, and Vittorio and I. We agreed to meet at the bookstore, then made our way to Piazza Navona.

When Ottavio arrived that morning, he had a wild, glazed look in his eyes. He was worried because he had lost his glasses at a university demonstration a few days earlier. They had been knocked off in the middle of a confrontation with the *carabinieri*, and he had seen one of them pick them up. He was worried they would somehow trace the glasses back to his address. He was terrified, not so much for himself, but for the unnecessary implication of his mother, who was visiting him at the time, and who knew nothing of his involvement with the Red Brigades.

It is difficult to say exactly how his wild worry that morning was fateful and how concern for the sufferings of his family was a premonition. Perhaps it was the worry itself which made him more vulnerable. Perhaps it was, simply, intuition of his impending death. But that was to be his last demonstration.

Many individuals carried pistols to these demonstrations, especially those with the group Autonomia, who seemed to glorify an orgiastic kind of violence, for its own sake. They were there that morning at Piazza Navona. Since we had been forbidden to be there, there were also many carabinieri. When we arrived there were a group of masked individuals sitting on top of the Four Rivers Fountain at the centre of the piazza, chanting slogans. We were still at a bit of a distance so we couldn't hear what they were saying. They were waving placards and the shouting was getting louder and louder. As we approached we saw a group of carabinieri ordering the masked men to get down from the fountain. The men refused to obey. They just kept shouting. Now we could hear them. "Organize your rage! Shoot the bosses!" They were saying, over and over. The police started inching closer, trying to force them off the fountain. Suddenly they just jumped off, pulled out pistols and started firing. The carabinieri shot back. Ottavio was caught in the crossfire, gunned down, a fatal blow to his head.

Lying in the pool of his own blood, I saw Antonio San D'Angelo, his uncle. I saw the scaffold break. I saw him fall from that great height, shattering to the ground, hardened indifference all around him. He was, after all, expendable, replaceable, only a manual worker. Likewise, who would grieve the loss of a terrorist?

A few months later, in the Fall of 1978, they came for me. I had no idea how they were able to connect me to the buying of the aviator caps, but they did. I was at my apartment in Trastevere with Vittorio, who was cooking dinner for us, eggplant *parmigiana*, my favourite.

They came. They asked my name, cuffed me, read me my rights, then took me away, Vittorio looking terrified and sad, as he stood in front of the stove, with spatula in hand.

There was no trial. I pleaded guilty to aiding and abetting the assassination of Aldo Moro. That is what I was advised to do. There was no one who could testify that I knew nothing about what the aviator caps were to be used for, no one who could testify, without implicating themselves.

* * *

During my prison years Vittorio visited me regularly, not as a lover in waiting, but as a friend, a friend who knew I had no one, a friend who knew I had unknowingly participated in the death of the president of Italy, and a friend who had, perhaps, in his own way, grown to love me.

The way I saw it, my seduction of Vittorio Levi was the best thing I did during that time. Those six month of passionate love carried me through my prison years, even though they had been surrounded by blood and terror, even though Vittorio was later to marry and leave me behind. Without them, I might not have survived those endless years of blue and grey.

At first, I was kept in the special prison for terrorists, a section that was extremely restricted, with very few privileges. I could only speak to visitors through a glass barrier, which made it impossible for Vittorio and I to kiss or embrace or touch in any way. But still, in those early years, he came almost every week. The sight of him through the glass barrier became the highlight of my days. At that point, I was not allowed access to any sort of media, so Vittorio updated me on the "situation." The movement was falling apart, he told me. The government had cracked down hard after the Moro affair. Countless arrests had been made, and people were talking in order to get lighter sentences.

"Too bad I didn't have any information to divulge," I said once, not knowing if I would have given names, even if I'd had them to give. If Ottavio had still been alive, would I have turned him in, in order to get a lighter sentence?

"No, you would not have done that," Vittorio said, with conviction. "You could have turned me in and you didn't." I looked at his earnest, handsome face through the glass barrier, and all I could think of was kissing him.

"The thought never crossed my mind," I said. "Never crossed my mind."

For the first few months, I was bunked up with a woman called Marietta, who had been charged and convicted of a car bombing in Rome, a bomb that had severely injured a judge and his wife. When she found out what I was in for, she kept applauding me as if I was some kind of hero. I put up with it for a while, but one day I exploded.

"Are you fucking crazy?" I shouted. "Are you fucking crazy? You think that's how we're going to get justice for the people?" Vittorio's words came back to me. "Those bodyguards were southerners, they were workers doing their job."

"Yes, the job of a fascist state!" she yelled back.

"And you think that assassinating the president of our country is going to serve the cause of revolutionary justice. Where does it end? Stalin? Mao? Brigate Rosse? How much atrocity has to take place, in the name of justice, before it becomes the very same thing you're fighting against? Tell me! Tell me! Tell me!"

She was seemingly taken aback, hadn't expected that from me. Frankly, I hadn't expected it from myself, till it came.

Marietta and I stopped talking after that, or at least, had very few exchanges. She turned out to be compulsively belligerent, getting herself into physical altercations with other inmates quite frequently, which to my relief, eventually got her moved to another section.

My strategy was to keep to myself. When I wasn't lying on my bunk, I was in the dingy room with books, which passed as a library. I stopped giving my opinion on anything. And I gravitated towards those who also seemed to be using silence as a strategy. For the most part this worked, except when it didn't. Still, I only incurred one physical injury during all that time in prison. And it was all about shampoo.

For a while, I befriended a woman called Clara. I confided in her what had happened with my father, about how Micola had accidentally pushed him to his death, about her withdrawal, her muteness.

Then one day, out of the blue, someone came up to me in the dining hall and accused me of stealing her shampoo, some fancy box of travel shampoos she had received as a gift. I tried to deny it, but she just kept yelling. "Did you take them as a present for your girlfriend, Clara? Did you? Was that it?" I didn't respond. She continued to taunt. "Why don't you get your murdering, lunatic sister to bring you shampoo, instead of stealing it from others? But then again, she's probably in a loony bin by now, or maybe they've put her in jail too." That's when I lifted my tray of food and threw it right at her. She stumbled and fell to the floor, food all over the place. When she got up, she tried to take a swing at me but missed. I punched her back, in the face, so hard, it fractured my hand. Didn't know I had that in me either, till it came. All that rage that had nowhere else to go, all that rage that had accumulated for decades.

That's the way it was behind bars. Small things became huge dramas when you least expected it, and betrayal a common currency.

After several years, I was permitted to sit in a room with visitors, for periods of time. I was allowed to receive books and other gifts, which was also a saving grace. The books, that is. And they came not only from my bookstore lover, but also from my teacher, Alfredo Negri.

If Vittorio saved my emotional life while I was in prison, then Alfredo Negri saved my intellectual one. He was my only other regular visitor. Until the end, he came on a regular basis. His commitment to the "struggle" was well known among the political prisoners, so his friendship garnered me some respect, which I used for all it was worth, to get people off my back, if necessary.

When Alfredo and I were allowed to sit together in the same room, we would discuss the books he brought me. Like a private tutor, or the father I had always wanted, he ushered me into the world of ideas, of literature, of poetry, worlds I'd always been drawn to, but somehow avoided. Because I had been persuaded that they were of no use to the class struggle. And though Alfredo was of that same political persuasion, he was wise enough to know that, at that point, the last thing I wanted or needed to hear was more ideological babble.

Initially, the extent of Alfredo's interest in me was perplexing. Why would he visit so frequently? Why did he seem so dedicated to helping me survive prison life? I assumed it was probably because he felt guilty about how I had ended up. After all, he had been the one to arrange my first meeting with Mario Moretti. But eventually, another story emerged, a story that better explained the mysterious draw between us.

It was a Christmas day. Maybe two years into my sentence. Alfredo had come to visit, bringing me lemon panettone and a thermos of espresso. We were discussing the poet Rilke, when I told him about my sister, Micola, who had been a singer, who had loved the poetry of Leonard Cohen. That is how we began speaking about the past. That is how I came to know what happened to Paolo's mother.

I was telling him what had brought my family back to Italy, the accidental death of my father, the birth, the adoption, Micola's withdrawal, and then Paolo. I was telling him about the shock of discovering that someone I had been so desperately pining for was gay. That's when I saw it, the way he ran his fingers through his hair, the exact same gesture, hand through his hair, sliding down the back of his neck, then pulling his hand forward and down again. That's when I saw the similarity in facial structure, and though in a different language, the way with words, the eloquence.

That's when he understood it too. "You said your friend lived in Westmount. What was his name?"

"Paolo Richards," I said.

He went pale, but then suddenly happy, as if some long-standing frown on the face of his life had just relaxed, and some great mystery had been decoded.

That is how I learned that Alfredo knew Paolo's parents. That is when he told me the story of his love affair with Marina Richards.

Paolo's father, Max, had been a diplomat, stationed in Rome during the 1950s, where he and his wife lived for several years. At first, Marina was excited about living in a foreign country, and as almost everyone is, enchanted with Rome's beautiful chaos. In "America" you had to go to museums to see art, but in Rome, you could just wander the streets, which she did, keeping herself entertained and occupied, for a time.

But, eventually, the loneliness caught up with her, even in Rome. She did not see much of her husband, Max, because he was always taken up with work. While this was not unusual, her husband's work habits being no different in Rome than they had been in Montreal, the isolation of living abroad, without friends or family, made it more challenging.

After a few months, Marina decided to take an Italian language course. She discovered that she was good with languages and was soon able to read newspapers and periodicals in Italian. When she felt confident that her Italian was good enough, she enrolled in a course in political economy at the University of Rome. This was an unlikely choice for a woman at that time. But her motivation was not so much interest, as it was hope, hope of learning another language, a language that might help improve communication with her husband, Max.

Her world was a landscape of the interior, a world shaped and coloured by the rhythms and nuances of emotion, slight gestures and muted tones, a poetic place only she inhabited. But while she could see that Max's world was different, he was completely blind to hers. For him the worlds of technical details, political analyses and scientific explanations were the only ones that existed, the only ones that mattered. Marina's concerns were not even mysterious to him, just the typical preoccupations of a woman, those things you tolerated in order to have beauty, comfort and security in your life.

Marina took the course in political economy, thinking she might be able to create some small bridge between herself and her husband. Her professor, as it turned out, was Alfredo Negri. At that time, he was not much older than she was, young, passionate and full of intense idealism. Negri noticed her immediately. She stood out to him not only because of her beauty but because she was a foreigner and because she seemed so sensitive. The way she moved, such grace and elegance. Unfamiliar. Unusual to him, who came from a place where hard labour, despair and the constant struggle for survival precluded such elegance; where sensitivity itself was a luxury not suited for survival. When he first met Marina Richards she seemed to him like the antithesis of everything he had known.

He watched her longingly for months, trying to figure out how he could spend some time with her. The erotic pull began to obsess him. He started following her after class without her knowing it. He discovered that she walked to Termini Station, took the Metro to Flamino, walked along the Tiber, then sat to have her lunch, which she usually brought with her. Often she stopped at Ponte Mazzini and sat on a bench along Lungotevere della Farnesina. After her lunch she would read for a while, or just watch the people go by. He stayed at a distance so she wouldn't see him. But finally, he decided he would walk by the bench near Ponte Mazzini, as if by chance.

At first she was shy and nervous at encountering him there. But when it happened a second time, and then a third time, she realized that she had started hoping for the encounters, started waiting for them, started wanting them.

She had never known someone like Alfredo, nor the thrill of what became their daily meetings at Ponte Mazzini. With Alfredo, she could talk about anything, poetry, philosophy, even economics, which had been a foreign subject to her, until she took the course with him. And though they were limited by Marina's Italian, the urgency of their desire to communicate with each other seemed to make it easy.

Marina's growing desire made her daring. She began fabricating reasons to be out at night, so that she and Alfredo could have dinner together at a restaurant, or go to a movie, or just walk, at night, without the glare of the sun, when he could reach for her hand and hold it, or stretch his arm across her shoulder as they walked, unnoticeably, as if it was normal, or as if it wasn't happening at all.

It was the sixth month of her clandestine intimacy with Alfredo when Max announced that he was being transferred back to Canada. On that night, the love she had been denying hit her full force, shattering the protective shield of fantasy.

She did not tell Alfredo until the last day they were together. She calculated with the precision of a mathematician, so that their last meeting would occur while Max was in Milan.

They spent the evening at an outdoor café in front of Piazza di Spagna. It was a chilly November night, a blustery wind tearing through the piazza, but they noticed none of this. Silence reigned instead of passionate discussion. She studied him, carefully, his raging blue eyes, his dishevelled, dark curly hair, the way he leaned with his face in hand, against the wall.

Later in the evening, he took her to his small apartment on Via Paradiso. She studied that too, its sparseness, the wooden table with a single chair, stacks of newspapers and periodicals everywhere, the single bed, a radio and nothing else, so antithetical to her own life, filled with opulence and emptiness.

It seemed too difficult to do or say anything. They just sat on the bed, close to each other, their backs against the wall. He gently stroked her hand. She took off her clothes and lay down. For a long time he just looked at her. Then he undressed and lay beside her, erotic tension taut between them. As if to prolong the agony, as if to preclude the end, they waited till morning before they made love.

And that was the morning that Paolo was conceived.

Alfredo did not marry until much later, not because of romantic attachment to Marina but because of political commitments. Though he responded to her letters at first, and saw her again, once or twice, his life came to have a different focus, one that did not include her. His politics became much more extreme and the memory of the beauty that had once ruined him was erased by an ideology that could never have justified an affiliation with someone like Marina Richards.

Alfredo's letters to her had been gentle, careful, for he must have sensed her fragility. Though he gave her no cause for including him in the fabrication of her private mythology, he did not take away the memory upon which it was built. He did become concerned about the constant flow of letters, year after year, decade after decade, letters so beautiful they sounded like music. But he never told her to stop. Only the declaration of his marriage, finally, accomplished that.

Marina sent a final communication, telling Alfredo what she was about to do. That is when he came to me with the suitcase full of letters, asking me to take them, and to find a way, somehow, of getting them to Paolo. I had been released by then, and had mentioned that, at some point, I would return for a visit to Montreal.

It might seem strange to build one's life on such a brief fragment of time. Yet, I understood it. I had done the same with Vittorio, though not for decades, certainly for years, I survived on that short interlude of love. Paolo's mother, it seems, could not survive without the possibility, or the sheer fantasy, of what Alfredo had brought to life in her, a threadbare lifeline, which finally just broke.

When Paolo and I first knew each other, in Montreal, I thought it was economic class that separated us. His mother's elegance, the beauty of their home in Westmount, the rooms full of books, the classical music, Erik Satie playing in the background. This is the chasm I thought was between us, a chasm that could not be bridged, because I had

175

nothing and he had everything. That's how I saw things then. My longing for him, a precious thing of beauty I could never have, was not entitled to.

But Paolo's mother's suicide taught me something different, that she had felt just as trapped by her social class as I had by mine. And that love just happens without regard for circumstance, or sexual orientation, or economic status. It happens without regard for anyone or anything. The problem is, that most of the time, we just betray it.

* * *

When I got out of prison in 1993, everything had changed. No one cared anymore whether you were a Marxist or a Leninist, a Maoist, or Trotskyite. The Italian government had succeeded in destroying the BR and were focused on trying to do the same with the Mafia. The Berlin Wall had fallen. Our cause had failed. Everything was about freedom and democracy and globalization. The idea of revolutionary justice had all but disappeared.

I truly hadn't known that my actions were supporting the kidnapping and assassination of Aldo Moro. I knew it was an "armed struggle." I knew that acts of violence were being orchestrated, and I had come to believe the justification for them. "Look at Chile," Ottavio would always say. "They're not going to let us change things democratically." That seemed true. So why did it all go wrong? I'm still trying to figure that out, still learning to live with the guilt and with the despair.

* * *

The first thing I did when I was released from prison was return to Volturino. I knew my mother had died; however,

I did expect Micola to be there. But the house had been sold and Micola was nowhere to be found. When I asked around about her, all I kept hearing was "*Ana purtato a chati paci.*" (They've taken her to the crazies.)—which I couldn't quite make out at first, and then it clicked. It was the florist, Lorena Vespa, who told me that Micola had been institutionalized in Naples since the mid-80s.

From the institution I learned that a nurse named Cassandra Caputo had taken my sister away years earlier, and that they hadn't been seen or heard from since.

I became obsessed with finding them. It took me several months of searches and dead ends. I returned numerous times to the Frullone Psychiatric institute in Naples and spoke to other nurses and doctors in hope of finding someone that might have known Cassandra or where she might have taken my sister. Then one day, one of the nurses came out with it. "I know Cassandra grew up in Amalfi. Perhaps they went there."

I took the bus along the Amalfi coast, along the narrow roads, limestone cliffs dropping precipitously into the sea. When I arrived it was not difficult to find them. They were well known to the locals. Micola, with her wild, black locks and ravaged beauty. The luminous Cassandra, with her blond, tangled tresses. Yes, everyone seemed to know them, their mythical aura and their magical potions. Their embrace of the open, their lack of need for traditional shelter. Their home was near a cave at the edge of the sea and their routines marked by the shifts and currents of elemental living. The cave of forever sorrowing, Cassandra later called it, when she sent me her written account of the years she spent with my sister. Their isle of weeping.

When I knocked at the green wooden door of their stone shack, it was already evening, and Cassandra answered tentatively. Even after I told her who I was, she seemed suspicious and afraid. Though after a few moments, it was as if she suddenly recognized me. And a warm, broad smile lit up her beautiful face.

Micola had already gone to bed, so we just sat at the kitchen table, had tea and talked about how they had escaped the hospital, about Micola's silence, about changes Cassandra had noticed after Micola had seen a dance troupe practising their choreography, outside a nearby grotto. About the small pieces of paper she had started writing phrases on.

I loved Cassandra immediately, earthy and intelligent, sweet and wise. What luck, I thought, that my sister had been found by someone like her. That night I slept on a foam mattress on their kitchen floor and, strangely, had the happiest dream I can ever remember:

I am in a cabin with a window facing the sea. Paolo's mother is standing beside me. I feel nothing of the old insecurity I always felt around her. It is as if we know each other very well. She is holding a suitcase. The letters. Her letters. It is a perfect day. It is hot, but not too hot. There are people lying out on the beach. I have the thought that we have travelled back in time, to a time before, before we had to fear the sun, before the water was a danger to our health, before Marina's unbearable loss, before Micola's silence, before Ottavio's death. There are people swimming, others just soaking in the sun. The breeze is gentle and caressing. We can feel it through the open window.

"Where is your sister?" Marina asks.

"She's on the beach, waiting for us. This morning, she heard someone say on the radio that isolation and loneliness is sometimes just a bad habit. So she decided to go out. She's waiting for us on the beach."

We walk out. She, with her suitcase in hand, and I too, with my notebooks in a basket. At first we can't find Micola. There are so many people around. But then we see her, at the far end, the far, more secluded end of the beach. She is sitting on a huge white towel, big enough for all of us. She has a brightly coloured, hand-made purse beside her, and that book, Handke's *A Sorrow Beyond Dreams*. When she sees us, she jumps up with joy, a joy I have not seen in Micola for a very long time. We stand on the towel, huddling together, as if dancing, a round dance.

Then Paolo's mother becomes distracted by a sight in the distance.

"It's Paolo, Paolo. Look. It's Paolo."

We all turn towards the water. There's a very small figure in the distance, which I could never have made out as Paolo. He is running, as if out of the sea, towards us. But then when he hits the shore and I can see his whole body, I too know it's him. He keeps running towards us and as he approaches I feel the old excitement, wild and thrilling. I'm happy it's still there, and the old dread is gone. As he gets closer I see that he is carrying something in one hand. Unidentifiable at first, and then I see it, a rose. A white rose. Then, just as he is about to reach us, I woke up …

I was filled with panic, for the thought occurred to me, for the first time, that I might never see Paolo again.

And just as I was trying to reconcile the joy in the dream with sad reality, Cassandra walked into the kitchen and offered to make me coffee.

"You seem different this morning," Cassandra said, as we sat, again, at the kitchen table, sipping coffee.

"It must be the dream I just woke up from. A happy dream, where everything works out, for everyone. The opposite of the life I've known, in fact."

"Well, you're here, now. That's a happy thing."

I was just about to answer that I agreed with her when Micola walked into the kitchen. She was wearing a tattered green nightgown, her hair wildly dishevelled. Still, that gaze of an enchantress, which could throw you off balance, that physical power I always envied. But this time it was she who got thrown off balance. I jumped up from the chair, and for a few seconds I met that gaze, before she started shaking uncontrollably. I tried to approach her so that I could hug her, but she started screaming, then fell to the floor.

Maybe it was seeing me so suddenly, maybe the flood of the past she had shut away. Whatever it was, it was clear Micola was not prepared to deal with me, then. The sight of me seemed to break down the walls she had erected against the past. My visit caused the turbulence to surface, a turbulence too great for her small frame. I knew it would be; I don't know what else I expected. Though it was painful to witness, in the end, I was relieved that she was with Cassandra, and that she had found a life that seemed to suit her.

"Perhaps if you come again, I can prepare her. That might make a difference," Cassandra said, after we had calmed Micola down, and stepped outside onto the rocky path, the waves slamming aggressively against the shore as we tried to talk.

"OK," I said, without too much conviction. "I think you're right. I shouldn't have come unexpectedly like this."

"Leave me your number ... I'll talk to her, maybe we can set up another time."

"All right, I can do that ... This has been very difficult, but I am happy she is with you, Cassandra."

"I am happy to have her, and she's fine, Francesca ... I know it's easy to say, but try not to worry about her."

She hugged me warmly and I left, up the countless stone steps to the main square, where I waited for my bus to Rome.

It was my turn now, I thought, to try and build a life for myself. I didn't have many skills. A couple of degrees in sociology from a Canadian university was not going to be worth too much in Italy. I had always followed Ottavio. Books were all I knew. So when I returned to Rome, I got back into book-selling. Vittorio, though married with two kids by then, still ran his bookstore near Termini Station. He had opened another store in the old Jewish ghetto, where he still lived. He was looking for a manager, so he didn't have to go back and forth between the two stores so much. The timing was perfect.

After Ottavio's death and my imprisonment, I wondered why we had paid such a price to accomplish nothing. Many of the high profile members of BR were arrested and collaborated in order to get shorter sentences. One of the founders, Alberto Franceschini, recanted his involvement with the BR, referring to that phase of his life as characterized by an addiction to ideology. "The worst possible drug," he had said.

It is painful to recall, now, how even my relationship with Ottavio had become reduced to nothing more than ideological exchanges. Everything was done to serve the cause, no room for personal emotion or doubt. Even so, I knew he cared about me. That was always a given we were supposed to take for granted, according to Ottavio. He would get angry if ever I challenged that, if ever I seemed to want more from him than these supposed givens, like some words of reassurance or affection. He stopped doing that altogether once we were in Italy. He always acted as if these kinds of emotional needs were a luxury we couldn't afford or some bourgeois inclination I hadn't yet over-come. Some part of me believed him, because I spent years trying to talk myself out of those needs, as if they were just bad habits, like smoking or eating too much cake.

And yes, ideology had become a prison for those of us committed to revolutionary justice. No one had time to stop and consider that, maybe, humans also had spiritual and psychological needs. But now, with everyone gone, dead or away, I could see that the malaise of mortality can never be appeased by power or wealth alone. This does not mean we should not fight for justice, but only that ideology cannot contain the complexity and creativity of human longing. Our own individual needs and desires should not have to be forfeited in the process of fighting for justice. Along with food and shelter and the right to work, beauty too is something we should all be entitled to. It's not just some frivolous, bourgeois construct. It's as necessary as air and water, and sometimes, the only antidote to the terrors and horrors of life.

Because when all is said and done, it is my memory of Paolo's beauty that remains. I didn't know at the time that I would never feel that way again. I did return to Mon-treal for a visit, though only once, after I found Micola in Amalfi and knew that she was safe. I went looking for him, but he was gone. To Toronto, Titiana had said, work-ing as the operations manager of a weekly magazine. But I wasn't up for that journey.

I went instead to that jutting piece of land, that slen-der peninsula, branching out from the St. Lawrence River, the one at the bottom of 75th Avenue and Lasalle Boulevard. Our private little woodland, suffused with the memory of my first erotic encounter with him, the one for which I paid, with a black eye for two weeks, the patch over my eye.

We had driven Titiana home to Lasalle. She hated it so much. Even long after her parents had moved there, she would come to N.D.G. to hang with the old crowd. We arrived at Titiana's place to discover her parents had gone out, and that she couldn't get into the house. We decided to drive down to the river with a six-pack of beer, which we bought at the local depanneur.

We sat by the river, laughing, talking and drinking. It was a hot and sultry summer night. We kept daring each other to take a swim in the polluted river, which smelled particularly bad on that night. Paolo almost pushed me in at one point as we chased each other along the banks, deliberately falling and tumbling into each other, enjoying that push/pull of innocent, physical yearning. But even as we tumbled around together, laughing and wrestling, I was aware of the sun going down, and the hell that would break loose once I got home. Even so, I could not say that I had to leave. Some part of me did not care, even as Ottavio decided that we should go walking in the wooded area of the jutting peninsula. I did not care. I had to be there with Paolo, surrounded by night and water. I had to be there with him.

The air sparked with our lust and longing. The trees swayed tenderly, magnetically, sounding and bending everything towards the electrical charge of our barely touching bodies, walking through the wood, on a sultry, summer night, adolescents searching for a hideout, just to be in the dark together.

When we reached the tip of the peninsula, we sat on the rocks and hung our feet in the water. Paolo was sitting right beside me and I watched as he fumbled with a piece of wood. His hands, so fine, so beautiful. I was transfixed as he slowly peeled away the skin from the wood, exposing its smooth, slippery surface.

Suddenly he dropped the piece of wood and abruptly stood, pulling me up towards him. We leaned against a tree and he stared at me for a long time. Then, tentatively, and ever so delicately, he brushed my lips with his finger tips. That was all. No more. Then he pushed me away, almost as abruptly as he had pulled me towards him. I stood there, stunned and confused, my lips throbbing from that tender touch, and nothing more.

I looked over at Titiana and Ottavio, who had fallen into some heavy petting. They were lying on the rocks, Ottavio with his hand up Titiana's dress as he kissed her half exposed breasts. We just watched them for a while, not knowing what to do. Then they noticed and it all stopped. But that erotic frame is still etched in my memory. Titiana's bare breasts, Paolo's hands, my throbbing lips, the whispering trees, the still, dark waters, the night.

Then we all broke into laughter.

Finally, we straightened ourselves up and brought Titiana home. Her parents had arrived. By the time you, Ottavio and I were driving home, it was past 11 pm. My first sexual experience mingled with dread and fear, as I prepared for battle with my father, who would ravage and rob my precious experience. But, not all of it; no, not all of it. Still. Today. Nothing remains so erotically charged for me as the memory of that first brush of my lips with Paolo's fingers. His beautiful hands.

Then I waited. I waited. For days, for months. For him to touch me again, like that. It never happened. He never touched me again with such tender erotic yearning.

Luckily, that tangled growth of lusty underbrush grew in a separate zone, a zone fenced off from the territory of our everyday affection. So I could hide it well, keep it silent. But then, there was also another territory which I inhabited, one with no wild growth or dense underbrush, just a barren wasteland of toxic refuse.

That is where I went the night I discovered Paolo and Ricardo in the bush, behind the meadow. I went to that barren land, which had slowly been taking over my life, that pull of darkness that long preceded Paolo, that I somehow inherited from that windy hill where I was born, from those buried there for centuries.

When I saw Paolo with Ricardo in the wooded expanse behind Titiana's cabin, the truth came tumbling forward, clear, clear as an avalanche, a hurricane or earthquake, clear as a natural disaster. The truth came circling in, in one clear swoop. I had no ground to hold it. Because Paolo had become my ground, my fertile ground, now contaminated.

I was still under the illusion, then, that someone else could be my ground.

For a long time I hated you, Paolo, hated the deception, the lie. Ridiculous, I thought. Men's and women's bodies are not that different. Flesh is flesh. If you love someone, does it make that much difference what sex they are? Petty, I thought, fixated, narrow. A cock-centred universe. So I threw you away.

But now, after all this time, I finally understand that you have always been my muse, an echo of unfulfilled, self-affection, some ancient piece of self-knowledge I had lost sight of, that only you had managed to mirror.

The truth is that the ideologically constructed world I let myself submit to was a purely male world, even if there were women who were a part of it. It was a world seen from the sterile lens of pure abstraction, inflexibly applied without concern for life or living. Purity of purpose, power and rage, that was all that counted. At the time, this suited me, because I too felt only rage and because I was trying to escape being haunted by the past.

But this is what I want now. I want my words to smell and taste of earth, with rivers and currents running through them, with sun and rain, intermittently, pouring out of them, with the dead, whispering in them.

The dead whispering, not pulling, as they often did, roaming the dry and dusty hills, surrounding Volturino. There, the dead seem to lurk from every corner, part of the very air you breathed, as if the place was theirs, occupied territory. There the dead surround you and envelop you, any time they please, voicing their laments, their complaints, their judgments, their sense of injustice, their pleadings.

Here, in Rome, they simply whisper. I can live with that.

In Volturino, the women carry the dead, as they carry their young, like a burden, like a duty, which they cannot escape. That is the unquestioned tradition, long and deep, women hold the grief and sorrow of their villages and bear the demands of the dead with their very lives. Those black-kerchiefed women. They are as much a part of those craggy, hilltop villages as the landscape itself, with its sprawling vineyards and olive groves.

Now, I want to listen, only for an elemental language, like the one that has pulled me back to you, Paolo, saving me from the oppressive pull of that sorrowful tradition, that history of miseria, that long dark skein. My memory of your beauty, an antidote.

Always,

Francesca

RAINY NIGHT
HOUSE

Some days the sea was all brute force. A throaty, roaring blast. It slammed its weight against the shore, almost reaching our doorstep, then receding, only to slam us again. On those days Mara sat on her red wooden chair, just outside the grotto, still as stone. The sea smashed and roared around her.

Surely, such concentration would bring her back, I thought at the time. But not yet, not then. She lived the life of the sea, submitting to its occupying force, almost like a lover, or maybe, a hostage. If you went near her on those days, her eyes would tell you she was a danger, the way all beauty can be a danger, a power that can singe and destroy.

Mara never tired of the roiling waves, the lapping and smashing, the wrecking and caressing. The moods of the sea suited her.

It was people she could not bear. The sea was her only love, then, her only tie to life.

When the sea was calm, Mara moved. She paced the rocky shore just outside our small stone house, several times a day, like meditative ritual. Sometimes she seemed to be humming quietly under her breath. Though I couldn't tell for sure, and I never asked.

I was sure Mara could hear the world even from our shore. Its grief and laments hounded her, pushing her, always, further in. At least that's what I imagined. I imagined that she was done with whatever it was that had happened to her, done with the inevitable harm humans cause each other, done with the indifference of the fates, their tangled weave of beauty and horror. She wanted none of it. She wanted to drown it out. She wanted to wash it away. In this, the sea was her only ally, smashing and clearing. In this, even I was an adversary, and love, a fractured thing she had discarded.

Or maybe, just maybe, I was only seeing myself. I, too, was trying to get away from the world, away from my visions of the planet burning, the rivers flooding, oceans dying and the boorish moguls rising.

That is what I saw. I saw my brother dying, too, I saw an earthquake coming, I saw the judge and his wife teetering, his bodyguards falling. But I didn't trust my visions, then. I was always getting lost in that thicket and bramble and dark wood of my sight. Then, I found Mara. She was the sensitive. She had the knowledge. That much I could tell.

I first met Mara when she was a patient at the Frullone psychiatric hospital in Naples and I was her nurse. I still had the vague notion, then, that maybe I could help cure souls the modern way. But I was not prepared for Frullone, a grim, dilapidated storehouse of tormented humans.

It had been 10 years since the *basaglia* law had passed, outlawing asylums in Italy. But it hadn't quite caught up to the South. A law is one thing, putting it into practice another. At Frullone they no longer electrocuted patients, or cut out bits of their brain, or chained them to beds for years. But the halls were haunted with the contorted expressions of broken souls, some half clothed, or crawling on hands and knees, some curled up in beds which they rarely left. There was Mara, with her torrent of black curls, seated as she always was, in the small alcove just outside the dining area, looking out the window, playing her silent part in this choreography of madness.

"Don't waste your time, Cassandra," I kept hearing from co-workers who saw me trying to engage her. "She hasn't spoken a word in five years. You're not about to change that now."

But I wasn't convinced. Mara's silence seemed to me to be an act of will. It was in her eyes, emerald green, deep and forlorn. Far, maybe unreachable. But I felt compelled to try.

Her file described peculiar hand movements which she used to make, repetitive hand movements, like those of a trumpet player, though when I met her, her hands hung limp by her side, as she stared out the window, overlooking a small courtyard, which had a couple of poplar trees and a gnarled olive tree. In front of the trees was a rusty iron bench that no one ever sat on; to the side was a statue of the Virgin Mary holding baby Jesus. Mary's nose was chipped and the baby's head cracked, missing half its face. At their feet was a mossy pond, birds flapping in and out, small lizards sliding around on flat rocks.

Her file referred to her as Micola Benvenuto, but to me she would always be Mara, the spiritual name I would eventually give her. Mara from the hilltop village of Volturino, a place where the wind never stops blowing, and people wander around with heads full of wind.

One such native came down from the windy hill in 1984 and brought Mara to the hospital, when her mother died. Her file mentioned a sister, Francesca, though nothing was known about her whereabouts. Mara had not spoken a word since she'd arrived, not about her mother, not about her sister, not about herself.

Because she did not speak, I began to speak to her. I would sit beside her at her window, in the mornings, make a cup of coffee for the both of us, and tell her things about myself. I told her that I had never married, that I had come to Naples from Amalfi to study at the university, where I had studied languages and then nursing. I told her that I missed Amalfi, with its lemon-scented air and cliff-side homes tumbling into the sea, that Naples was wearing me down. I told her that my parents were dead and that I'd had an older brother, who was killed in a car bomb in Rome. I told her that I had a house on the coast of Amalfi, which my parents had left to me, not a big house, more like a couple of stone rooms, where my father used to stay when he went out to fish. It was close to the sea, hidden by a stone wall, which my father had built himself, shrouded by ancient cedars, that you couldn't see the house at all unless you knew it was there. My father was a hermit, I told her, so he built his refuge away from all the other fishermen's cottages, away from the sandy beach with its rows and rows of deck chairs and brightly coloured *ubrallini*.

Mara flashed me a look for the first time, her fiercely sad look, which startled me and left me breathless. Prescient, feral. That's when I knew she could hear me.

A very old man came to visit her one day, dishevelled and skinny, wearing a black suit and a fedora, a suit way too big for him, as if he had borrowed it for the occasion. Mara got agitated at the sight of him. The man became upset too, and left, when he saw that Mara didn't want him there. No one got a chance to ask who he was or what he knew. He never came again.

We had no personal history. We did not even have fragments. Except for the reference to trumpet playing, and her ancestral roots on a windy hill, we knew nothing.

I tried to find her sister Francesca. It did not help that I had no idea what part of Italy she lived in. About a year after I met Mara, I made a trip to the windy village, in the mountains of Apulia. At that time of year, in early November, it was filled with toothless old people who seemed to have no interest in speaking to me about the Benvenutos. Finally, someone directed me to Lorena Vespa, a round, hefty woman, with the face of a beauty queen, owner of the local flower shop in the central piazza. When I mentioned the Benvenutos, Lorena gasped and went pale, expecting the worst, I could see. But when I told her who I was, her eyes softened and she let out a sigh of relief.

"I loved that girl," she said. "They never should have taken her away from here, not even when her mother died. I tried to find her sister in Rome to ask her to come back, but she didn't seem to be anywhere. When she left, she said she was going to Rome to meet up with her cousin Ottavio, who was going to help her get a job. We never heard from her again. We heard that Ottavio died in 1979, gunned down at a demonstration. Turns out he was a member of the Red Brigades. We never knew. We just saw it on the news. I think that's what killed the mother. She couldn't bear it anymore, a daughter who had stopped speaking and another who had disappeared, involved in God knows what."

"When did Micola stop speaking?" I asked.

" I don't know. They immigrated to Montreal, and then came back in 1977. Micola was already mute, then, and they never said anything about it, just that the father had died and that's why they had returned."

"What is your relation to them?"

"No blood relation. Everyone comes through my shop, at one time or another, birth, death, love, marriage. Micola liked flowers. Her mother would bring her here, sometimes. She would sit with me for the day." She pointed to a small wooden chair parked in the corner of the store beside a red Oleander bush. "There, she would always sit there, just in the corner."

I asked about the old man in the fedora. She said that was the uncle, the mother's brother, but that he had died, recently, as well. No one else in the village was related to the Benvenutos. The rest of them were all in Montreal.

"Why didn't Micola stay with the uncle when the mother died?" I asked.

"He felt he was too old and couldn't handle her care, but then I think he felt bad about it afterwards."

"Yes, that's probably why he came to visit. But Micola did not take it well. She refused to see him, or at least became too agitated to have any visitors. "

"I'm so glad you decided to come," she said, "so at least I know she's OK."

"Yes, I'm glad I came too," I said, though I was no closer at all to understanding what had happened to Mara.

When I returned from Volturino I decided to take Mara away from Frullone. If there was any hope for her, she needed to be away from that place. I too, had become demoralized by the hospital, and tired of the frenzy and chaos of Naples. I had my savings, my small house on the coast, and a twist in my heart that was pulling me back to an ancestral calling I had been resisting.

I packed Mara's things. There was very little, a few items of clothing, a copy of Let Us Compare Mythologies by the poet Leonard Cohen, some photographs that seem to have been taken in Canada, somewhere in the woods, pine trees all around, a lake. There was a jade necklace with some matching earrings wrapped in some red tissue, a pair of sandals, a leather case with some money in it, some blank notebooks and a vinyl copy of Bob Dylan's Blood on the Tracks.

I know I should have gone through the proper channels, but they would have resisted or not allowed it. I knew it was the right thing for both of us. So in the dead of night, we left, like two escaping criminals. We waited at the train station till morning, then took a bus to Amalfi, along that narrow, nerve-wracking, cliff-side road, with its tiny villages and hotels, precariously clinging to the rocky slopes, past silvery groves of olives and leafy vineyards, past forests of lemon and wild cactus fruit.

We made it to Amalfi in the early afternoon. Though it was December, it was warm, the air almost sultry. We stopped at Piazza Duoma, Amalfi's central square and picked up some groceries at the fruit and vegetable market, then stopped at Bar Cortina to have a cappuccino and *sfoilatale*. Sandro Petrilli, a middle-school friend of mine, was still working there. Not a great time to be running into people, I knew, but there he was.

"Cassandra, *che surprese, sei returnato*?" (What a surprise, you've returned).

"Ah si," I said brusquely, not wanting to engage his curiosity at that moment. Then he looked over at Mara and said, *"Ciao, Bellissima."* But she didn't answer.

"E stanche. (She is tired)," I said, just as another customer came in, distracting him from us. We slipped outside to have our coffee and pastry on the terrace. Then we made our way down the long *scalatinella,* carved from the cliffside rock, zigzagging down through tangled shrubs, right down to the clump of cedars that hid my father's house.

When Mara saw the house, she took a deep breath and exhaled very slowly, then sat on the red, wooden chair just outside the door, a rickety old chair, left there by my father, the chair that would become her spiritual prop, her anchor.

"My father has a boat. I could take you to Capri, sometime," I said enthusiastically. She didn't respond, completely indifferent to the idea of an outing. But when I took her to the grotto, where my father kept his boat, the expression on her face changed, from the usual stony vacancy to a slight smile, or a release of some tension. I couldn't tell exactly what it was, but for the first time I saw feeling in her face.

At first, Mara continued her mute existence as before. I cooked and cleaned. She slept and sat on my father's red chair, which she took to the seaside grotto everyday. The path to the grotto was rocky and treacherous, not easy to manoeuvre. My father had left it that way to keep away the tourists. But it did not deter Mara. She wandered down, through rugged stone and wild shrub, carrying the red chair into the sheltered cave opening on the rocky cliff, where she sat surrounded by wild cactus fruit. She placed the chair in, slightly, so that that if you did not know she was there, you could easily pass by without noticing. Though it was rare for anyone to pass there. There was no sandy beach, just a small stretch of rough pebbles outside the grotto.

At high tide, the sea almost reached her feet, but she did not move. At night, when she came in, she was always damp and smelling of salt. Only if it stormed did she move the chair further in. In winter, I had to bundle her up before she left, or she would simply go, without a hat or coat, as she seemed to feel nothing, as if nothing mattered, except sitting and watching the changing moods of the sea.

I returned to my magical arts, which I had abandoned when I left for Naples to study nursing. In the summers I would forage for herbs in the bushy surrounds of Piazza Duomo. My favourite spot was through the white-washed passageway that led past Piazza Spirito Santo and the Museo della Carte over to Via Paradiso. Just beyond *via Paradiso*, the way gets stony and wild as the cliffs close in, and past the forests of lemons and wild figs, you can also find wild valerian, nettle and thyme, and sometimes even wild roses.

I chopped and measured and mixed and brewed my herbal remedies and potions, which I sold at the local market, where I was known, as that is where my father had sold his fish. Sometimes I took the boat over to neighbouring Atrani and Minori and sold my concoctions there. Soon everyone knew I was back, and a stream of locals began to trickle down to our stone house by the sea. Ailing old people, mostly, looking for herbal treatment or looking just to talk.

One of my most frequent customers was the matriarch of the family know as *i buciardi*, the liars. In the villages and towns of the South it is common for families to not only have official last names, but also clan names, names that they and their ancestors would have been known by, for who knows how long, and who knows why. Some of the clan names were extremely bizarre, with origins impossible to fathom, like "pigeon shit" or "small holes." But it seemed easy to imagine why "liars" might have attached to the Monacos, one of the wealthiest families in town, some say the region. They owned many of the grand, lemon terraced homes with their lush gardens and trellised belvederes, with magnificent views of the sea, which they rented out to the rich and famous. They were not well liked in town, though everyone feigned respect, while behind their backs they told a different story. The most popular refrain was that they should really be called the "stealers," because their ancestors had been pirates and that was how they had originally come into their wealth.

Teresa Monaco wanted me to break a spell which she believed had been cast upon her son, Salvatore Monaco.

Salvatore was tall, rich and handsome. Some said he looked like Sylvester Stallone. No one could imagine why he would choose to marry the short, round, though pretty, Pina Stella, least of all his mother. Rumour had it that Pina had got a witch to cast a spell on Salvatore, the only reason people could come up with, including his mother. I told her many times that I had no experience with the business of breaking spells, that my concoctions were mainly to help with wellbeing, to change moods and emotional states. But she persisted, each time she came offering more and more money, to break the love spell on her son.

I suggested fennel or rosemary tea, then lavender oil or nutmeg. Calming the nerves was bound to be helpful in any situation, I figured. But she didn't like my recommendations. Eventually I told her that Salvatore should be able to marry whomever he wanted. And that Pina Stella was a wonderful person, in any case, that he was lucky to have her. That's when she stopped coming.

But despite my refusal to break spells, they began to refer to us as the *strega* and the mermaid, which I did not mind, and which Mara was oblivious to, as she was to everything, other than sitting and watching the sea. She never went into the water, never swam, not even in the sweltering summer heat. She was indifferent to heat or cold. Only storms seemed to move her, cause her to shift her position or retreat, deeper into the grotto. But when the rains became torrential and hard as they did over the years, I had to go out and get her and bring her back. Or she would just stay out and return at night like a sea creature from the open wild.

One summer a dance troupe from Germany, called Tanztheater Wuppertal Pina Bausch, came to perform in the neighbouring village of Ravello. They showed up at our cove one morning, not by local ferry but with their own boat. And despite the jagged rocky path and swaths of wild cactus, one of them made their way to our house to ask me if they could practice in front of the grotto. I looked over at Mara who was sitting at the kitchen table, still having her coffee. She gave no response. I figured if she was opposed to it she would have given me some sign.

"Sure," I said, "but how in the world are you going to dance out there? There are no flat surfaces except for that small, rotting dock, which couldn't even hold a cat."

"No worries, we need to practice for a piece that is going to be danced in water. We wanted a deserted place, though, away from all the tourists and travellers," he said with his German accent. Suddenly aware of his lean, muscular body, I realized he could probably dance anywhere, even on the jagged, rough stones, certainly in water.

"Well, I guess you've lucked out," I said. "You may have found the only deserted spot in the area, certainly at this time of the year."

"Yes, we know, we've been circling the coast in our boat for a few days looking for the right spot."

"Well, I might have been exaggerating about the dock. It can certainly hold a boat, so you are welcome to dock there if you like."

"*Gracie mille, gracie mille*," he said, and left me with his broad, warm smile.

"Looks like we have some entertainment for the next while," I said to Mara. But again, no response.

I wondered if Mara would avoid going to the grotto while the dancers were there, but she did not. She continued with her daily ritual, and watched as the dancers, with their feet in the shallow tide, flung themselves about with sinuous abandon, expanding, reaching, then retreating and hurling themselves back, like a dagger in the chest, or a wave of sorrow in the heart. Each morning they did this, I saw Mara move her chair outward, away from the cave, slightly closer to the dancers, so she could see them better. This was the first time I saw her visibly respond to anything around her.

One day they showed up with a couple of blue chairs which they planted in the gravelly beach just outside the grotto. When they began dancing with the chairs, I felt certain there would be an accident. But no, they were just testing. The goal was to place the chairs in the water and dance with them there, which I had the marvellous opportunity to witness from a distance, out at sea. I was returning from the market in Atrani, when I saw them against the verdant limestone cliffs, flinging their bodies off and on the chairs, as if the chairs were extensions of themselves, picking them up, lifting them above their heads, then planting them back down again, with a dexterity and fluidity that made them seem like they were sea creatures, themselves. In their blue leotards and with blue chairs, they navigated the waves. When it was windy or stormy, of course, they did not come. Only when the waves were relatively calm.

On the first morning that the dancers failed to return, I saw a slightly sad look on Mara's face. She was always so opaque, expressionless, except for that depth in her green eyes, that wild unreachable inner shore. But when the dancers left, I could swear I saw something else on her face, if not sadness, a feeling of some sort. Then I began to find small bits of paper left around the house, torn from the blank notebooks that had been among her few belongings.

Peculiar behaviour, I thought at first, before I noticed that the bits of paper had things written on them. One had the word "black" written on it three times. Another had the sentence, "I told you when I came I was a stranger," scribbled on it. I assumed at the time, that she was trying to communicate something to me.

Another note said. "He gave up all the golden factories, just to see who in the world he might be." It was then I knew that this was not about me at all. That these were fragments, fragments of a story that was trying to put itself back together, fragments of some former life.

The most frustrating thing about our living arrangement, at first, was that everyone was constantly questioning me about Mara. My friend Sandro, from the Bar Cortina, was particularly annoying, asking me to bring Mara to the Bar again, so he could ask her out.

"*Ma dai, Cassandra, chi e questa mica tuo? La vogle ancontrare un altra volta? Da dove vienne?*" (Come on, Cassandra,who is your friend? I want to meet her again? Where is she from?) To which I always responded, "None of your business."

"*Ah, ta voi tenere solo per te. Ma sei lesbica?*" (You want to keep her just to yourself. Are you lesbian?) Then I would get really pissed off and tell him to fuck off.

For obvious reasons I did not want anyone to know that I had taken Mara from the hospital. Yet what could I say about my silent roommate that wouldn't sound strange or invite unwelcome gossip? I finally decided on making her my cousin from Benevento, who had come to live with me because her parents had died, which was, in a way, true.

This did not stop people from creating their own mythology. Teresa Marco, a frequent customer, started referring to Mara as the ghost of Parthenope. Some of my favourite comments, which I overheard, while selling my wares at the market or shopping at the piazza, was that she was a mermaid, caught between land and water, or a broken-hearted soul, whose lover had drowned at sea, or Persephone herself, brought back from Hades, longing for the underworld.

But after a while, Mara simply became a part of the landscape, like the rugged cliffs and churning sea, or a moonlit night in early autumn.

One summer evening in 1993, there was a knock at my door. Mara had already gone to bed. A tall, lanky woman with short black hair and dark, penetrating eyes stood at my door.

"Hi," she said. "I'm Francesca Benvenuto. I was told that my sister lives with you."

I hesitated, thinking at first that it was some kind of devious plan to take Mara back to the hospital. How could she have found us? But then I saw the family resemblance, the high cheekbones, a certain way that she tilted her head, that faraway sadness echoing in her voice, despite her hard, brittle manner.

Francesca seemed secretive and did not reveal much about herself that night. Where had she been all this time? Why was she showing up now? She did tell me that she had gone back to Volturino and that Lorena Vespa directed her to the Frullone in Naples, where she heard that I had taken Micola away with me. With that information she had managed to track us down. She did not seem angry or upset, just relieved that she had found us.

Since she did not want to talk much about her own whereabouts, I tried to update her about Micola, what little there was to update. I mentioned the words and phrases written on the bits of paper, and Francesca's stony face softened and became wet with tears.

"Those are words to songs she used to sing," she said.

But when I probed for more details, Francesca simply shook her head and said she couldn't talk about it.

She slept the night on a foam mattress laid out on our kitchen floor. In the morning I made coffee for us and, as we were sitting at the table drinking it, Micola came out.

"Micky," Francesca blurted out with an anguish that seemed almost unbearable.

At first Micola just stood there and did not respond at all. Then she started shaking and convulsing as if she was having an epileptic seizure or something. She fell to the floor and we ran to her trying to calm her down. I put a tea towel in her mouth just in case it was a seizure.

"I don't think it's a seizure," Francesca said, sadly.

"Oh, OK, what then?"

"I think it's just seeing me."

"Why would she react like that to seeing you?" I asked, knowing I was stepping into some minefield.

"It's not me, exactly. It's what I am reminding her of, the past, our past in Montreal. It was a difficult time."

"I see. Well, she's told me nothing."

"She's still not speaking?"

"No, not at all."

We managed to calm Micola down, placed her on her bed. We went back to the kitchen table to finish our coffees. What was it about the past that Micola had not wanted to remember? Francesca never told me. She simply thanked me for taking Micola out of the hospital and caring for her all these years. She said that she had come with the intention of bringing Micola back to live with her in Rome. But now, she was not so sure that would be a good idea.

"She probably really likes it here, doesn't she?" she asked.

"Well, Francesca, it is hard to say," I said. "She has her routines and rituals and appears to love the sea. But

I can't engage her in anything else. I used to ask her if she wanted to go to the market with me, or take a boat ride to one of the neighbouring villages, but she never responded in the affirmative. A few years ago, one of the locals, Pina Stella, got married in Duomo di Sant'Andrea, the cathedral in the centre of town. I thought she might be interested in seeing the inside of a 13^h century cathedral. But again, no. So now, I just let her be."

"Yes, I hear you. So maybe a bustling city would not be the right place ... I don't want to leave her, but I think, maybe, she is better off here, with you," she said, tentatively, looking away to hide her pain. "Are you OK with that?" she asked, after a brief silence.

"Of course," I said. "I was actually afraid you were going to take her away."

"I have a good feeling about you," she said.

Then we hugged.

We stepped out onto our rocky path and talked a while longer. It was a tempestuous, windy morning, the waves so loud we could hardly hear each other.

"If it wasn't so windy I would offer to take you to Ischia or Capri in my boat. But that doesn't seem possible, today."

"No problem, I am not really in the mood for sightseeing."

She left soon after, did not see the point of staying longer. She did not want to agitate her sister further.

I suggested that she leave me her phone number, and that, perhaps, we could arrange another visit, that if Micola was prepared, she might react differently.

Micola never got up from the bed, never came to sit with her sister, and did not answer when Francesca went in to say goodbye.

After Francesca left, Micola changed. She refused to go out, lay on her bed, restless with pain. One night she leaped out of bed and started screaming like a crazed person. I tried calming her down, but it was as if I wasn't there. Nothing was getting through. I didn't know what to do. I was frightened. I started thinking that, maybe, the situation was too much for me, that I would have to call Francesca, or take Micola back to the hospital. But gradually, she changed, returned to herself again, but in a different way.

At first it seemed like a tangled, twisted thing, an indecipherable mix of fear, anger and sorrow that came out of her, as if Mara had decided to let herself remember the past, but did not know how to navigate it. She stayed in her room, lying on her bed in a kind of shaking, weeping state. Perhaps some of my concoctions could be helpful to her, I thought. Each morning I brought her a teapot full of oat straw, nettle and valerian. Initially, she refused to drink or eat, but gradually she began to drink the tea and it calmed her down. Eventually she began to eat again.

When the tremors and fears subsided, the weeping began. It would go on for years, a weeping that became her life's ritual, in the end, hers and mine.

When the weight of the *Thing* diminished, and she could walk again, Mara resumed her daily retreats to the grotto, taking her chair more deeply in. If you didn't know she was there, you could not see her, though she could still look out. Mostly, she just cried, with her head in her hands. She let the *Thing* that had silenced her return in all its sadness. Sometimes I imagined that she might want to talk to me about it, that this would help her piece it together. But it was never so. By then I had concluded that it was probably a question of a broken heart. So each day I brought her a potion made with rose petals, lavender, lemon balm and hawthorn berries, which she drank. This was encouraging to me as it suggested a certain willingness to heal and trust in me, or at least in my remedies.

I brought her the tea at midday, along with some lunch, and then another pot of the tea, later in the afternoon. It was my way of checking up on her, making sure she was OK. She was always in the same position, head in hand. She would lift her head when she saw me, but then resume her crying when I left. Sometimes I would sit quietly outside the grotto and listen to her wordless song of melancholy. Then it seemed I could not tell if she was old or young, if she was crying for herself or for someone else, if it was her pain or the pain of the world that was finding its way out.

I let Francesca know of the changes in Mara. She answered the phone at the bookstore where she worked the first time I called.

"She's coming back," she said. "This is what it means. She's willing to remember. I can't tell you how happy I am. I'd given up hoping for that, long ago."

I expected she might fill me in on what exactly had happened, what it was that Mara was remembering But nothing. All she said was, "I'm so grateful to you, for your work with her."

"Well, I haven't really done anything, except take her out of the hospital and give her a place to live."

"And you call that nothing! That is everything, that is everything." I could hear her voice tearing up on the other end. But then she abruptly cut the conversation off, promising to call. I learned no more of what ailed the sorrowing mermaid who was living with me.

Strangely, my clientele really increased at that time, keeping me busy and less focused on Mara. The terrain around our house was very rocky with little earth for growing herbs. Mostly I grew them in pots around the house or foraged for them in the paths surrounding the town. Then I had the idea to turn my roof into a garden of potted herbs. I bought a ladder which leaned against the side of the low house. So began my project, which took a year to complete.

And then she spoke. I was harvesting my first batch of lavender and lemon balm when I heard a voice calling out to me. I looked down and there she was staring up at me.

"I'm sorry," she said. "I'm sorry." Those were her first words. I almost tumbled off the roof. I climbed down the ladder and met, for the first time, her wild green eyes. I hugged her, and all I could think of saying was, "No worries, none at all. Just do what you have to do. That is OK with me."

I thought perhaps that it would have been a turning point and, while it was a significant moment in Mara's saga, it was not a turning point. The ritual weeping would go on for years. I lost track, really. It stopped becoming an issue. It just became a way of living, by water.

"My husband won't make love to me anymore."

"Ah, here we go, some …

"I've had insomnia for two months. I don't know what's wrong."

"OK, that's an easy one. Take some of this tea, every night, half an hour before you go to bed."

"My Chiara got stung by some bug. Look! Her arm is all swollen."

"Here's a cream to draw out the toxins and help the swelling go down."

Sometimes the issues were more serious and I would recommend the hospital, such as when Marco Ferrara, the local butcher, showed up with a cut on his hand which had caused it to swell up to twice its size, or the time Anna Pizzuto, the hairdresser, showed up with chest pains and nausea.

Once, even Pina Stella, who, spell or no spell, had married Salvatore Monaco, and was now Pina Monaco, came to me. She had not stopped being harangued by the unhappy Monaco family. After three years of marriage Pina and Salvatore were still childless. The rumour was that the marriage was childless because it was cursed.

Pina came to me for fertility herbs. But that was not all. Salvatore wanted to move to Rome, where he had work in construction and Pina did not want to leave Amalfi.

"I figure that, if I get pregnant, he will stop pressuring me to move to Rome," she said, clearly in an anxious agitated state.

"Well, first of all, we should calm your nerves," I said, "since stress can affect fertility."

"Oh really," she said, "then no wonder I am not getting pregnant. That family is driving me crazy."

"Yes, I can imagine. Isn't that, maybe, a good reason to move to Rome, to get away from his family?" I said, without being certain I should be interfering in this way.

"You have a very good point, there. But I've lived here all my life. I won't know anyone there. Rome is kind of crazy and wild and loud."

"Yes, but beautiful and magnificent, too."

"I'll think about it some more."

"For the time being, then, I'll give you some herbs for the stress and some to increase fertility. I also recommend focusing on your diet more. Eat less carbs, more fibre, foods rich in anti-oxidants like fish, and eat a big breakfast to start the day."

She left, a more satisfied customer than her mother-in-law had been.

Though I had not been fully conscious of it at the time, one of my reasons for studying nursing was because I wanted to know all forms of medicine. I knew that herbs were slow in their cure and that magic was difficult and sometimes missed its mark. "Everything has *la lena*," my mother's mother, Nonna Nicola, used to say, who was from Benevento, the town of the stregas. So much effort is required to work magic. So much concentration and visualization. "*Devi volerlo davvero tanto* (you have to truly want it)," was her constant refrain.

My mother had wanted nothing to do with her strega legacy. She hated dreary Benevento, as she called it, and felt she'd hit the matrimonial jackpot when she met my father during *Ferraugusto* festivities in Naples. A handsome fisherman from *Amalfi*. What more could she ask for? Away, away, from Benevento. That is all she wanted, or so she thought.

But I was naturally drawn to my grandmother's secret knowledge and took every opportunity to spend time with her in Benevento, until her death in 1979.

She told me about the walnut tree where the witches used to dance and make their magic, about the liquor and nougat which the town still produced in their honour. She brought me once to Lake Nevi, where the temple to the Goddess Diana had once stood. "Even the most important literary prize in Italy is called 'the Strega'," she once said with pride. "Though in Italy, we love and fear our witches. Love them for their beauty and fear them for their power. Beautiful and powerful like you. I can feel it. It skipped a generation, as these things sometimes do."

"I am not beautiful," I said.

"Ah yes, those who have the beauty rarely seem to know, or it gets destroyed by other people's greed and neediness, made shallow and powerless."

This is what I started to believe about Mara, that her beauty had been wrecked and maimed by others, that she had been unable to recognize and protect the power she had. Or maybe she was simply a sensitive, born in the wrong time, a sensitive crushed by circumstance.

I could hear the subtle changes in her weeping.

At first, the sorrow sounded like it had just escaped a huge dam, threatening the surround, a volatile eruption, spilling all around her. She was frightened, then, I could tell, but determined to no longer hold it back, or perhaps was simply unable, its force literally greater than her resolve.

After a while it seemed to come from the heart of her, and was no longer just a wild force of nature. Those were the inconsolable years, when the sorrow seemed more personal.

I began to doubt that Mara's sadness could reach its end. I did believe, in principle, that it could, but I started to wonder if Mara would ever allow it. She seemed to have fallen in love with her own melancholy during those years.

But then my fear went away. I let it go, cast it to the wind, the erratic and unpredictable wind that had become our daily companion. Mara's weeping became the backdrop of my life, a heart-wrenching, beautiful music, that I, too, could not imagine living without.

And so we lived, for many years, side by side, each doing what we had to do. I tended to all the domestic responsibilities and the demands of my growing business, and Mara wept. She had little capacity to do much else in those days. If I did not somehow budge her out of bed, she could stay there all day, and if I did not encourage her to bathe, she could go for months without washing, wearing her night clothes as day clothes and her hair, a long knotted mane, wild as her eyes. I periodically sat her down and combed it, taking out the knots. I braided it for her so that it would become less tangled. But she seemed to like it free, without restraint. Perhaps she liked the way the sea wind blew through it. Perhaps she simply did not want to care about anything, least of all the state of her hair.

I took up reading the tarot again, along with the sale of my teas and potions. I put a small round table with two chairs at the far end of the room, with the window facing the wild swath of cedars surrounding the house. I put potted geraniums and some lavender on the window sill and a lace tablecloth over the table, the cards at the centre, my Earth Magic cards, not the traditional Waite deck which I found too cumbersome and dated in its symbolism.

Before I changed things around, when people made the long trek down the winding *scalatinella* to our secluded house, I would sit them at the kitchen table, which was usually strewn with canisters of herbs, tincture bottles, in addition to teapots, cups and plates. But when I set up the tarot table it gave me the idea of moving our domestic life as much as possible into the adjacent room, which was our bedroom, and turning the main room into a full-fledged shop. I organized the herbs into neat packets with directions for their use and laid out a variety of tinctures also labelled and marked with their curative use. I set them all out displayed at the kitchen table in different sections. In the centre I put a bowl of lemons.

Dario Mancini, a local carpenter I had known since childhood, made some wooden shelves for me, so I could store all the large canisters. I organized and shelved the books inherited from my grandmother and set them up like a small local library, which became as popular as the potions and teas. Dario painted me a sign which we hung on the front door. It read "Tea and Lemons" in green cursive lettering against a shimmering gold background.

When my clients wanted to talk I would take them over to the tarot table. If they wanted a tarot reading, I would give them one; if not, I would simply listen to whatever they had to say.

Sandro's 15-year-old daughter, Mina, came to me once because she thought she was a lesbian, and wanted to know how she could tell for sure. Then I knew why Sandro had lesbianism on his mind.

"Well, sweetheart, I'm afraid I don't have any herbs for that, but I could do a reading for you and see what happens."

"OK," she said, somewhat timidly. "Actually, I'm just afraid of my father's reaction, that's my real problem."

"For that I can help you," I said. "Give you some herbs for anxiety and fear. But let's still see what the cards say."

The wolf card came up which correlated exactly with what I thought was at issue.

"Mina, I think you need to listen to your instincts, in order to break out of the straitjacket of your religious and paternal upbringing. I know it's hard. The herbs I am going to give you will help calm your nerves about it. Defying parents and religion in order to be true to yourself is not an easy thing."

"I know, I know," she said, suddenly a little more perky. "But I am going to university in Rome next year, so that should make it a bit easier."

"Yes, exactly, Mina, that will help you sort things out. You cannot live a lie. The body will eventually rebel, one way or another."

Sometimes the ailments were physical, yet seemed to have psychological origins. Despite the fact that I sent the butcher away with his infected hand, without being able to help him, he returned. This time with acute tendinitis in his shoulders, which made it impossible for him to reach for or carry anything. What I learned, as we sat at the tarot table talking, is that, in addition to being our local butcher, he sometimes also took jobs in construction. He and his wife had just had a fifth child and he was worried about finances.

"My wife's parents have offered to help, but I absolutely cannot take money from them. I cannot," he said, almost shouting.

"Why not?"

He didn't have much of an answer. "It would show that I am weak, and that I can't properly provide for my family."

"It is not weak to know your limitations, it shows self-knowledge and wisdom." The idea seemed completely foreign to him.

"Look, you may not want to take the money, but your arms are saying otherwise. They don't want any more responsibility; they can't carry anymore. Are your in-laws well off?"

"They are, they're very wealthy," he said. "I just didn't want to have to depend on them."

"You're not depending on them. You're just going through a rough patch. It happens. You need to relax your machismo. I can give you something for that. In any case, they'd be helping their daughter and their grandchildren, not just you. Consider yourself lucky that you have a wealthy family you can turn to in a time of financial crisis. Most do not." This seemed to shift things for him, being able to think of himself as lucky, rather than weak.

I gave him a concoction made of passionflower, valerian and lemon balm and sent him on his way, up the *scalatinella*, to his butcher shop in Piazza Duomo.

That is how we passed the years, me in my shop, and Mara in her cave, as the waters rose higher, the storms grew stronger, and Mara's weeping got more wild. It turned into a kind of wailing or a dark roaring, at times indistinguishable from the sea.

When I heard her in that state, I was certain she was no longer crying just for herself, but for the sorry state of the world. She was raging at the gods. That's what I heard in her dark roaring. And I understood exactly how she felt.

After he completed the building of my shelves, Dario started coming round more and more. Even in middle school I had found him disarming, with his brash sexuality yet soft demeanour, a combination that felt dangerous to me at the time. At first I was resistant to his overtures. I hadn't been in a relationship since my college days. I loved my solitude and sex always seemed difficult to navigate and, in the end, not really worth the trouble.

But I had known Dario forever, and I was in my mid-forties. Surely I could handle his sweet masculinity by then, I thought. He was a little older, in his fifties, though still pretty well-put-together. Strong and soft. A man of few words, which also suited me well, as he didn't ask too many questions about Mara.

Dario lived in a small golden house with silvery green shutters, folded into the rocky cliff-side. It had four bay windows overlooking the terrace, with rows of potted lemon trees, from which he made his own limoncello, and a trellised fence smothered in morning glories. Beside a green wooden bench he had made himself was a large, red oleander. The great turquoise of sea below, boats bobbing up and down at the jetty.

The first time he invited me over for dinner, we were sitting on his green wooden bench, a haunting, melancholic voice singing in the background. Lhasa de Sela, he

214

told me later. We were talking about how much we loved the winters in Amalfi, because it was so quiet, without the throngs of tourists. It was then that he said it.

"*Ti ho sempre voluto.* (I always wanted you.) *Anche quando eravamo ragazzo.* (Even when we were kids.) *Ma sempravo sempre lontano, nel tuo mondo.* (But you always seemed far, in your own world.) *Difficile da raggiungere.* (Hard to reach)."

"Maybe I was difficult to reach," I said in English, because English felt less intimate, more distancing. And I knew he spoke English, as I did. "I always found you a bit scary."

"Scary? Really?" he said. "What could be scary about me?"

I looked a him sitting beside me, with his 50-year-old, muscular body, grey black hair slicked back, the ever so relaxed way he was sitting, with his legs splayed apart, black jeans and a light, white T-shirt. Then I said it. "You were too sexy then."

"Oh, and now I'm not," he said.

"No, I'm just more of a risktaker now than I was when I was 16." Then I leaned over and started kissing him.

At first I was nervous about leaving Mara alone when I stayed the night at Dario's. But the fear passed when I realized she was fine with it. I left my cell phone number by her bedside, and told her to call anytime, though she never did. But in the end, whether it was because I took a lover, or not, things began to change.

Once I found Mara sitting outside the front door, as if waiting for me. One day she was seated at the coffee table where we now ate most of our meals as the kitchen table was being used to display my wares. She had made some coffee and had set out a cup for me. I was delighted to see this, as in the time we had been living together, I had always been the caretaker and she the invalid. It was almost miraculous to witness this first offering to me.

During the years of Mara's passionate sorrow, she did not want to hear about the world at all. We had no television, just a CD player which had a radio, so I too, was a bit on the edge of things. But still, the news always reached me, often through clients, and later through Dario, who was a regular reader of every newspaper around. But it was clear that Mara wanted none of it. So in the 90s, when anti-Mafia prosecutor Giovanni Falcone and his wife, along with three bodyguards, were killed, I did not tell her. When the singer Fabrizio De Andre died, and I too had to retreat into a week of grief, I said nothing. When an earthquake struck Umbria, killing four people and causing extensive damage to the Basilica of St. Francis of Assisi, I was silent. And when the century turned and the Western world shook and trembled as the financial pillars of America were crashed into by Islamic terrorists, I thought it wise not to mention it.

After that, many other things changed too. The rising sea flooded the grotto and Mara's rituals had to change. She could no longer "live" in her cave. She brought her red chair, now worn and discoloured from the salty smashing of wind and waves, and set it up outside our front door. This, in some ways, was the first sign of Mara's willingness to return to human society. Though I cannot say whether she truly chose to return or whether she simply chose to submit to the command of the sea.

Dario was always worried about us being so close to the water. He had read alarming reports that predicted the rising sea along our coast was going to, eventually, swallow up Pompeii and Herculaneum, and that the ancient Greek ruins at Paestum were also under threat.

"We're all in danger in these coastal villages and towns, Cassandra," he would say. "Maybe not soon, maybe not in our lifetime, but if things don't change, we're going under." The thought of my beautiful town under water was more than I could bear. I decided I did not want to think about it, and I was not ready to leave my home either. Nor was Mara.

She continued to sit just outside the front door, on the faded red chair, like a sphinx, as my trail of clients trudged down the rocky *scalatinella* in order to see me. Eventually another chair materialized out of nowhere, and was placed right beside Mara's. After seeing me, my clients would sit and chat with her. She was in her early fifties then, but still a ravishing beauty, with eyes that pulled you to a depth, even though she said very little, if anything at all. Mostly she just listened and responded with compassionate looks and expressions.

Sandro Petrilli from the Bar Cortina became a regular visitor. He had always had his eye on Mara. He had shown up at my shop once to complain about the advice I had given his daughter. "You pushed her into being a lesbian," he said. "What's it to you? Why did you do that?" I assured him that's not what I had done, and that if I had encouraged anything, it was for his daughter to be true to herself. He remained disgruntled, though I don't think he really thought I was responsible. Maybe he just needed to vent and knew I could handle it. Then he went out and sat beside Mara and started chatting her up. His mood changed immediately. After that he came, just randomly, not to see me, but to see her.

The butcher, Marco, was also very fond of Mara. Though he had accepted financial help from his in-laws, he seemed to still suffer from a lot of anxiety, mostly about his masculinity, for which Mara was a perfect antidote. Her beauty and her attentive kindness bolstered his confidence. He showed up once with a bouquet of purple aster, which he had picked from his garden. She was taken aback, but accepted it graciously.

Mara listened to people's troubles with rapt attention. What a great hunger people have to be listened to, I thought, when I treated them for all their aches and pains, the body calling out, sometimes screaming. That is the great wish that humans have, to be met and heard in their singularity. They do not wish for the marriage of man and machine, they wish for the marriage of heart and mind.

My clients began opening their hearts to Mara in ways they had always longed to do, with someone, with anyone, sometimes for just 15 minutes, sometimes for hours. After receiving their treatments from me, they stopped and talked to Mara. At first, I worried that this was a pressure that Mara wouldn't want. I can't say that she enjoyed it, but she didn't seem bothered by it. After a time, she became part of the healing practice. Before Mara took up her post outside our home, talking to my clients had been an integral part of figuring out what truly ailed them. Then Mara took up the talking part of the cure. She seemed to insert herself into the process, without even thinking about it, simply because she was there.

When Mara and I first moved to our seaside home, the troubling visions that had plagued me most of my life stopped. It was as if my psychic energy expended itself in the extreme focus I needed to envision what was wrong with people and what they needed. Because often, what ailed them was not what they thought they were coming for. Their symptoms were simply a symbolic entry point to some elemental imbalance. At least that is how I eventually came to view health and wellbeing. My task was to figure out the imbalance, its source, and its remedy. Some people were too full of air, their minds billowing too far into fantasy and thought, under-nourishing their bodies and souls. These people needed earthy remedies and the strength to bear their reality. Others had too much fire, which burned everything around them, like Sandro, the bartender, or Marco, the butcher. These people needed water remedies and the fluidity to soften their will. Then there were those who were too fluid and could not define themselves at all, always getting lost in things, in others. Mara herself probably suffered this imbalance, which is why she had to retreat so far away, for so long. These people needed the firmness of earth and also the fire of will to stand their own ground.

Eventually the disturbing visions returned. They seemed to coincide with the rising sea levels and the loss of our grotto, and Mara's entry into my healing practice. A kind of re-balancing of our own lives seemed to happen then. Perhaps it was Mara taking up some of the psychic activity of my practice which left me more room for other mental activity. Perhaps it was, simply, as Mara saw it, that the sea itself was making its will known.

Sometimes the visions came as nightmares, where I felt as if I was suffocating and woke up in a panic of breathlessness. I thought I was dying. At first it happened only occasionally, but then it started happening at least once every week. I wondered whether all those years of working with peoples' problems had created some imbalance in me, that the cumulative effect was taking my breath away, that I needed some lightness. I thought too, of all those years of holding and witnessing Mara's pain. But why now, I thought, when Mara actually seemed to be improving? I had no answer, but eventually it came.

It was early September in 2005 when a boat anchored at the harbour, near the ferry docks, west of where we were, along the more touristy side of the shore. There were several people on the boat, which was on a research expedition of the Mediterranean. It remained docked there for several weeks, while its crew made daily treks along the narrow, twisting cliff-side roads and cobblestone alleys around Piazza Duomo. The rumour was that they had stopped their research for a while, in order to enjoy the rugged, limestone beauty of the Amalfi coast.

One of its handsome crew members found his way to Mara's chair. He had been looking to get away from the throngs of people, he said to her, the first time he sat to talk.

"What a secluded little spot you have here. I never would have guessed there was a house behind all these wild cedars." Mara nodded and said, "Yes, we like to be away from the crowds too ... You should come in winter. It's more quiet then."

"Something to consider."

He was more inquisitive with Mara than my clients, who were mainly looking to be seen and heard by the enchanting woman with green eyes and hair like the mother of the wind.

Through the open window, I overheard the man say that he was a marine biologist, researching the ocean. When he asked Mara about herself, she hesitated. She ran her fingers slowly through her tangled bush of grey-black hair, as if she was going to tie it back, or maybe even just get up and leave. Then I heard her voice, that soft, deep, tender voice of hers. "I too have been researching the sea."

"Ah," he said. "And what have you discovered?"

"That is difficult to put into words, and I have been very far away from words, for a long time."

"Far away from words?"

"Yes, the sea took my heart and my words. I was trying to understand why."

"And did you figure that out?"

"No, I did not. I found only sorrow."

"Ah, maybe you were sorrowing for the sea?"

"Yes, it seemed that way, but for myself too.

"Such sorrowing sounds like a kind of praying."

"Yes, it was. Yes, it was," she said with a liveliness I had never heard in her before, as if she was being understood for the first time.

From the window I could see Mara's body had relaxed and that she had turned towards the man, who was looking straight at her now. It was a damp, drizzly day, with the wind picking up momentum, maybe calling in a storm. But the two were oblivious to the weather, like two sea creatures, in their element, smelling of water and salt.

One day the boat was no longer anchored near the ferry docks. His co-workers had gone to explore the rest of the coast, we heard, while marine biologist Tom Banks had taken a room at a *pensione* in town. Every day, the tall, denim-clad figure, with his unshaven face and long blond hair tied back in a man bun, made his way to our secluded rocky cove and sat with Mara. Sometimes I brought them cups of tea, which Tom seemed to greatly appreciate.

"This is not one of your magic potions, is it?" he said, the first time I brought them tea.

"You got anything against that?" I asked.

"No, absolutely not. I just like to know what I'm drinking."

"Fair enough. It's rose hip and chamomile. It may just relax you a bit."

"That's exactly my mission," he said as he looked out at the jagged, rocky path leading from our house to the sea. "A bit treacherous for you, isn't it? Not very easy to go for a swim here."

"Neither of us is big on swimming, and we know how to navigate the rocks pretty well by now. This place was my father's fishing cottage. He was a hermit, didn't like being around people much. It worked for him, like it works for us. Except that my business keeps a steady stream of people coming here now."

"Oh, I hope I haven't been intruding," he said.

"Oh no, not at all," Mara said, before I had a chance to answer.

"Clearly, Mara enjoys your company," I said, "so maybe I'll just go in and leave you to it." As I turned to leave, I caught a look on Mara's face, which made me wonder if she wanted me to stay. I knew that Tom probably wanted me to leave. So I went in, though it didn't make a great deal of difference, since I could hear them pretty easily through the open window.

The waves were crashing loudly against the shore that day, and the scent of autumn was in the air. My favourite time of year. The leafy vineyards clinging to the hillsides were almost ready for harvest, the hills were slightly tinged with gold, and the gardens, dense with autumn bloom, oleander, marigolds, aster and geraniums, scented the air with floral magic. The crowds of tourists were thinning out, too. I felt happy, and was happy for the changes in Mara.

"Mara, why do think the sea took your heart and your words?" I heard Tom ask one day.

"That is the mystery of it all, isn't it? Because it could."

"Could it be that, maybe, that was the sea's gift to you? If your heart was broken, maybe that was the sea's way of protecting you, from the state of your heart. It took your words, so you wouldn't be reminded, so the silence could help you heal."

Tom had figured out how to enter Mara's reality. When I listened to him I couldn't help feeling guilty for not trying harder to engage Mara in conversation. But maybe it was just a question of timing. She was ready, then, to re-enter the world of humans, a world she had abandoned long ago.

Mara looked up at him and smiled but didn't say anything for a while.

"It could be," she said. "I never really thought about it that much, until now. The sea was like an angry god that was punishing me, and yet, also, my only true friend. I let it dictate how I was to be. I had done something terrible. I felt I deserved whatever punishment it gave."

"I can't imagine what terrible thing you could have done."

"Well, I'm not going to talk about that. Though now that I am thinking about it, I can say that, maybe, the sea relieved me of my guilt. It took my guilt and my pain into its waves and carried it far away from shore. While that was happening, it seemed I had lost my heart and my words, like I was at the bottom of the ocean, surprised I could even breathe. But I trusted the power of the sea. It was the power I trusted."

It had never occurred to me that Mara might be guilty of some transgression. I had always assumed it was something terrible that had happened to her. And like Tom, I could not imagine what she could have done that would have caused her so much torment.

Tom was becoming enamoured. But Mara's view of the sea troubled him. "You know," he said, "I understand that your experience of the sea is very personal and part of a long mythological history, but it bothers me."

Mara looked confused, stood up abruptly, as if to leave, then reconsidered and sat back down.

"I didn't mean to offend you by saying that. Please don't be angry with me."

"I'm not angry. I just don't understand what you meant to say."

"You are right. I did not make myself clear ... I am a scientist, Mara."

"Yes, but why does my experience of the sea bother you?"

"Because your view of the sea implies that the sea is some kind of God, that it's a force that cannot be reckoned with, that it's eternal. Because of its vastness, people have always believed that the sea is indestructible."

Mara listened.

"Or people saw the sea as simply surface, an expanse to cross, to get to other lands, for colonial exploits and self-serving expansion and acquisition of wealth, or a limitless resource for industrial fishing. They were wrong there too."

"They do not see that the ocean is the Mother of Life," Mara said, tentatively, yet with a kind of assurance that surprised Tom.

He looked at her with delight.

"Yes, Mara, that is true, even from a scientific perspective. The ocean is the Mother of Life, which means that planetary life cannot continue without the ocean. The fate of life lies with the ocean."

"I know this is not exactly scientific, but all these years that I have been living by the sea it was as if the sea called and I followed, the only faith I was capable of having. The sea kept me alive. All its fury, depth and beauty eventually put my sorrows in perspective. But then, my sorrow changed, it got wider, somehow ... I have been far from the world of news and science all these years, but I could feel that something was changing, the sea was rising, getting more fierce, angrier. It swallowed up our dock, took over the grotto where I used to sit."

It was then that I heard him say: "I love you, Mara."

"Now, you are changing the subject."

"Don't worry, don't worry," he said. "I just mean love in a platonic sense. You are a beautiful person, and I am fortunate to have crossed paths with you."

"You have no idea how fortunate I feel that, that of all places, your boat docked here. You have absolutely no idea."

One evening, in mid-September, shortly before the marine biologist took his leave of us, I was playing a CD by Lhasa de Sela, the one I first heard at Dario's place. He was a music lover and was always introducing me to new music. In addition to carpentry, he sometimes drove a bus for his cousin's transit company. He drove people to other European countries, then sometimes brought them back. He was exposed to people from all over the world. In addition to English, he spoke Spanish really well and French too. He was a worldly man, in his own local way, much more than me, in any case, who had only ever been to Naples and Rome.

I was sitting in the main area where I usually see my clients and Mara was in the bedroom area. I was playing the CD, not too loud, so as not to disturb her, when I heard her softly enter the room.

"Who is that?" she asked. I often played music, but she had never asked me about any of it before. Her facial expression had a life in it I had not seen till then, something approaching desire, maybe a delicate kind of lust.

"It's Lhasa de Sela, a Mexican American, who lives in Montreal, now."

She seemed startled, but said, "I lived in Montreal, a long time ago."

"Yes, I know."

"How do you know that?"

This was not a conversation I had ever expected to have with her, so I wasn't sure what to say. I hesitated and then opted for the truth.

"When I met you at the hospital in Naples, I made a trip to Volturino to find out anything about what had happened to you. I found out that your family had once lived in Montreal."

She looked at me as if she might run away, but pulled up a chair and sat beside me. We listened to the music, together, without saying anything, for a long while.

When the CD was over, she looked over at me and said, "I used to sing, you know."

"That I did not know. No one told me anything about your past. Though when your sister was here, she did mention that those fragments of paper you wrote on were lyrics from songs you used to sing."

Her face twisted into pain at the mention of Francesca.

"Yes, I was going to be a singer." Tears started to stream down her face. "But then, some terrible things happened. I couldn't recover, until you took my hand and brought me here."

"Funny, somehow, I always thought it was you who brought me here."

The next day Tom returned to have tea with Mara.

"What kind of research do you do?"

Tom looked at her and hesitated, uncertain of how to answer.

"My area of specialty is plankton."

"Plankton? Tell me about plankton."

"It's a small micro-organism, sometimes plant, sometimes animal, an essential part of the ocean's eco-system, and as it turns out, the planet's eco-system."

"OK, tell me more."

"Well, it's crucial to the ocean food chain. Everything depends on it. But because of climate change the ocean chemistry is changing, becoming more acidic, inhospitable to the life of the ocean, plankton in particular. The coral reefs where much of the plankton lives have been dying at an alarming rate. Last year, one of the hottest years on record on the Great Barrier Reef, birds were dying en masse. At first everyone thought that the birds were dying because of the extreme heat. But later we discovered it was because the surface water of the ocean had became so hot that the plankton moved to cooler places and the fish followed. So when mother birds went foraging to feed their chicks, the little planktons weren't there. The birds were dying of starvation."

He took a deep breath, and continued.

"But here's the really alarming part. Plankton actually creates fifty percent of the oxygen that we humans breathe on this planet. The plankton is not just the bird's lifeline. It's also ours. And it needs to live near the surface of the ocean because it has to catch the sun's rays in order to photosynthesize and create the oxygen. If the surface water gets too hot or too acidic, it won't survive. So we're pretty much choking ourselves to death. How's that for a gloomy prediction?"

Hearing this from the open window, I gasped, as if reliving the recurring dream of waking up out of breath. Yet I felt strangely calm, as I often did, when I understood what my visions meant.

"Why is the ocean becoming more acidic?" Mara asked.

"Well, it's because of the excess carbon in the air. The carbon simply traps the heat around us, creating a warming of the planet. But when absorbed in the ocean, it reacts chemically with other elements, changing the PH balance in the process, resulting in more acidity. That's partly what's killing the reefs."

Mara stayed in her silence for a while, that full, poignant silence of hers that I had grown to love. Then she said, "So what is to be done?"

"Ah, a Marxist/Leninist, that I never would have guessed." And he chuckled.

"I have no idea what you are referring to. Though my sister probably would."

"You have a sister?"

"Yes, her name is Francesca. She was always more intellectual and political. Not me, I was only into singing."

"You're a singer?"

I could hear the pain in her voice now. But she continued, not about the singing so much, but about Francesca, whom I'd never heard her speak of before.

"Yes, I used to sing, but my sister, Francesca, she was the smart one. She always wanted to know what was going on in the world, always kept herself informed. I just ran away, like I always did, away from her, away from everything."

"Where is your sister now?"

"I don't know. That's the horrible thing, I don't even know. I think she's in Rome."

"Rome is not that far away," Tom said.

"Yes, maybe at some point, I will try to find her."

Mara waited, again, for a while, in her lusty, sensuous silence, and Tom stayed with her.

Then it came, her revelation: "I know what I can do, I can sing, I used to sing, so I can sing again."

"Ah, that is perfect, perfect for you. Music is always a solution to something, why not ecological problems?"

"I'm glad you agree," she said.

And I liked the idea too. Finding the energetic balance needed to foster people's health was very much like discovering their unique musical composition.

Two days later Tom's colleagues returned and their boat left for good. Mara did not even seem sad. Just determined. Tom thanked me for my daily tea and told Mara that he was glad she hadn't been singing when his boat passed our shore or he might have crashed and died. She chuckled and then stretched out her arm as if to shake his hand. But he leaned in and kissed her instead. He was the sad one, now.

"Listen, Mara, if your singing ever takes you to Portland, Oregon, please look me up." He passed her a piece of paper with his address on it, which she folded and put inside her bra cup, on the side of her heart. And Tom Banks was gone.

We passed another winter together, Mara and I, a difficult one, with snow and wind and ice bellowing at our doorstep. As used to it as we were, we could see that the weather was becoming more extreme, the water coming closer, with more punch, more recklessness, and the wind ferocious, like we'd never seen it before. Some nights we became afraid, as we peered out at the slamming sea, as if we were in the middle of it, in some precarious boat, sure to be swallowed up.

Dario had been asking me for some time to move in with him.

"You're in danger, down there. You have to get out, Cassandra. I know it's your father's cottage and there's a history there, but is it worth your life, and Mara's?"

"I know, I know."

He offered to build an addition to his house, so I could have my shop, a continuation of Tea and Lemons. He knew that I would never leave Mara, so he offered to have her move in with us too. There was an extra bedroom she could have. But I was reluctant to leave my life by the sea with Mara. It had been so unexpected, illuminating and rich, even if painful, at times. And my father's house, the only remaining tie to my past.

I didn't speak about any of this with Mara, but of course, she always had that uncanny ability to feel everything.

We went through that difficult winter together, always a little bit on edge, but happier somehow. Mara had clearly stepped out of her sorrowful place and I, with her, was happier. Dario too made me happier.

Spring came, finally. The fear and danger lifted. I thought perhaps we might go through another summer together. But one morning, a clear crisp and sunny morning, I woke up to find her gone. Her things were gone, everything was gone, including the leather case she kept under her bed with money she had inherited from her mother, which she had always refused to deposit into the bank. She had taken some of it and put it in an envelope, left it on the table. She had tried to give me some of that money before, but I had always refused it, telling her that if we needed it, I would let her know. And gone was Francesca's phone number, which I had pinned on a bulletin board near the phone, just in case she ever wanted to call.

On the table, beside the envelope was the note:

Cassandra,

Please forgive me for leaving like this. I am not very good with goodbyes. And I never would have been able to say all that needed to be said. I am going to Rome to find Francesca. So please, don't worry.

Forever in your debt, my Angel.

Micola, from the Windy Hills.

And that was the last I ever saw of Mara, my beautiful sea priestess.

IF YOU WAIT

IT TOOK ME SEVERAL DAYS to read all the letters and notebooks Paolo had given me. When I was done, I sat there confused and alarmed. I picked up my cup of coffee and noticed that I was shaking. I took a shower to try to calm myself down. Got dressed, without thinking, put on my running shoes. It was November, but it was 30 degrees. I felt nothing, instead I still seemed to be shivering. I ran without direction, without destination, down Logan all the way to Eastern, then across, all the way to Bay, through the 5 pm traffic. I felt that if I stopped I would fall flat on my face. I was running so I could keep standing, so I wouldn't fall. No, it was actually so I wouldn't kill someone. I wanted to smash someone's head against a wall, banging and banging, till it was dirt. I was running so I wouldn't kill someone, running so I wouldn't call my parents in that state.

When I got to Bay Street I turned up and ran to Queen, then kept going west. I realized that I was heading towards Daniel's place. That made me stop for a moment to wipe away tears I hadn't noticed were falling.

Finally I found myself down by the ferry docks at the bottom of Bay Street. I crossed Lakeshore, walked over to the Lakeside Park and sat on a bench. Out of breath. Tried to think, but all was blank, blank as a clean slate.

That's what I was, a clean slate. That's what I always was, what I always wanted to be. Nothing, nobody. But my parents would never allow that ... what the fuck was I thinking? I wasn't making any sense. Nothing was making sense.

The inside didn't match the outside, like a trans person, that's how I had always felt. All wrong. But I could never articulate it. Just a vague sense of displacement and detachment.

The fucking November heat. Why was it 30 degrees in fucking November. I jumped in the lake and started swimming. I knew someone who lived on Ward's Island. Maybe I would swim across and visit them. I swam for about 10 minutes and realized that I was losing my mind, that I shouldn't be swimming across Lake Ontario in that state. I turned back, crawled up to the shore and threw myself on the grass. I lay there and didn't move for a long time. Then someone came by, looked down at me and asked, "Is everything OK, my dear?" Was it that unusual to lie on the grass? An old woman with blue-tinted hair was looking down at me. "Yes, yes, I'm fine," I said. She kept staring down at me with her concerned look, till I finally said, "Please leave me alone. I want to be alone. Is that not obvious?"

"OK, OK," she said, and moved away reluctantly.

I lay for several hours, listening to waves smashing against the shore. Felt so exhausted, I didn't know how I was going to get myself home. Maybe I would stay there all night. No, I couldn't do that.

I got myself up, slowly, gradually. It was dark by then. Luckily I had some cash in my pants pocket. I took a cab to the liquor store on Danforth. Bought a bottle of gin and some tonic water. Walked home through Withrow Park. I remembered the *Thing*, the first time it happened, walking home along the park, the mysterious images of someone tumbling down stairs, blood, broken glass.

I walked in the door, put on Chilly Gonzales and drank myself into oblivion, something completely out of character for me.

The next day I ended up sleeping till noon, also out of character. I had my three coffees and headed out to Leaf and Bloom, my head throbbing as if it was going to explode. I couldn't work in that condition. But I had to see Paolo.

When he saw me he sat down on the chair near the cash register, as if he could avoid me by doing that.

"I think I'm going to need that chair," I said.

He immediately got up and let me sit.

"You look terrible," he said.

"Oh really. How did you expect me to look?"

"I don't know, Chiara. I don't. Was I wrong in giving you those notebooks? "

"Well, it's hardly a question of right or wrong, now is it?"

"I guess that's true."

"Why would they never tell me? I can't believe it. They send me to see a kid psychiatrist, but they never tell me something like this?"

"I guess you have figured it out, then."

"What? That my real mother was insane and my aunt was a terrorist?"

"She wasn't insane. She was highly sensitive, musically talented, beautiful."

"I don't know what to do. I don't know what to think."

"Well, if it's any consolation at all, those notebooks brought shocking news into my life as well."

"No, it is not a consolation of any sort."

"OK, you're furious. You have a right to be."

"I don't know what to do. Tell me what to do."

"Well, I guess you have to speak to your parents."

"Which parents are we talking about now? It's too much, Paolo. I can't deal with this."

"Yes, you can. There is no doubt in my mind about that. You can or I wouldn't have given you the books and the diary. Look, I'll lock up for a while and we can go sit in the cactus room. It will calm you down."

"I don't think I can talk anymore today. My head is splitting. I need to go buy some Tylenol."

"I've got some Tylenol. Let's go sit in the cactus room. I don't want you going home like this."

I took the Tylenol and we went to the cactus room. Mara's grotto surrounded by cactus fruit came to my mind, the grotto I was always trying to get to, that exotic grotto in my mind, that symbol of exquisite solitude which I longed for. Can memory reach back like that, in the dark, without maps, a net catching stray objects, missing pieces of a life you never even knew you had?

"Where is she now, do you know?"

"Micola?"

"Micola, Mara, I don't know which."

"I knew her as Micola, so she will always be that to me," Paolo said.

"But she later became Mara, it seems."

"Yes, so it seems. I'm not sure where she is now, Chiara. I got those notebooks from Titiana in the summer of 2012. She just sent the package without a word. I knew that Micola had already left Amalfi, because after I received the notebooks and letters, I did manage to contact Francesca. She told me that Micola had come back to Canada, maybe even Toronto. Micola knew that your adopted parents had moved to Toronto. I think she is looking for you."

"Do you know my parents?"

"Only casually. They lived in my neighbourhood. Our parents knew each other, so I had heard that they were looking to adopt. I helped set it up."

"You know my fucking parents!"

"Not really, Chiara. I have never been in touch after they left for Toronto. I thought of looking them up when I moved here. But I felt it best to leave the past behind. And then you walked into my store, and I knew immediately who you were. You look exactly like her, except more feisty, more confident."

"This is too much to take in, Paolo. I really can't do it, not today. I need to go home."

When I stood up Paolo took me into his arms and held me in a tight embrace, gently stroking the back of my head, almost like a father. Paolo would have been a good father. I broke away and looked into his moist, sparkling blue eyes.

"I can see why Francesca was in love with you," I said.

"Thanks, I guess. I loved her too, though not in the way she would have wanted."

"OK, I think I really need to go now."

"Alright, but just call me at any time if you need to."

I walked away from the shop, then turned back to look at the store's green awning. The swaths of bright yellow forsythia that had been lining the front of the shop that day I ran for cover from the rain seemed to reappear. A random act that brought an emotional avalanche. Was that magic?

My splitting head was swirling; love, hate, rage, tenderness, panic, relief, sorrow. And that was something, since for most of my life, I seemed to feel very little, except for random bouts of inexplicable anger, I was always kind of blank, indifferent. That is until I met Daniel and until the *Thing* started happening, which now seemed to be connected. Cohen, Daniel Cohen, the same last name. OMG, what if I was related to Daniel? The panic got worse with that thought.

I couldn't call anyone, then, not even Jo. The headache was subsiding, but I needed to be still. I lay on my bed and started breathing, just focusing on my breath, aiming for stillness, that calm blank centre that had been natural to me, before everything started to crack.

I needed to see Peter Allen. He was the person to talk to. Luckily he had time available that same day. When he saw me, he looked alarmed. I don't pay much attention to my physical appearance at the best of times. I guess I hadn't paid any attention to it all for a few days.

"What has happened, Chiara?" His calm, gentle voice was almost unbearable. So I started there.

"I think I can't bear it when people treat me nice. I've never known why. It's as if it touches some great sorrow I didn't even know I had."

"My voice touched a great sorrow?"

"Yes, I think I know where it comes from now, and who it belongs to."

"Oh, it's not yours."

"No, I don't think so."

"Whose is it?"

"I think it belongs to my mother, or maybe it's an ancestral sorrow, from before my time, an epi-genetic memory, as they call it these days."

"This is new, Chiara. I feel compelled to ask you what happened?"

"Well, I just discovered that I was adopted, and not from my parents telling me, but from reading some letters and diaries, given to me by a friend, my boss, actually, who knew my real mother. How's that for a mind blower?"

"That is a mind blower ... and your parents don't know that you know."

"No, they don't. At this point, I don't know how to talk to them about it. I figure a talk with you is a good place to start."

"Yes, that seems wise under the circumstances."

"And, I've already gone through the drinking myself into oblivion phase."

"You survived that, obviously."

"Barely."

After my session, I called Jo. She came right over, always my dependable friend, since forever.

"I could feel this coming, Chiara. I can't say why or how. But I always knew there was a depth to you that seemed unreachable, even to yourself, and it was somehow starting to surface, in the last few years, since you met Daniel, and you started having those weird episodes."

"Well, you might be on to something there, since my father's name was, guess what, Andy Cohen."

"OMG, are you saying you're related to Daniel?"

"I don't know, Jo. I don't know. Cohen is a pretty common Jewish name. It doesn't have to mean anything, except that I am half Jewish, and half Southern Italian."

"I can see it, Chiara. I can see it all in you. Somehow I feel happy, I feel that you've been needing something to crack you open."

Jo's positive take on events helped a little, but as soon as she left I was adrift again. One thing was becoming clear, though, that the emotional chaos I had been trying to avoid by leaving Daniel was this, this broken-down, lost at sea, without anchorage, kind of feeling. The desire that filled me whenever I looked at his face threatened to break me up or push me off a cliff, or ruin me in a way. I was trying to escape being ruined.

The thought that I could be ruined by a man was against my moral grain. It wasn't possible for me to live with that kind of risk. How is one supposed to love under such conditions? If desire breaks you up, there is no self. How are you supposed to be in a relationship without a self? Psychologically impossible.

These thoughts were comforting. They mitigated the guilt I had felt in breaking up with Daniel. They made me feel that I had done the only thing I could do, the only thing that was possible. Yet, yet, at that moment, the only thing I was aware of wanting, really wanting, paradoxically, was to see Daniel's face, to hear his voice, to watch his confident gait as he walked towards me, to see that pleasure in his eyes as he greeted me.

But there was no hope of that, I knew. It had been many months since I'd sent that e-mail from which I never got a response. Still, it felt good to be able to acknowledge my longing without feeling threatened. That was probably because the *Thing* I had dreaded no longer had to be kept in check.

There was only one thing to do, one more dread to confront, talking to my parents.

"What the fuck were you thinking?" was the first thing I said. First time ever I had spoken to my parents in that tone. "Why did you never tell me? As a kid, I can understand. But I'm thirty fucking seven." I was shouting by then and they were mute, not knowing what to say. Finally, my father braved a response.

"Chiara, maybe we were wrong, but we were trying to protect you. The events surrounding your birth were tragic. We thought, I know, maybe stupidly, that you'd be better off not knowing. We knew the Benvenutos, not well, just through Paolo. And there were lots of rumours about how things had ended up for Francesca and Micola, after they left Canada. We figured that if you knew, you might look into things, and that what you discovered would cause you a lot of distress."

"Oh yes, just better to send me to a child psychiatrist for being abnormal!"

My mother piped in. "Chiara, you father is right. Those are the reasons. We didn't decide never to tell you. When you were having troubles as a child, we did think that maybe we would have to tell you. But then the years passed and you seemed to be doing so well, we didn't want to disrupt or interfere with that."

"Well, it's become one major, fucking interference now. Everything is falling apart. I can't function."

Father: "Yes, I can imagine, and we are very, very sorry, for our part in it."

Mother: "Chiara, we loved you as much as anybody could, and still do. I hope that with time, you will be able to forgive us. We meant no harm. You must know that."

"I suppose. I guess I thought that educated persons like yourselves would have known better. You've been ignorant in your way of handling this."

I knew this would hurt them and I didn't care. I just slammed the door in their face and left, and didn't speak to them for several weeks. But that is as long as I could sustain my anger towards them. They were right. I knew they didn't mean me harm. But harmed is how I felt, and I didn't know who to blame.

"For some things there is no one to blame," Peter Allen said. This comment irritated me.

"What? And you don't think the decisions people make bear upon what happens to them in life?"

"Yes, of course, but the fact that you were born into this set of circumstances is mysterious or accidental, don't you think? You've studied philosophy, 'thrownness', right, do you know that concept? That we are thrown into a world that is not of our own choosing, but we still have to contend with it. That's where choice comes in."

"I don't fucking need a philosophy lecture from you, right now, Mr. Peter Allen. Even if I am not to blame for the circumstances I was born into, others are. Other people's choices have impacted me. And I have feelings about that. That's what I am trying to figure out. Your pithy philosophy is not helping"

"OK, you're extremely angry, and you need somewhere to direct it. It's coming to me right now, and that's OK. I can handle it."

"Great, aren't I the lucky one!"

A few minutes of silence passed. I thought I saw a little discomfort on his face, but then his gentle, kind expression returned. This time it didn't frighten me or bother me. I seemed to be able to relax. His return to kindness, no matter what I said or did, was starting to become an anchor.

"It's just too much. It's all too much. I just don't know where to go with all my thoughts and feelings."

"You'll get through this, Chiara. In a way, now your therapy can truly begin."

"Great consolation."

For days I became obsessed with the idea that maybe I had slept with my cousin or even my brother. I kept trying to remember if Daniel had ever referred to his father by name. I'd felt so at home with the Cohen family, that much I remembered, a sense of déjà vu, as if I'd known them before. Was that it? Were we blood relatives?

Paolo and I met at Allen's back patio, the only place that had a willow tree larger and older than the one that had been destroyed in my courtyard that summer. It was

November, but it was still warm enough to sit out. As I waited, I contemplated the willow. There's something about willows, I don't know exactly what, their strong trunks contrasted by their draping willowy foliage. Or maybe, Jo was right, it was just trees in general. Some people love animals more than they love people. I loved trees.

Paolo arrived, looking his usual, handsome self, though seemingly agitated. I was feeling angry and confrontational.

"I'm sorry, Chiara. I can imagine how difficult this must be for you. I'm not sure I did the right thing."

"Look, I'm a neo-philosopher. Truth is always the right thing."

"OK, that makes me feel better."

"I just have some questions and you better answer me directly and honestly."

"OK, go for it."

"Did you know my father?"

"Only briefly, we went to the same high school, Westmount High. He was a musical prodigy, at least that's what everyone said about him."

"Where is he now, do you know?"

"He died, Chiara, from a heroin overdose, in 1980."

I was relieved and yet I could sense an unbearable sinking in my chest, a paradox of feelings that left me speechless. I wanted him dead, and yet, I wanted him alive at the same time. Then I was immediately plagued by the thought that I was not out of the woods yet. Daniel could still be my cousin.

"Did he have any brothers or sisters?" I asked.

"No, he didn't. He was an only child"

How devastating it must be to have your only child die of a drug overdose. Or was I just projecting my own devastation, so I could distance myself from it?

Again. My heart felt torn up with wishing he was alive and glad he was dead. Well, at least this heart was feeling something, I thought, remembering how Pat had once accused me of having a heart of steel.

"They were Russian Jews. His father was a classical pianist. He and his wife defected to Montreal in the mid-fifties when he was there for a concert."

"Why are you telling me that?"

"I just thought you might want to know something about the Cohens."

"So my father was born in Montreal?"

"Yes, he was."

My heart started aching, then, with the wish to have known him. Or was this, too, just a way of avoiding the thought of my mother, who might actually still be alive? She seemed to be the most difficult to keep in mind. The thought of her was like a raging fire I was trying to escape, a raging fire I knew I had to go back into, to recover things I hadn't even known I'd lost.

"How strange, Paolo, that of all the flower shops in this city, I walked into yours, looking for a job. How do you make sense of that?"

"Ah, there's my neo-philosopher. Why neo, anyhow?"

"Well, I work in a flower shop, don't I? I like to think about things. But I'm not cut out for academia, especially not these days."

"Well, you're right about that, I think. I can't quite envision you as an academic ... The way I see it, Chiara, Mystery is both meaningful and arbitrary, and we have very little means of figuring out the difference, not until after the fact, I guess. Looking back we are sometimes able to distinguish between fate and chance."

"How?"

"Wow, you're really putting me to the test today, aren't you? I would say it's about feeling. Fate feels different from chance. But it's often hard to identify that in the moment. But you know, now that we are speaking about this, I did somehow feel, though I wouldn't have called it fate at the time, that I was fated to meet your mother and her sister, Francesca. It felt like I had to have them in my life, that these were friends I had to have, people whose lives I had to be a part of. I didn't even feel that way about Ricardo, your mother's cousin. He was the one who introduced me to the Benvenuto sisters, as they were known then."

"OK, I think I know what you're getting at. That's how I felt when I first met Daniel."

"Yes, yes, that makes sense, Chiara, and also why he was such an emotional trigger for you."

"I never told you that," I said.

"Well, let's just say I'm a perceptive person."

"I guess you are, yes you are."

"You know, Chiara, love is just a rare confluence of factors, a thing that happens of its own accord. We can either go with it or run from it. Though it's rare, I think, to be able to run from it. I think you tried to."

"Well, I didn't really get too far, did I?"

Several months passed and it was winter again. My anti-social inclinations were less conspicuous in winter. I could stay indoors and no one wondered why or commented about it. My fear of bad weather remained, though. I rarely went out. Except for going to work, I holed up in my apartment watching past seasons of *Rookie Blue*.

The shock had worn off, somewhat. I was able to start thinking about the events that had led up to my birth, and everything that happened afterwards. It seemed easier to think about my aunt, Francesca, living in Rome. It was her voice that went through my mind, her love for Paolo, which I could totally understand, her indignation, her rage, her commitment to social justice. I guess they really did believe they could change the world. Still, taking to violence did not sit well with me, even though I knew that power never seems to yield otherwise. A conundrum I couldn't sort out. Would society really have been better off with a dictatorship of the proletariat? Is the killing of infidels by ISIL really all that different from killing the enemies of the people?

I was filled with despair, at times, when I thought about how impossible it was to create a fair and just world, even more now than before, with the world ruled by thwarted geeks who have more money than god, who are intent on replacing man with machine, as if defeating our carbon-based bodies was some obvious and necessary feature of human progress.

I wondered about my aunt, how it must have felt to give up 14 years of her life, for nothing, for a revolution that never happened, for a murder she didn't commit. Somehow I understood her, her idealism, her wish to believe in the ideology of the worker. Like a faith in the earth, the roots of things, the labour that builds the world we take for granted, a wish to join the body with the mind, to believe in their union. But we are far from that now. Submissive minions, orchestrating our own demise. That's what I saw. We had stopped believing that we could subvert anything. Those of us who could just tried to build our lives outside the digital grid of our disappearing world. I was in the middle of trying to figure out how I could do that, when the past came crashing into my life.

It was extremely difficult, at first, to think about my mother—Micola, Mara, whoever she was. I felt a kind of revulsion at the thought of her, a sickness in my stomach, something impossible to hold in mind without making me nauseous. It took a long while for me to even think of her as a person, instead of just a wound I couldn't bear. But then, gradually, I started to see her, a phantom, that hovered around my life. A phantom who wanted to speak to me, but couldn't. I too had no words, yet, to say to her. So we wandered around together for a while, in and out. When I went to the flower shop, she came with me, and when I came home, there she was. I let her be. I let her stay. That was my first version of a relationship with my real mother, a sad ghost that had moved in with me.

I didn't tell anyone about this, not even Jo, and especially not my parents, who had became balls of anxiety, constantly worrying about me, like when I was a child, afraid of what I might do, maybe afraid that I would disappear from their life. I was capable of that. I could disappear, maybe the way Mara had. I had the capacity to shun the world. I could go elsewhere. I could be completely alone, become another person, even, someone no one knew. Briefly, I entertained this possibility, but the ghost kept me put. Had she not appeared, my parents' fear might have been justified. The ghost started to become a comfort I was afraid of losing. I stayed.

Those winter months of 2015 were the most difficult of my life, the past an unstoppable flood I couldn't contain. Outside it was cold and snowy and bitter, but inside it was hot and stormy, and the flood waters would not stop, levelling the signposts of who I had been. The ghost hovered, and tried, at times, to hold my hand, though I wouldn't let her. I wanted her there. That was all, that was all.

"I think I'm a nut case," I said one day to Peter Allen.

"Why?"

"Because my life is falling apart, and all I can do is binge on episodes of *Rookie Blue*. I hate cop shows, I hate law and order, but I have become completely sucked into this fictional world. I just discovered the show by chance, one night when I was flipping through channels, looking for escape. I didn't know it was in its last season. So I've been renting out all the previous seasons and spend my evenings watching multiple episodes of this fucking cop show."

"Well, it's understandable that you might need some escape right now."

"It's not that," I muttered.

"What is it then?" he asked, with that gentleness that kills me.

"Stop it! I can't stand your kindness." He didn't say anything after that. He waited for me to say something. About five minutes passed.

"I'm not sure what it is. Maybe it's the camaraderie of these cops working together, having each other's backs. It's something I would be completely incapable of. Yet I envy it. I've always been such a fucking loner ... and the show is set in my neighbourhood, so that's kind of cool. Even though its just a police procedural, somehow the characters and their relationships with each other are complex and interesting ... see what I mean. Why am I so engaged with these fictional characters as if they were real people? Daniel used to say that I talked about characters in books as if they were real ..."

"We've talked about this before, haven't we? You like relationships at a distance. Maybe fictional characters move you more deeply than real people can."

Then the dam broke. I was muttering and sobbing about McNally and Sam Swarek, how everyone could see that they were in love, but they were always running away from each other, afraid of getting singed or broken or abandoned, and how they were always missing each other, in every sense of that word.

"I'm finding it a bit unbearable, the dynamic between these two."

"What is it exactly that is causing you pain?"

"It's that the chemistry is so right, so obvious, so beautiful. Yet, one of them is always running away from it."

"And what does this have to do with you?"

"I'm a fucking loner, didn't you hear me? It has nothing to do with me."

"OK, but why have you become so obsessed and moved by this fictional relationship?"

I couldn't talk because I was crying so hard.

"For someone who never cried as a child, or in my whole adult life, I'm sure making up for it now, aren't I?"

Peter Allen looked at me quizzically but said nothing, just waited. He always waited. I was beginning to appreciate that.

"I had a mother, who apparently did nothing but weep and wail for decades." I had told him the basic story, but not the details, until then. When I described what I had read about my mother, he looked a little bit stunned, or surprised, or something else I couldn't make out. But then I got overwhelmed, and decided to go back to *Rookie Blue*.

"Can you see, now, why I have decided to bury myself in episodes of a police procedural?"

"Well, somewhat, as an escape, yes."

"Have you ever watched it?"

"No, I haven't. But I do get a sense, on the surface, of why it would appeal to you. But there is something else going on with you and this show."

"Yeah, Sam Swarek's eyes."

"No, I know you're not that superficial."

"Maybe I am."

"Come on, now, someone with a Masters in philosophy. Who are you kidding?"

When I got home, for the first time in a long while, I had a strong urge to phone Daniel. It had been over six months and he'd never even responded to my e-mail. Was it possible he didn't get it? It can happen, sometimes, for no particular reason, just some inexplicable computer glitch. But I couldn't talk myself into it. I called Jo instead, who wasn't answering either. Then I called my parents, who were just getting ready for bed. Dad had some kind of conference the next day, had to be up early, so Mother joined him in his early-to-bed. That's the kind of relationship they had, a kind of symbiotic thing that never really appealed to me, now that I think about it. It never really felt like love, more like a dependency, or a need, or just a habit.

And what was love, anyhow? How was I to know? A beautiful terror I had no capacity for.

I said good night to my parents and put on season five of *Rookie Blue.*

It was early spring, the full moon, just before Easter. It was my day off, so I hadn't been in to the flower shop. I was sitting on the slope of a hill in Withrow Park. It was wet and muddy, but I didn't care. I lay on the slope under my favourite maple tree, my power spot, as Daniel had once referred to it, when my phone rang. The only people who have my cell phone number are Jo and my parents, so I answered. It was Paolo. Yes, I had forgotten that I had given it to him as well. His voice sounded stiff, a bit ragged. Holy fuck, what now? I thought.

"Chiara, I need to talk to you."

"OK, talk."

"No, in person. I know you are not supposed to be in tomorrow either. But I'm wondering if you can just come in, some time in the afternoon, maybe."

"OK, but what's going on?" I said, a little panicked.

"Don't worry. It's nothing bad. I just think it would be better to talk in person."

When I walked in the next day, Paolo looked pale and haggard. Something was wrong. The first thought that came to my mind was that he had been diagnosed with some serious illness or something.

The store was empty, so he locked the front door behind me and suggested we go to the cactus room.

He pulled up a chair in front of the bench that I like to sit on. He drew closer and cupped my face with his hands. "You look so much like her, it's quite remarkable."

"Not like my junkie father?"

"You have his smoldering brown eyes." I was taken aback by the use of that word. "Well, that's a first," I said. "People generally think of me as a bit of a cold fish."

"Your mother was a green-eyed mermaid."

"Yes, I guess she probably was."

"Chiara, she's here."

"What do you mean here?"

"Here, in Toronto."

I stood up abruptly, as if leaving could erase everything. That had always worked for me before, just getting out, running, getting far, leaving behind, away from the tangles, away from the blues, or whatever was hounding me.

But that day, I sat back down and put my head in my hands.

"How about some mint tea?" Paolo said, moving to sit beside me on the bench.

"No, I don't want anything. Nothing. Just my old boring life from before. That's what I want. Is there anything you can do about that, Paolo?"

"She's living at the Cameron House."

"What?" I shouted, in a voice that sounded quite unlike my own, like some freak.

"She's been living there for a couple of years. She's been performing there, singing again."

"OMG, this can't be. I've been going to the Cameron for years. Jo's father practically lived there, had friends who played there regularly. Maybe I saw her perform and didn't even know it was her."

"Probably not. It's only been fairly recently that she started singing again."

"How do you know all this? You don't seem like a Cameron House type."

Paolo had gotten the rest of the story from Titiana:

When Mara left her home at the edge of the sea she went to Rome, looking for her sister. She found Francesca managing a small bookstore in the old Jewish ghetto of San Lorenzo. The bookstore was on a small, cobblestone alley off Via Portico d'Ottavia, the neighbourhood's main drag. It had been an art gallery selling Jewish-themed art before Francesca's friend, Vittorio, took it over and converted it into a bookstore. Right beside a hotel and busy Portico d'Ottavia with all its shops, restaurants and cafés, it did extremely well. Except for the winter months when there were fewer tourists, the small store was always teeming with people, browsing, putting in orders or just chatting with its charming manager.

At first, it was extremely difficult for both Micola and Francesca. Their separation had helped keep the past at bay, but together they had to finally confront it. Both had felt abandoned by the other, and had to emotionally wrestle with that. But gradually, the love they'd always had for each other came back, in small ways, through joking, cooking together, speaking their scramble of dialect and English which always had them in stitches.

Much of Mara's time was spent walking along the Tiber. She could not stay far from water. It was during one of those walks that she decided she had to find the daughter she had given up for adoption, though she wasn't quite ready yet.

For a while she helped Francesca at the bookstore. Francesca did most of the conversing with the customers and Mara worked the cash, took care of other administrative tasks. It helped that she had worked in a bookstore, long ago. It helped that it was her sister who managed it. It helped her re-enter the world, a world which was very different from the one she had left behind.

At first she refused to have anything to do with the computer. But since it was impossible for her to be any help without using it, she agreed to learn. She drew the line at smart phones, though. Said she had no one to call and there was no one to call her. Though she had to give up that resistance too, once she left Rome, in the summer of 2012.

Just before the world was supposed to end, she returned to Montreal, the city where everything had taken place. She had the suitcase with the notebooks and letters, and the diary which Cassandra had sent to Francesca, after Mara had left. Francesca's instruction was that they be given to Paolo, if she could find him. But they ended up with Titiana, who found Paolo and sent him the package shortly after Mara arrived in Montreal.

As always, Mara moved at her own pace. She was not ready to see Paolo, or me, when she first arrived in Montreal, so she stayed with Titiana. Titiana was married with a husband and two grown children. They lived in the

Plateau area and owned a grocery story in Little Italy. Mara spent her days in St. Louis Square staring at the fountain and feeding pigeons. After a few months she mustered up the courage to go to the old neighbourhood, Melrose Avenue, the tunnel, N.D.G. park, the spooky lane they had used to get to school as kids. To her surprise, she felt little. She realized that all the sorrow had flowed out of her. It was with the sea now, and she was clear, clear that none of it had been her fault, the betrayal, the freak accident that had sent her father tumbling down a flight of stairs.

In order to save money to get to Toronto, Mara worked for a few months at Titiana's grocery store. Titiana had mentioned the Cameron House because of its bohemian history. She had had some musician friends who had lived there for a time, when they first moved from Montreal to Toronto in the early 90s.

In Toronto, Mara went straight to the Cameron House, got herself a room, in the midst of a musical world again, surrounded by music, her one true love. Somehow, it had waited. It had waited.

She knew then what she had to do. She got herself hired as a cleaner for the bohemian bar, so she could afford to stay there indefinitely, and she began writing her own songs again. There was another project which she decided to embark on, to sing the songs of Victor Jara and Violetta Parra. She already knew *Gracias a la Vida*, which she used to sing back in Montreal. And she had always loved Victor Jara, from the very first time she heard him. It was at Paolo's, the only time she and Francesca had ever visited him at his Westmount home. Paolo, who had discovered her and convinced her of her talent. She needed to call him. She would, when she was ready.

That was the end of the tale, as told to me by Paolo. I was speechless, bereft, did not know what to say or feel. A vast longing overtook me, one I knew could never be satisfied, a longing to have been someone else, someone who knew what Mother was, what Mother was supposed to be, who believed in her existence, someone who did not hate herself, someone who could love. Because after all was said and done, I hated myself. I had been well armoured against it, with a clear and lucid confidence. But beneath it all had been a wild self-negation, a roaring darkness that wanted to annihilate me.

"I'm not going to fucking see her. I'm not going. She's been here two years and she's never even tried to contact me."

"Look, she just called me a couple of days ago. She didn't say much, except that she was singing at the Cameron, and she talked a bit about what she was into musically. She didn't mention the past. I called Titiana who helped me piece together what happened after Mara left Amalfi."

"I'm not going, Paolo. I'm not going to see her."

"That's OK. You don't have to, or maybe, you can just wait and see, if you change your mind."

"I won't change my mind."

When I was walking home down along Withrow Park, I remembered that, before Lhasa de Sela died, she was planning to do a CD of songs by Victor Jara and Violetta Parra. But she never got to do it, because she was diagnosed with breast cancer and died soon after. A dog chasing a frisbee ran in front of me and I stumbled, almost falling.

"Sorry, sorry, sorry," the owner said. But I was oblivious. I continued walking to the bottom of the park, and then up the hill to my power spot, under the maple tree.

257

I sat down and started crying. A young man approached, a concerned look on his face, asking if I was alright.

"I'm good, I'm good, just a bit overwhelmed today, that's all."

Under the protection of my maple, I sat and had a long cry, about everything, about the past, about the present, about the future, about the *Thing* that had come crashing into my life, dismantling who I had been. When I was finished, I clambered down the grassy slope, slightly wet with spring dampness, and headed home.

And there he was, my green-eyed fish man, hair long and dishevelled, sitting on my front steps, gazing at the brave, purple crocuses, always hopeful, asserting their fragile beauty, against the spring chill. For a brief moment, it was as if a wind had swept through my mind, and cleared everything. A wide, open gladness, an uncontainable fullness. Was this joy? How was I to know? He stood up when he saw me. All smiles. He seemed taller, more muscular, somehow, more of a man. He moved towards me as if to embrace me, but then stopped himself.

"Hey, good to see you," he said.

All I could muster was: "What are you doing here?"

"Well, I figured you probably wouldn't respond to any of my phone calls or e-mails, so I decided to just drop by to see you. I wanted to see your face."

"Look who's talking. You never responded to mine. It's almost a year, now,"

"OK, let's get something straight, Chiara. You are the one that left me, aren't you? Without so much as a word of explanation, and then never responded to any of my desperate pleadings to talk. So I don't know where you get off, now, getting all uppity and rejected ... In any case, I never got any e-mails from you."

"You didn't?"

"No, but then it depends when you sent it. I have been away for a long while."

"Oh, where have you been?"

"I was travelling. Europe and Asia. After school ended last year, my friend Jake and I just decided to take off and see where we ended up."

Then silence. Neither of us seemed to know where to go from there. But he sat down again, on my stoop, which made me feel relieved. He wasn't planning on going anywhere, not for a while anyhow.

"Oh yeah, I actually discontinued my e-mail account when I left, so if you e-mailed me after August 1st, I wouldn't have got your e-mail."

Again, relief, he hadn't written me off, yet. That thing called joy, or whatever it was, was spreading through me again. Like an antidote to all the breaking, it was pushing everything else away, making clear, making one, a fullness, a lightness. I wanted to grab him and kiss him, but I didn't. Why couldn't I? Why not? Why couldn't I have what I wanted? A battle was taking place in the moment. Then the answer came, out from under the fullness, not light but heavy as brick, that raw hatred of myself, the unworthiness, the beast that had no face.

Daniel was staring at me with a puzzled look. He was expecting an answer that wasn't coming. Lost in my struggle, I had forgotten what we were talking about. Then I remembered. "Yes, yes, it was after August 1st that I e-mailed you."

"So how have you been?" The question I was hoping, somehow, he wouldn't ask.

"Oh boy, that's a hard one to answer," I said. "Have you got some time?"

"Yeah, actually I do. Do you want to go for a drink or something?"

"I was thinking more along the lines of maybe sitting at the picnic table under my battered willow tree, over there. I have some beers upstairs. I could go get them. Also just want to put on a warmer jacket."

"Sure, sounds good."

But when I was getting my jacket out of the closet, I heard his footsteps running up the stairs. When I turned around he looked all flushed and out of breath. Then he moved towards me and said, almost tentatively, "Chiara, I've really missed you." I looked at those green eyes of his and I thought I saw a yearning in them.

This is the cue I thought, this is the cue. I went over, grabbed him and kissed him. He seemed happy about it. He didn't stop, kissed me back, pretty passionately. But then, abruptly backed off and went to sit down at the kitchen table. He pulled over the vase of yellow roses on the table and smelled them, hesitated for a few moments. "OK, Chiara, it's not that I didn't want you to do that, believe me. But you wrecked me. I'm not going through another round of this without knowing what the hell went wrong, why you just callously dropped me, without a word."

"OK, Daniel, fair enough."

I pulled out the beers from the fridge and sat down at the kitchen table across from him. "It's still a bit chilly outside, anyhow, so let's do it here. It may take a while."

And so I told him, everything, that I was not a WASP after all, that I was actually part Italian and part Russian Jew, like him, that my father was a Cohen, a musician, a junkie, who had callously broken my mother's heart, that my mother was some kind of mystic, and that my aunt had been a terrorist, that they were still alive, both of them, and that my mother was here, singing at the Cameron House.

I told him about how I had been afraid that he was my brother or my cousin, about how the *Thing* had started to hound me even before I had read any of the diaries or letters, that there was something about him, the way he had made me feel, the look in his eyes, the way he moved that seem to correlate with the *Thing,* and so it had frightened me, that I was trying not to fall apart, that looking at him made me want to fall apart.

"Now, in retrospect, I think I was just calling up a past I didn't even know I had, and so it was kind of crazy-making for me at the time." I stopped, thinking I might be overwhelming him.

But he looked solid, attentive, compassionate. He turned over to smell the roses again and then said, "You know, this complexity suits you. You make more sense to me now. You're a bit of a mystic and a terrorist yourself, you know. An emotional terrorist, that's what I thought of you, for a long time. You can be cool, calculating, indifferent, but then there's your love of trees, nature, solitude."

That's not quite what I was expecting from him. But it was fine. He still sounded a bit angry. I could let him have that. If he had done to me what I did to him, we wouldn't have been sitting here having this conversation. We'd never have got that far, and I wouldn't have cared the reasons why.

Then he backtracked. "Pretty mind-blowing, though. Difficult thing to be going through, I must say."

That still sounded pretty cool to me, though I wasn't quite sure what I wanted, or what I was expecting. Actually, I did know what I wanted. I wanted to fuck. I wanted that wild, shattering sex with him. Escape sex, was that what it was? No, not entirely, partly that, partly just the sight of him moved me in that way. That's just how it was, the truth of it. I didn't know how else to tell him how happy I was that he was there, that he came back. But there was no chance of sex, right then. I knew that. He was still wary, trying to process everything I had told him.

"Yes, it's been mind-blowing. I seem to be in a constant state of overwhelm with it. But Paolo's been great. I don't know what I would have done without him. And Jo, too, of course. My parents, that's another story. They're not handling it well. They seem to be in a perpetual state of anxiety about what I might do, which is not at all helpful. I guess they're weren't expecting that I would find out in the way that I did."

"Listen," he said, suddenly. "I'll go with you. I'll go with you to the Cameron House, if you want to see her. I mean, we could just go see her. She doesn't even have to know who you are."

Until then, I had been convinced that I would not go. Not a chance. Then, the sound of his voice, saying those words, with such enthusiasm and care, it turned things around, all the way around.

"OK, OK, with you, I can do it. Let's do it." I couldn't believe I'd said that, that I'd let myself feel that kind of dependence. But everything was in shambles then, including my defenses.

In the end, I decided I wanted Jo and Paolo to be there, too. But with Paolo there was no chance of just going incognito, because she would recognize him.

Her night was Tuesday nights. So for several weeks, every Monday night I became ill, headaches, nausea, just couldn't move. But eventually, I built up the nerve. It was early May, it had been warm, so the lilacs were early. I spent part of the afternoon just walking around the neighbourhood, and passed by the small lilac grove near the east end of the co-op several times. That scent seemed to make everything OK. How could anything go wrong? What could go wrong, anyhow? It was hard to imagine, since this was not, exactly, like something I had ever done before. I thought of the blank place inside my head, or more accurately, the desert place, where I lived most of my life, the flat plane of nothingness, where nobody really mattered, and safety was the only consideration. I couldn't really go back there now, could I? Even if I wanted to, that ground had cracked and was safe no more. I didn't have much of a choice, did I? I stayed with the lilacs for ten more minutes, and suffused myself with that beguiling scent. Then I went home to get ready.

It was the six o'clock matinee show, so Daniel had asked if I wanted to get a bite to eat beforehand. But I told him I couldn't eat. He came to pick me up, even though I had insisted that we meet at the Cameron. He just ignored my request and came over anyhow, around 5 pm. We took the streetcar over and got there a bit early. It was good that we had, as there were already hardly any seats left. The Cameron is intimate and it can get crowded pretty fast. But we were able to save seats for Jo and Paolo, who arrived shortly after us. We ordered drinks, and everyone was quiet, as if afraid to say anything.

Paolo spoke, finally. "You know, I haven't seen Micola in almost 40 years." Everyone nodded. "She was a remarkable beauty, back then, and super talented." We nodded again. The anticipation was unbearable and Paolo's chatter was not helping.

The place was packed, people sitting at the bar, and the entrance was crowded, standing room only. My mother had a following, already.

I felt like I was shivering, yet I knew it wasn't cold. Without my asking, Daniel took off his jean jacket and threw it around my shoulders. The place was getting rowdy, noisy. Then they came out, four of them, a piano player, an accordion player and a guitar player. And she, Mara, with a long black dress and a green shawl wrapped around her shoulders. She was wearing beads of all sorts, on her wrists and neck, and her hair, a torrent of gray/black, wildness.

Without a word of introduction, she began to sing. The first song was "Gracias a la Vida," the only song I recognized, from the first set, of the songs of Victor Jara and Violeta Parra. But then, when she introduced Victor Jara's song "Plegaria a un Labrador," she said: "This is for my sister, Francesca, who I'm sure, would have loved to be here." As she said it, I saw her glance at Paolo.

Her voice immediately hooked into my heart, and transported me to some kind of place I'd never known. Some mountainous region surrounded by sea, a rugged world that only my bones knew, bones that had been divorced from my mind. I had a body that knew things my mind was opposed to, a body of knowledge that felt like it could kill me, and yet I wanted it, like the way I had wanted Daniel, yet somehow felt that it could kill me. But there he was beside me now, and there she was, before me, a mystery maker, a sweet sorcerer. I was still alive. I was surviving.

After the first set she did not come over. I noticed that her musicians went to the bar to get themselves some drinks, but she retreated to the back room and returned only when the second set started. Paolo looked over to see how I was doing. His face was streaked with tears.

"It takes some people a very long time to get where they are supposed to be, but they do get there," he said. I nodded, but felt speechless.

"Her voice sounds a bit like the lead singer from London Grammar," Daniel said. No one seemed to know who that was. "It's an indie pop group from the UK."

"I am wondering what her connection to Lhasa de Sela is," Paolo said. "She's singing a project that Lhasa had meant to work on before she died."

"Maybe it has something to do with her Montreal connection," I said. "Wait, wait a minute. Didn't Cassandra play Lhasa de Sela for her once in Amalfi?"

"Yes, that's it," Paolo said. "I think you're right, Chiara." And then said: "If there's one thing Micola always had, it was an ear for music."

The musicians were getting ready for the next set, so we settled in for the second round, songs of lament about the sea, its beauty, its danger, its peril. Exquisite poetic incantations, of heartfelt protest and longing for our origins. Her sea of heartbreak, her vision of the deep, the loss of our beginning and our end. Songs of lyrical pleading to open up our hearts to Her distant voice, Her roar, Her murmur, Her imminent death.

Some songs were in Italian. And though I couldn't understand the words, still, they reached past everything, to the heart of things, things long lost and long forgotten, long forgotten to me, for sure. A heartache that had no choice but to believe in magic, a silence beyond the beauty and the terror.

Then it was I who was tear-streaked. I cannot say how those songs went into me, and turned my heart of steel into an ocean of feelings. But they did. Every word was wrought of love and sorrow, despair and hope, fear and determination. Every word, a paradox.

I did not want her to stop singing, as if her voice could save me, save me from myself, save me from the world, save me from everything I couldn't handle. Oh Mother, where have you been?

The music ended and the trance broke. She went into the back room. But she came back out with an envelope in hand, walking towards us. I started to shiver in earnest, and knew I wouldn't be able to stop. Daniel reached for my hand and held it tightly. What a miracle that he would know

265

to do that, because it worked. The shivering stopped and I was able to centre myself just as she arrived at our table.

Paolo stood up and embraced her passionately. He was crying but she was not. She kissed him on both cheeks and stood back and looked at him for a while, then just said, "Paolo, Paolo, I can't believe it's you. Francesca will be jealous when I tell her I saw you."

"I can't believe it's you, either ... both sets were amazing. You did it, you made it."

"I suppose that's one way of putting it."

Then she turned in my direction. Her deep, green eyes washed over me, like the sea that was Her heart. At that moment she seemed sad. But I just focused on Daniel's hand, still holding mine firmly.

"Hello," she said. Her speaking voice was quite different from her singing voice, softer, more tender.

Then Paolo spoke. "Micola, this is Chiara, and these are her friends, Daniel and Jo."

She nodded, but did not take her eyes off me.

"I cannot say how happy I am that you came."

I nodded, not knowing what else to say.

Then I muttered, "Yeah, your songs are wonderful, and I am also a Lhasa de Sela fan."

"Oh wow, what a coincidence." She smiled widely. She did not seem to know what else to say.

She remembered the envelope in her hand.

"I have something for you," she said. "Just my attempt to explain where I have been, and why it took me so long to get here."

"The long obedience," I said.

She looked puzzled.

"'All great things take a long obedience.' Nietzsche said that."

"Oh, I think I understand," she said and smiled her enchanting, wide smile.

She turned to Paolo and hugged him again. "Don't be a stranger," she said.

"I think maybe that applies more to you than to me," he answered.

After she nodded, kissed him again, she came over to me, opened her arms tentatively, as if she wasn't sure I would want to hug her, but I did. Then she disappeared into the back room of the Cameron House.

* * *

Dearest Chiara,

If my heart had been my own, I never would have let you go. I never would have let you go. But it was broken or occupied, frozen or shocked, or lost at sea on a voyage I did not choose, or scattered in the wind, the windy hills of my origins. I felt like a sketch on a cave wall, an ancient memory of ochre shade, a blood-red hope from another century, trapped in the tangles of time.

A time that had forgotten me, my muted life behind a wall of pain. I did not want to escape. I could see no place in the world for someone like me, not knowing which way to turn, where to put my feet. The ground was gone. Was I a ghost or a phantom? I could not tell. I could only be still. That was all I could do, live my muted life, against the cave wall, waiting.

I could not grieve for you. I could not hope for you. I could not look for you. How could I look for you without a heart? If it could have been otherwise, it would have been. But the events that led to my leaving were kind of like a whirlwind that swept me up into its path and left me speechless.

I always had the thought that, somehow, I couldn't live in this world, even before everything happened. Like a leaf in a storm,

I could not hold my own. Could I bend, every which way, and still survive? I thought not, but yet, here I am, writing to you, my dearest, my innocent one.

All I can say, in my defense, is that I was a motherless child, myself. The only comfort I knew was Fear, my Mother was Fear, always present, ever strong, a dark cloak, a kind of beauty, in some strange way, that I hid behind, until your father found me. Ah, he was a magician, that swooped in, or was he a bird of prey? I will never know. But at the time, he took off my dark cloak and ravaged me, then pulled me back from the edge of the cliff, where with one hand, I held back the sea, and with the other, a sword. And for a brief period, I set foot on this earth, as if I belonged. Love swept away all psychic debris and took me into its orbit, as if it would rule the world. And why shouldn't love rule the world? Who better?

That was the alchemy of your birth, my dear, love and magic. She caught you in flight and brought you to us, the Mother of Days, the one we all want, the one we all deserve, the one who is always leaving and always arriving, shrouded in Mystery, and barred by hate, indifference and violence.

I am always taking flight in mythos. Forgive me for that. It is how I survived the muted years, after the devastation, after love disappeared without a word, after I killed my father, accidentally, after everyone left me. I created a world in which I could live.

In the end, I was rescued, not by a man, but by an angel, who took me to the sea, where I belonged, to the cave of my origins, where I waited for my lost heart to return. There, finally, I could relax. I put down my sword, and let the sea ravish me. She was the Mother of Days, the one who took it all away, but then, the one who brought me love and the one who brought me back to you.

At the time, it did not seem possible that I could ever find you, so I gave myself over to the silence that rose. To the silence I could belong. The world could always use more silence, I thought. That would be my contribution, my revenge against Time, against the Noise.

I had once believed in music, but then, all of a sudden, it was all Noise. No one was speaking properly, no one was speaking the truth, and what had seemed true, withdrew without a word. Without a word. How desperately I had longed for word from your father. But that word never came, and so I took my revenge against the Noise, against Time.

I am sure you are wiser than I, to know that revenge gets you nowhere. It was my only luck, in a sea of misfortune, to choose the right weapon. Silence. Though it only took me so far, and in the end, could not hold back the tide of sorrow, which eventually came. But that is what saved me, for though I had been mothered by fear, I did not fear sorrow. When it came I let it stay. I made it my home for as long as it wanted. My Angel allowed it, she let it move in, the one who could see, in a world gone blind. She let the rain come as far as it could, as hard as it wanted, until the floods came, and then we had to move. But at that point, I knew what was happening, and I was ready to leave.

Since I've been gone, the Noise has gotten worse, and the Silence, a bygone whisper that no one can hear. This much I have been able to determine, that I was lost, but now I am here, and I bring with me a fragile silence that the world is forgetting, that my revenge, though useless, was not in vain.

And though there is nothing, I'm sure, I can say, that could ever take back the loss I have caused you, I give you this, that your origin was love. It was the sea's peril that reminded me of that.

How could we destroy the origin of life? I wondered. I always knew we could not know the origin but only dream it. But I never dreamed we could destroy it. Lay waste to the Source, to the Beginning. And as I thought the unthinkable thought, I remembered you, the passion of your origin, and of how I had laid waste to that, even if not intentionally. I let it happen. I let them take you away from me, and completely forgot the love that had conceived you.

But now, from the far side of sorrow, where earth and sky are still married, I can at least bring you this. Love rains.

Acknowledgements

While *Love and Rain* makes use of certain historical events and personages, the characters and story lines are fictional. For the part of the novel set during Italy's 'years of lead' I would like to acknowledge research drawn from Robert C. Mead's *Red Brigades: The Story of Italian Terrorism* and *The Aldo Moro Murder Case* by Richard Drake.

I would like to thank Mark Anthony Jarman for his editorial mentoring. His rigorous and thoughtful comments helped shape the book into its present form.

Thanks to Barb Milroy, Camilla Burgess, Liz Kalman, Mark Czarnecki, Steven Carter, Katy Petre and James Fitzgerald, for reading early drafts of the novel and providing me with support and encouragement to move forward with the project. Special thanks to Mark Czarnecki for his sharp eye on the timeline of events in the novel.

Thanks also to Raffaela Carlone for her help with the Italian and dialect phrases in the book.

And much gratitude to Guernica Editions for agreeing to publish my first novel. Thanks to Michael Mirolla and Julia Roorda for their fine editorial work. Thanks to Rafael Chimicatti for working so diligently on the cover design, which in the end, was exactly the cover I had envisioned.

About the Author

Carmela Circelli was born in the region of Campania, Italy, but grew up in Montreal. She moved to Toronto to study philosophy in 1976. Since 1990 she has been teaching as an adjunct professor of philosophy at York University. She also works in private practice as a psychotherapist. Her philosophical memoir *Sweet Nothing: An Elemental Case for Taking our Time* was published in 2014. *Love and Rain* is her first novel.

Printed in April 2023
by Gauvin Press,
Gatineau, Québec